Praise for *In the Shadow*

'My girlfriend's dad was [...]
get onto the Piper Alpha a [...]
graphs one of his workmates secretly [...]
In the Shadow of Piper Alpha is not just another, much needed
representation of the human costs resulting from the unceasing
and capricious chase for profits. It is also one which explores
the long-term effects which go on behind the horrible headline
of "167 killed".'

Gregor Gall, Visiting Professor of Industrial Relations
at the University of Leeds,
editor *Scottish Left Review*,
director of the Jimmy Reid Foundation

Praise for *The Waves Burn Bright*

'A cauldron of a book, bubbling with anger and magma which
might at any moment spill over and bring further devastation. It
is both particular to this tragedy in 1988, but also universal; a
compelling story exploring how a father's trauma sends shock
waves through a family, changes the pattern of lives – particularly
his daughter's – and makes love risky. However, as well as being
about damage and running away, it is also about healing.'

Linda Cracknell, author of *Doubling Back*
and *The Other Side of Stone*

'A compelling and highly engaging story, told with insight
and compassion, this novel deserves a wide readership.'

Alison Miller, author of *Demo*
and Scots Scriever for Orkney

'The characters are well drawn and believable; the tortured survivor, struggling with dreams and the need to blot out memories with the bottle; the child damaged as much by the implosion of her parents' marriage as the disaster; and the guilt-ridden mother who has positioned herself outside the close unit of father and daughter but who still wants to revel in Carrie's achievements. The night of the disaster is sensitively and evocatively handled... Digging through a hard exterior to explore the layers beneath can be a dangerous and explosive exercise, whether that's the earth's crust or a human's weaker shell. In this novel both are explored in equally compelling ways.'

The Scotsman

'He's crafted a powerful portrayal of how the consequences of such a disruptive event can reverberate through people's lives for decades afterwards...his characters are consistent, making believable, relatable choices.'

The Herald

'Iain Maloney has done it again. He has written a book that simply must be read...Maloney leads us through the tale with great sensitivity and understanding. In this, he is masterly. It is an astonishing tour-de-force. It is an object lesson in how an author of fiction should approach the telling of a real-life tragedy of this kind, where 167 men lost their lives in a horrifying inferno. It is really difficult to find the words that are adequate to the task of praising this book. If you want to understand modern Scotland, this book is necessary. If you want an insight into the nature of trauma, this book is essential. It is not an easy read, but it will make you care deeply. That can only benefit you.'

David Kenvyn, *For The Joy of Reading*

'Iain Maloney's best book to date, not only an entertaining and thoughtful one, but, I would suggest, an important one... Maloney not only pays respect to the memory of that terrible event, he offers fresh insight into how individuals and their families and friends cope – or more often fail to cope – with trauma, and the humanity behind the headlines.'

Alistair Braidwood, Gutter 15 and Scots Whay Hae

'Takes you on one of those rare, utterly enjoyable literary experiences where you find yourself disappointed to have to close its pages.'

Nothing in the Rule Book

'It reminded me a little of Iain Banks and his interwoven families – a Crow Road sort of a book – loss, distance, redemption.'

Simon Sylvester, author of *The Visitors*

'The pouer o Maloney's tale-tellin is fair winnersome whiles ...it wul be lang or it eilies awa frae your mynin.'

Derrick McClure in Lallans 89

In the Shadow of
Piper Alpha

Iain Maloney

TIPPERMUIR
· BOOKS LIMITED ·

The moral right of Iain Maloney to be identified as the author of
the Work has been asserted by him in accordance with the
Copyright, Designs & Patents Act 1988.

This edition published and copyright 2022 by
Tippermuir Books Ltd, Perth, Scotland.
mail@tippermuirbooks.co.uk – www.tippermuirbooks.co.uk.

ISBN 978-1-913836-16-0 (paperback)   978-1-913836-17-7 (eBook)

A CIP catalogue record for this book is available from the British Library.

Editorial and Project coordination by Dr Paul S Philippou.

Cover design by Matthew Mackie.

Editorial and Project Support: Molly Greenshields.

Text styling, layout, and artwork by Bernard Chandler [graffik].
Text set in Sabon LT Std 10.5/13pt.

'Fit means thon word survivor?' from "At the Piper Alpha Memorial,
Queen Mother Rose Garden" by Sheena Blackhall, collected in
Hairst O Thorns: Poems in Scots and English (Lochlands, 2004).
Used with permission.

'Did we forget we're tectonic?' by Rebecca Sharp, in *Rough Currency*
(Tapsalteerie, 2021). Used with permission.

Printed and bound by Ashford Colour Press, Gosport, Hampshire PO13 0FW

For the one hundred and sixty-seven
For the survivors
For the families
For Aberdeen

Fit means thon word survivor? -
Sheena Blackhall

Did we forget we're tectonic? -
Rebecca Sharp

Incheon Airport, Republic of Korea,
June 2013

I need to run.

The ground beneath my feet, granite hardness, taut muscles stretching out, flexing and tiring before the next flight, eleven hours of stasis, the world circling below, night and day passing. Already the fatigue like mercury in my veins. My hand against the shower wall, I grabbed an ankle and pulled, feeling the strain in my thigh. Maybe I could run through the terminal, run against the travelators, run from gate to gate tracing the outline of the airport. The urge like electricity. Run.

Maybe not. With terrorism and whatever's going on with the North, someone running could be a threat. The firepower on display. How did people ever get used to being around guns? I asked Ash, she's American, she should know.

'You rationalise it, Carrie. You push it aside, try not to think about it. Humans can get used to almost anything given enough time. Given enough pressure.'

Pressure turns carbon into diamonds; given enough time anything can happen.

She was dozing in the lounge. She could sleep anywhere and in Seoul they made you comfortable. Each time I came through Incheon I thought about moving to South Korea. I loved Seoul, loved the food, Seoul food. I could live on *samgyetang* chicken every day for the rest of my life, but I could never leave our home in Hawaii, the house I shared with Ash, the view of the sea from the front, the mountains at the back. For the first time in years I had a home, a fixed centre even when I was in Japan, in the Philippines, in Chile doing my research, when Ash was in New York. There was always a conference, an invitation, a seismic event. Jetsetters, both of us. But Hawaii was our heart. Where we met. Where we fell in love.

Take this time. She'd been in Hawaii, I'd been on Aogashima, a volcanic island south of Japan. So we met in Tokyo, her direct, me by taxi, boat, aeroplane, my suitcase snaking behind me on a broken wheel, then onto Incheon, Amsterdam then Aberdeen. Scotland. Home.

From Hawaii to Scotland, every way is the long way round.

I wrapped up in a fluffy white towel, fabric-conditioned into cloudlike softness, and towelled my short red hair, pulled on cargo pants and a strappy top, gave my hair a quick muss with mousse, spiking it loosely, dumped the wet towels in the basket and swung my new backpack into place. It didn't sit right, too high up my back, the straps too narrow.

It was a birthday present from Ash and I didn't like it. I hadn't been ready to call time on the last one, a khaki canvas bag I'd had since I was a PhD student in Durham sixteen or so years before, a present from a girlfriend, Anna. It was stained and smelled of rot and damp, the stitching frayed, but it had circumnavigated the Pacific Ring of Fire, scaled active peaks, been buried in ash and was once stolen by a boy on the back of a motorbike in Vietnam before being dumped minus valuables in a puddle. We'd been through a lot together and when Ash presented me with this new backpack...over the years I've become good at suppressing emotions.

She gave me a sleepy smile, 'Hi.' Her long auburn-tinted hair was all scuffed around by the chair. I loved it when she was relaxed and scruffy, when sleep brought her to my level of grooming. She was my first partner of either sex whose fashion sense wasn't some variation of 'grunge' or 'nerd'. She was a lawyer, expensive suits and salon hair. Me the scientist, practical hair, tomboy clothes. Somehow we worked.

'Feel better?'

'Yeah.'

'It'll be fine.'

'I swore I'd never go back.'

'You swear too much.' She sat up and lifted an eyelash off my cheek. I blew it and wished. Kissed her, the scent of her, coconut.

'Let's find our gate.'

2

Ash would be asleep before we crossed Chinese airspace. She viewed sleep like an accountant views money: *profit and loss.* Long-haul was her way of making up the deficit. Some parts of life are worth sleeping through, she'd say.

I can't sleep on planes so I had prepared ahead, my backpack full of work-related good intentions. Papers to read, marking, draft correspondence, funding applications. One thing they never tell you when you start out in academia: for every rung on the ladder you climb, the level of correspondence doubles. I spent more time writing *unfortunately at this time...*than I did talking to my PhD students. I padded down the aisle, slipped my laptop and folders into the seat pocket, wrote a post-it to-do list and thought how much more organised my life would be by the time we landed.

They closed the shutters and turned the lights off, like it was nap time. In the window seat, Ash took a Valium with her wine and closed her eyes. The aisle seat was taken by a middle-aged Japanese man who plugged in his iPhone headset and also fell asleep, little trills of maybe Schubert counterpointing the thrum of the engines.

The carbonara sauce sitting badly in my stomach, not mixing well with the coffee, I opened two files on my laptop. The first was my paper for the conference at the University of Aberdeen. The paper was fine and if it were to be delivered anywhere else I wouldn't even look at it again. Aberdeen was where I'd been an undergraduate, where the oil industry was everything and the oil industry reps, many of whom would be in the audience, would be asking questions, hostile, loaded questions, about my conclusions.

This wasn't an average conference. This wasn't an average paper.

Aberdeen was where I grew up. Where my father was.

Dad wouldn't know I was there, didn't follow research anymore, wasn't in the academic loop. He wouldn't be there. He wouldn't. But maybe Harry Boyle had told him? Dad was old friends with the Head of Department. Maybe they still drank together.

I watched Ash sleep. She smiled, her lips tight together, dimples and laughter lines. She hated the lines, showing despite her care regime. I loved them. Contours and gradients were my field, I knew how to read them. Perhaps that was why love became simpler as I aged.

The second file was a report a colleague at Aogashima had given me about research at Mount Ontake. I'd already run it through Google Translate and now had to turn the gibberish into grammatical and scientific sense. I felt breath on my arm, stale and smoky. The Japanese man had woken up and was reading over my shoulder. 'Can you read?' he said, pointing at the original report.

'No,' I replied. 'It's too difficult.'

'Yes, even for Japanese people I think.'

'It's a scientific paper. About volcanoes.'

'You study volcanoes?'

'And teach others.'

'That's good. A good job. In Japan we have a saying – there are only four things that scare us.' He counted them off on his fingers. 'Volcano. Earthquake. Tsunami. Father.' He laughed at his joke, and I smiled. He was probably a father himself. Did his children make the same joke? 'This is Ontake-san.' He pointed at a couple of symbols. 'Have you been?'

'No.'

'It's very beautiful. Sunrise from the top is wonderful. I grew up nearby. Very good skiing.'

'I'll try and go. I like skiing.'

'You must have been to Sakurajima though?'

I nodded. Volcanoes and Fathers. Sakurajima.

Kagoshima / Sakurajima, Japan,
September 1980

Mummy didn't like it there. She wanted to leave.

She hated being sticky and sat puffing and fanning herself with the map. Daddy had been there before so maybe he was used to it, or maybe he didn't mind sweat so much. His beard must have made his face really hot but he never complained like Mummy. I didn't like it at first but then I got used to it a bit. It was cooler when we were in the north, on the island called Hokkaido. Kagoshima was south. South is hotter but only if you're in the north. If you're in the south, like Australia or Chile, south is cool and north is hot. Daddy went to Chile. He went to a lot of countries when he was younger. When a country he had been to came on TV he said 'I've been there' and Mummy rolled her eyes. Now he only went to America. He went to places like Houston, Texas for business. In America you have to say the name and the state because Americans aren't so good at geography and you need to help them, like London, England and Tokyo, Japan. I looked up Houston, Texas in the atlas. It's in the south of the north so it must be hot too. Maybe that was why Mummy never went with him.

Mummy was in the next room and Daddy was out on business with Taka. He told me on the plane that Taka was an old friend from university and Mummy laughed her mean laugh and said she thought all his old university friends were women. After university in England Taka came back to Japan to study earthquakes. If I knew no one was going to die I'd like to feel an earthquake. It must be so weird to feel the earth moving like a bouncy castle. Taka tried to guess when earthquakes would come. He told me in the car from the airport that he'd never been right yet. I said he should study more and he laughed. When he laughed you could see he had lots of fillings in his teeth so maybe he ate too many sweets when he was little. Mummy told me not to be rude.

Everything about this room was different from home. My bed wasn't a bed, it was a mattress on the floor, called a *futon*. There was no carpet. Instead, the floor was covered in straw mats called *tatami*. They were nice and cool under my feet when I walked back from the bath hot and already sweaty again. It was summer but it wasn't like summer at home. At home we sat in the garden and had a barbecue, swatting wasps and watching the sky for signs of rain. The clouds came in quickly over the hospital where Mummy worked and dropped their water on our washing. Here there were no clouds all day, just hot blue sky.

We'd been in Japan for a week and we'd seen temples and castles and mountains and lakes. We flew into Tokyo and then flew straight out again. I only saw it from the air. When I told my friends I was going to Japan they all said 'Tokyo?' because it was the only place they knew. I was going to take a map home and show them where I'd been.

Next to my bed was a lamp. It was made of a dark wood Daddy said was cedar. I could switch it on and off without getting out of bed. At home I didn't have a lamp next to my bed and Mummy switched the light off for me, which was nice when I was tired, but if I wanted to read, I couldn't. Here, if I wanted to read, I could.

Daddy bought me two books for the holiday: *A Journey To The Centre Of The Earth* by Jules Verne and *How Volcanoes Work* by Kenneth Murphy. He gave them to me as a surprise. Mummy bought a book for me in the airport. It was called *Goddesses* by Jane MacMillan. It was about all the different cultures around the world and the goddesses they prayed to. I liked this book because the pictures were funny and interesting. You could look at them for hours and keep finding new things. Jules Verne had no pictures because it was a book for grown-ups and grown-ups don't like pictures. Kenneth Murphy put pictures in his book because it was for children like me but because it was science and not fantasy the pictures were not so exciting. The pictures were of volcanoes erupting and volcanoes that had been cut in half so you could see the inside and underground and learn what happens to make a volcano erupt. The photos of real volcanoes erupting were amazing but most of the pictures weren't real.

I was going to see a real volcano. When we arrived at the airport it was dark and I couldn't see Sakurajima. Most people could only drive around Sakurajima and look at it from far away but Taka had made it okay for us to go close because he was friends with Daddy.

I flicked the switch on the lamp and the room went dark. I lay back and listened to the fan whirring and clicking. It turned its head like a person watching a very slow game of tennis and when it reached the end, it clicked three times, like it was trying to turn further but couldn't. Then it turned back.

Maybe it wanted to be an owl and turn its head all the way round. Without the fan I couldn't sleep, it was so hot and sticky. I didn't need any sheets. I closed my eyes and imagined walking on a volcano. Would I feel it boiling under my feet like a pan lid when Mummy was boiling potatoes? Taka said that smoke always comes out of the crater like someone was burning their barbecue up there. Would we be able to breathe? Would I see lava?

Mummy and Daddy were in the room next to me and there was a door between the rooms so you didn't have to go out into the corridor and knock. The door was closed but it was very thin. Doors and walls were all thin in Japan. At the hotel in Hokkaido some were made of paper. I lost my balance putting my shoes back on and put my thumb through a wall. The walls here weren't made of paper but they were still thin, not like the granite walls in our house in Aberdeen, Scotland. (You have to say Scotland because of the other Aberdeens – there's one in America and one in Hong Kong and another in South Africa.) At home we couldn't hear our neighbours, Mr and Mrs Galloway. But I think they sometimes could hear Mummy and Daddy.

Daddy came back from his meeting with Taka and he was very noisy. It sounded like he kept dropping his key in the corridor and then there was a bang and he said a bad word. I woke up thinking it was morning and time to see the volcano but it was still dark and maybe I'd only been asleep for ten minutes or maybe two hours. It was so hard to tell time in the dark.

I put my head under the pillow but I could still hear them.

'You stink of whisky.'

'Not polite to say "no" in Japan.'

'And the state of you. Your shirt untucked and…God, your fly is open.'

'Ah, he wants to come out and play.'

'If he sticks his head out he's getting whacked with my hairbrush.'

There was one thud, a pause, then another. His shoes.

'Be quiet. Caroline's asleep next door and there are other guests, you know.'

'They won't complain. Too polite.'

'No, go and have a shower. You're not getting into bed reeking of alcohol and smoke. Where the hell did you get to? You said it was just a couple to catch up.'

'Lots of catching up to do.'

'Well I hope you weren't causing havoc in the hotel.'

'No. Went out. Hit the town.'

'It looks like the town hit you. Where did you go? I can't imagine there are too many bars open at this hour.'

'Taka knows a place.'

'Taka always knows a place. I'm serious: shower. And don't wake Caroline. We have to get up in a few hours to see this damned volcano.'

'She wants to go.'

'Like she has a choice. I'm sure if you asked her she'd much rather go to the beach or a theme park than all these museums and geologically *fascinating* places.'

'Fine. Let's ask her.'

'You are *not* waking her up.'

'She loves geology. Been reading those volcano books.'

'Only because you wouldn't let her bring any others.'

'She has others. She likes the volcano ones.'

'She has one other and that's because I bought her it in the airport.'

'Stupid book. Ghosts and pixies and nonsense.'

'She's eight, Marcus.'

'You say that like it's a handicap. Her age is only relevant as a stage in her development. You say she's only eight. I say mentally she's nearly twelve.'

'Shower.'

'No.'

'Shower or floor.'

Next time I woke it was sunny behind the curtains. I was sweaty and the sheets under me had come out and got pushed into one half of the bed. The bed was wet with sweat. I could hear Mummy was awake next door.

I tried to pull back the curtains but they were fixed on the runner and I realised you had to pull a cord on the right side to open them. They slid apart like the curtains on stage at school and there, over the tops of the buildings, I could see the volcano.

Sakurajima was a stratovolcano, Kenneth Murphy told me. That meant it looked like what people think a volcano looks like. There were other kinds of volcano but these are the most well-known. It was like a pyramid, the edges uneven and curved but about halfway up the top was missing, like it'd been ripped off and the crinkly edges were still there. It was actually three volcanoes all joined together. It was on the other side of the water from Kagoshima and looked like an island and in fact it once was but Taka said that one time so much lava came out that it made a bridge to the other side, you just couldn't see from here. Dark grey smoke was coming out of the right side of the mountain like it was on fire and rising high into the air, drifting towards us. It was beautiful but I felt a little scared. Maybe it was going to erupt like Vesuvius and cover us all in lava and ash and people in the future would dig us up and put us in museums. I looked down at the streets but no one was panicking so maybe this was normal.

'God, look at the state of your bed.' Behind me Mummy came in, fussing. She kissed the top of my head and sniffed. 'Shower.'

'Look, Mummy,' I pointed, 'it's a stratovolcano.'

'That's nice.' She was straightening my bed and didn't look. Mummy's a heart surgeon. She says after you've taken out someone's heart and put a new one in, nothing much can surprise you.

'Come on, shower then breakfast.'

I was looking forward to breakfast. The hotel had a buffet so I could choose what I wanted. In Hokkaido there was no menu and every meal was decided so if you didn't like it that was tough. Some of it was nice but some of the vegetables were too bitter and there was too much. At home I had cereal and a slice of toast with marmalade and a piece of fruit. In Japan they have fish and vegetables and rice and soup and pickles and if I ate all that I'd have to go back to bed and sleep again.

When I came out of the shower Daddy was awake and sitting on a blanket on the floor rubbing his face. Because he was on holiday he'd stopped trimming his beard and it was getting bigger. It was strange because Daddy had brown hair but his beard was red.

'Did you see the volcano, Daddy?' He nodded. 'It's smoking.' I showed him with my hands, the smoke rising into the clouds.

'It must smell like Daddy then.' Mummy was making coffee with the tiny kettle. While Mummy dried my hair Daddy had a shower. When he came out he was happier and messed up my hair.

'What kind of volcano is it, Carrie?'

Mummy rolled her eyes. She didn't like him calling me Carrie. 'Stratovolcano.'

'What other kinds of volcano are there?'

'Compound. Somma. Caldera. Shield.'

'Good girl. Breakfast?'

'What time is he coming?' Mummy was putting toilet paper in her khaki backpack.

'Taka? He'll pick us up out front at half nine.'

'I want to get some juice and snacks from a shop. If we're going to be out in this heat all day we're going to need plenty of fluids.'

'I'll get him to stop somewhere.'

Full of bacon and orange juice we got into Taka's car. It was an old Honda but the air conditioner was powerful so it wasn't too hot. Mummy and I sat in the back. In the streets you often couldn't see the volcano so I opened Jules Verne. Professor Lidenbrock, Axel and Hans were about to begin "The Ascent of Mount Sneffels".

'Don't read in the car, Caroline, you'll get sick.' Mummy was counting money. 'Taka, I'd like to stop at a convenience store, please.'

'No problem, Mrs Fraser.' Taka swung the car sharply and we bounced over the kerb and into a 7/11 car park. I went in with Mummy. I didn't need anything but Japanese shops are full of strange things and I liked to try and guess what they were. I stopped to look at a comic but Mummy pushed me by all the magazines because she didn't like the ones at the end with the naked women on them. We bought juice and nuts and dried fruit and the old woman at the till smiled at me so I smiled back.

'Mummy,' I poked at the car park ground with my feet, 'what's all this black dust?'

'It's ash, Caroline, from the volcano.' I looked up at the tower of smoke. One bang and we'd be covered in ash, like Pompeii. We got back in the car and Taka bounced over the pavement and into the traffic.

'Did you buy any candy?' Taka could see me in the mirror. He had smoked while we were in the shop and the car smelled bad. I wondered if the volcano smelled the same like Mummy said.

'No,' I closed Jules Verne because it was rude to speak and read at the same time, 'sweets are bad for my teeth.'

'And they'll give you diabetes.' Mummy was holding her hand over her mouth and nose because of the smell. 'People need to be careful what they put into their body.' I could see Daddy look at Taka and they both laughed. 'Were you as drunk as Marcus last night?'

'Now dear,' Daddy turned round in his seat so he could see Mummy, 'in Japan what happens at a drinking party is never discussed the next day.'

'How very convenient.'

Taka looked embarrassed in the mirror but Daddy laughed.

We drove onto the ferry and got out of the car. I took my books with me and followed Mummy up onto the deck. The ferry was old but had been painted recently and the white parts reflected the sun like mirrors. The water was dark blue, almost black which meant it was very deep, and as I looked over the edge of the ferry I felt like I wanted to jump in, like a rope attached to my stomach was pulling me over the edge and down. I pushed myself back from the side of the boat and walked to the front. We were sailing in a straight line to Sakurajima and as we got closer the volcano appeared higher and higher. I got my camera out of my backpack. It was a red one with an automatic flash that I got from the bank when I opened an account for birthday and Christmas money. I had five films but I'd already used two in Hokkaido. Each one took twenty-four photos. I put the new film in and clicked it shut hard because films need darkness and if any light got in it would ruin every photo. It was very bright so I didn't need the flash. I looked at the volcano and the smoke through the viewfinder and made sure I could get the smoke in. I took two, just in case one didn't come out. There were a group of girls posing for each other, holding their fingers up in a peace sign. They were older than me but it was hard to guess their age. They wore short skirts and brightly coloured tops. Daddy and Taka sat on a bench facing the girls.

Mummy was still angry about last night. At home when she was angry she went running in Westburn Park but she couldn't do that here. Maybe she could run around the boat. She came over to me. 'Do you like your book about goddesses?' I showed her how far I'd got through it, my boarding pass stub as a bookmark.

'Is there a chapter on Pele in it?'

'Pele? He's a footballer.'

'Not that Pele.' She took the book from me and flicked to the index. 'Pele was a volcano goddess in Hawaii.' She showed me the picture. Pele was sitting cross-legged in a red dress holding fire in her cupped hands. She was sitting inside the volcano, or more like she was the volcano. Her long wavy red hair made the sides and a wreath on her head was the summit. Underneath her a lake of magma rippled deep red and yellow, smoke rising around her. Her eyes were open wide, staring straight at me. She looked fierce, beautiful, dangerous, proud but there was sadness in her eyes.

'She's very volatile. When she is angry the volcanoes erupt and destroy everything in their path. She has to be placated with sacrifices and prayers.' She looked at Daddy who was looking at the girls posing.

The whole island was much bigger than it looked from the hotel and even when we drove off the boat we weren't there yet. Kenneth Murphy said under the car, under the road, miles down, magma was bubbling away. It travelled in underground rivers and when it found a way up, a volcano was formed. Places like Hawaii wouldn't exist without volcanoes. There was a vent of magma under the plate at that exact spot. As the plate moved it created new volcanoes. Hawaii was only the current volcano. If you looked under the water there was a chain of old Hawaiis like a necklace across the ocean floor. 'Mr Taka-san,' I closed the book and look at his eyes in the mirror, 'why is it called Sakurajima? What does it mean?'

'It means Cherry Blossom Island. *Sakura* is cherry blossom. *Jima* or *shima* means island.'

'Like Kagoshima?'

'Yes, that means, um, Baby Deer Island.'

'Can I see the cherry blossom?'

'Not now, Carrie-chan. It opens at the start of spring. It's too hot now.'

I liked being called Carrie-chan. *Chan* is a friendly word used for girls, like 'Carrie, dear'. Boys get called *kun*.

'When the *sakura* opens it's very beautiful.' Taka was watching me in the mirror and not looking at the road. There weren't many cars so maybe it was okay. 'But it only lasts for a very short time, then it falls to the ground. In Japanese culture the beautiful but short existence of the *sakura* is a metaphor for our lives. It is a very important reminder to us.'

'Carpe Diem.' Daddy had been listening too.

'Is that Latin, Daddy?'

'Yes. It means "seize the day". Enjoy life now because it doesn't last forever.'

'Eat, drink and be merry for tomorrow we die.' Taka nudged him across the handbrake.

'Amen.'

We drove past some girls on bikes. Daddy turned as we went by. Mummy slapped the top of his head.

'There are two observation points,' Taka stopped but left the engine running, 'and that's as close as people get. This is a private research facility.'

One old building that looked like it would fall down if you pushed it stood under the shadow of the volcano. Fences ran from either side of the gate north and south. We waited in the car as Taka took another set of keys from his pouch and unlocked the padlock. We drove through, stopping on the other side to relock the gate and then drove up to the building, parking in the shade. Up close the building looked even worse. It might have started out white but it was sort of yellowy now, and some bits were even green or black like there was mould growing. The ground was bare dirt like the bit in front of the hockey goals at school but it was all covered in black ash. There was no grass anywhere but there were lots of shrubs and trees. It looked like a cowboy movie. Hawks floated above. In the sunny blur the wind kicked up the ash and it stung my eyes. I took my sunglasses out of my backpack and put them on. The dust still got in the sides. I needed my swimming goggles. A grain of ash crunched between my teeth.

'We have to walk from here. It will get a little hot.'

'A little?' Mummy was already wiping her forehead. 'Leave the books in the car, you can't read and walk at the same time.'

'I can.'

'Okay, you're not going to read and walk at the same time.'

I took one last look at Pele, held the picture up with Sakurajima behind it, then placed it on the back seat. 'Are we climbing to the top, Mr Taka-san?'

'No, Carrie-chan, it's too dangerous that close. We're not even supposed to be here. There's a small cave where they do experiments. We'll go that far.'

I was disappointed but tried not to show it. That would be rude. We followed the path that zigzagged up the mountain. I slipped a few times when the rock moved and there was a small landslide behind me and I had to grab onto thin bushes to stop myself, black powder bursting into the air. Taka went first, then me, then Mummy, then Daddy at the back. Taka walked slowly and I had to watch his heels or I'd step on them. I looked back and Daddy was taking a picture of us. I hadn't taken a picture since the ferry. I took my camera out, jumped round and snapped a quick picture of Mummy and Daddy before they could pose. Maureen, a friend of Mummy's from work, told me not to let people pose. It wasn't natural and natural photos are the best. She could take great photos while the camera was resting in her lap so no one knew until they heard the click or saw the flash and by then it was too late.

'Caroline, you'll fall.' Mummy looked cross. Was it me, the heat or Daddy? I was never sure. They argued last night but they argue every night. I could always hear them. Sometimes they argued about me and that made me cry. I didn't want them to argue about me. I didn't want them to argue at all. Sometimes when they argued things got broken, like cups or ornaments. Once a door.

Taka stopped and I crashed into him. He was out of breath but making it look like he was waiting for Daddy. Daddy had stopped too and was drinking from his small silver bottle.

'What's that?' asked Mummy.

'Hair of the dog.'

'At this time of the morning?'

'It wouldn't be hair of the dog if it weren't this time of the morning.'

'This was your idea.'

'What?'

'This volcano. This hike. All of it.'

'I know. And I'm enjoying it.'

'By abdicating all responsibility to me?'

'Who's abdicating anything?'

'You'll get pissed, by yourself, and leave me to look after Caroline and sort out lunch and do everything.'

'I'm on holiday.'

'We're all on holiday.' Mummy turned her back on him and started walking again. She passed Taka and me. 'I really appreciate this, Taka-san, organising this trip, getting us onto the volcano, I know it can't have been easy. I'm sorry to expose you to our bickering.'

Taka bowed. Mummy kept on walking. Taka looked sad but I couldn't think of anything to say so I followed Mummy. She was walking fast and I almost had to run to keep up. 'Mummy, wait.' My boot caught something and I fell. Slowly a piece of rock came up to meet me, sharp, volcanic, pitted with holes. I had time to notice that, the holes all over it like a million tiny mice had been nibbling it, then everything sped up again and there was deep white pain and I was crying and someone was picking me up and someone was shouting at me because it was all my fault and I couldn't see out my left eye and I thought I was blind but then I could because it was only blood and Mummy said it was just a cut so stop screaming while she cleaned it and put a plaster on it and because Mummy was a doctor I had to listen so I tried to keep very still but she was rough and prodded and poked my head like it was dough and she was baking bread and I wanted to scream and push her away but I didn't and eventually it was over.

'Glad I brought this,' Daddy was holding out the silver bottle, 'she looks like she needs a stiff drink.'

'That's it. Come on, we're going.' Mummy started going down the way we just came. Taka looked lost.

'Hannah, calm down.' Daddy watched her go by. 'You said yourself it's just a cut.'

'It could've been her eye.'

'And that's my fault? Come on, we're nearly there, aren't we, Taka?'

He nodded. 'Five minutes. Ten.'

'Mummy, it doesn't hurt anymore. I want to see the cave.'

Defeated, she came back to us and snatched the bottle off Daddy. 'I need this more than you today. You've had enough fun for one holiday.' She drank long, coughed, put the bottle in her pocket. 'Right. Cave. Let's go.'

It was a small crack that opened into the kind of place cavemen might live. The three grown-ups sat in deck chairs surrounded by scientific equipment, fanning themselves. No one spoke. I wanted to sit down too. I felt dizzy, but the atmosphere around them was bad. I wanted to know what the machines were doing but it wasn't a good time to ask. I left my backpack next to Daddy and looked around. My head ached and it felt like there was an egg under the plaster. I wondered if there would be a scar. I had a scar on my leg where the front gear cog on my bike ripped out a chunk when we were camping at Loch Morlich. We had to go to hospital then because the cut was full of oil and grease. The scar looked like cling film instead of skin. I touched my forehead and there was blood.

I wished they'd stop fighting. At home they both worked and after school there was only one or the other, usually Daddy who could get away from work more easily except when he had to go offshore. They argued at night but I could shut them out from my room and it was only when it was really bad that I could hear. I had a tape player and headphones and I listened to tapes when it was like that. I had a couple of Carl Sagan's, and one called *Women of Science* which was all about female scientists like Marie Curie and Lise Meitner, and another which was about Darwin's voyage on the Beagle. I liked imagining him finding these huge turtles on the Galapagos islands. I'd like to go there one day. I wasn't allowed to bring my tapes with me. Since we came on holiday it had got so much worse. In the airport, on the plane, the hotel and now up a volcano.

I tried to work out myself what the experiments were. I guessed the scientists wanted to know when it would erupt, like Taka wanted to know when earthquakes would come. One machine drew squiggly lines. Another was full of some kind of liquid. Everything was dusty and ants crawled up the sides and over the top of the machines. Maybe Daddy and Taka used machines like that in their work, although Daddy said his job was mostly paperwork now, except when he had to go offshore. The pay was good, he said, but it wasn't real geology. Maybe he'd prefer studying earthquakes with Taka.

At the back, the roof of the cave came down almost to the floor. It was so low there were no experiments there, nothing. It was too small for grown-ups. I lay on the dirt and looked through the gap. I wished I had a torch. It felt nice and cool there out of the sun, resting on the ground. My eyes adjusted to the darkness and I could see a burnt red glow. I crawled forward, squeezing myself under the rock, through the low gap. It scratched my back and I knocked my head again but I made it through.

It was another cave. There was writing all over the walls, words and pictures done in charcoal like we did in art class. The red glow was coming from further ahead. I edged forward and there was a cliff. Below me was a lake of magma, scarlet and gold, boiling gently like toffee. Rivers ran into it and ran off again disappearing below the cavern walls. It smelt of barbecue and crackled like a steak on a hot plate in a restaurant. I was inside the volcano, inside the heart where all the power and heat, all the volcano's secrets were stored, waiting to erupt. In Pele's world. Her home. Her church.

The heat was different from the heat outside. The sun tried to melt you, to force all the water out of your body and leave you like a raisin. This heat warmed me like cocoa in winter, inside my heart, inside my head. I lay at the top of the cliff letting the fire wash through me and I relaxed like in a bath, like in the hot spring in Hokkaido. I could sleep there, forever.

Up above me was the dome of the mountain, the flat roof, the underside of the crater, a hole, flickering when the smoke shifted enough to let in daylight. In the smoke I saw her, Pele, the fiery, passionate goddess who controlled this, who decided when it burst, when all the bubbling magma could pour out, who decided how long it stayed locked in. She was stern and beautiful, hard and warm. She looked at me, smiled at me. The magma flared for a second, a jet fountaining up, then the surface settled again, calm. For the moment.

I woke up on the cave floor, Mummy pouring water into my mouth, over my face. She was putting a proper bandage on my head. Daddy picked me up, carried me down the mountain. The car was hot and sticky and I slept as we drove back, slept on the ferry, waking up lost, falling under again, all the while a heat in my heart, in my head, Pele's heat still with me. There was a hospital, a bed, Mummy, Daddy, Taka translating. 'I'm fine,' I tried to tell them. I just needed sleep. The heat was fading. I was too far from the volcano and as I cooled the pain returned, the pain in my head, in my heart.

I had concussion from the stone so it wasn't too serious and they let me leave. Taka wasn't there and Mummy and Daddy weren't talking. We got a taxi back to the hotel. Apart from a headache I felt much better but Mummy wouldn't let me go to the restaurant for dinner. She ordered room service.

'It was an accident. You said yourself she's fine.'

'She is now, no thanks to you.'

'How was it my fault? She was running after you not me.'

'We'd never have been on that bloody thing if it wasn't for you. I wanted to take her swimming and get some ice cream but you drag us up a volcano that's so dangerous it's closed to the public. What did you think was going to happen?'

'She's had an adventure. She can go swimming anytime she wants back home. How many volcanoes can she climb in Aberdeen?'

'Why has she got to climb volcanoes? How many other eight-year-olds are being dragged up volcanoes during the summer holidays?'

'Exactly! She's already had experiences none of her peers have had.'

'And she's got the scar to prove it.'

'I'd have killed for a father who took me to places like Japan when I was a kid. Every year we went to the same caravan site, took the same pitch, ate the same ice cream and fish and chips, swam in the same bit of the sea and it was soul-destroying. I was the only kid in my school who looked forward to term starting again. I won't have Carrie suffer a childhood like that.'

'Fine, but you don't have to go to extremes. How many kids in her class have been to a water park in Japan?'

'Kim's going to Disney World in Florida, USA.' I was starving, I hoped the food would come soon.

'Thank you, Caroline. What I'm saying, Marcus, is this is supposed to be a holiday for all of us. Spending even a few hours of that inside another bloody hospital is not my idea of a holiday. We've got one full day left in Kagoshima before we fly back to Tokyo. We're going to the water park in the morning, then we're going to have lunch in the big department store and get some souvenirs to take home. No, Marcus,' Mummy put her hand up and cut him off, 'you are not taking us to the Kamikaze museum. If you want to go you can go yourself.'

'But—'

'No, Marcus.'

'Okay, but if we're doing all that tomorrow, can we do something else tonight? Why don't we go down to the bar for a drink?'

'Caroline can't go to the bar.'

'She can stay here. You can stay here, can't you, Sweetie?'

'No, she can't, she's got concussion.'

'I'm fine, Mummy. I can read until I fall asleep.'

'Come on, Hannah,' Daddy pulled her into his chest, 'a drink will do you good.'

'On one condition.'

'Anything.'

'Flirt with one waitress and you'll be wearing your drink.'

Daddy raised his arms like he was innocent but Mummy had her doctor's face on and he dropped them to his sides. They hit with a slap.

I ate dinner and got into bed. I thought the *futon* was too hard at first but now I liked it. My body was tired all over. I lay on my side, my cut facing up, and looked again at the picture of Pele. Jane MacMillan said in her introduction that we are taught to think of men as powerful and women as weak but all through history some of the fiercest and most dangerous deities have been women. Pele could make fire and lava pour down onto villages. The Hindu goddess Sarasota gave humans the gifts of speech, wisdom and learning. The Roman Diana was goddess of hunting. I knew by then I hadn't gone into a second cave, that I'd fainted and had some kind of dream, but it didn't feel like a normal dream. The heat stayed with me long after, the smell and the sounds, and the smile Pele gave me through the smoke. Maybe it was a dream but that didn't mean it wasn't real.

I left Jane MacMillan open at Pele's picture, propped against the cedar lamp, and opened Jules Verne. They were about to climb down into the volcano. Harry was scared but he wouldn't admit it. The chapter was called "The Real Journey Commences".

Somewhere Over Russia,
June 2013

The scar was still there on my right temple, just under the hairline, hidden from the world. History written on the surface.

The face of Scotland is scarred by glaciers, geological wrinkles gouged by rivers of ice advancing, retreating for millions of years. Over enough time these scars will disappear, worn down by weather, wind and rain turning rocks to sand, washing it into the sea, washing Scotland away.

Given enough time everything erodes.

The glaciers are still retreating, global warming melting the permafrost. Each summer more and more of Greenland is exposed. The scars, the wounds. Consequences.

The end of the world.

Not that climate change is the end for the planet. We're creating the conditions for our own extinction and no geological scientist would ever confuse the two. I'd delved deep enough into the Earth to know it would get on just fine without us crawling across its skin. Better, perhaps.

Human extinction. Thirty-five thousand feet thoughts. My carbon footprint. Bigfoot.

We destroy the planet. Justify, rationalise. You push it aside, try not to think about it. Humans can get used to almost anything given enough time. Given enough pressure.

I reached over Ash and slid the shutter up a little, the clouds ivory in the twilight. Somewhere below us families were preparing for bed. All it would take was a pocket of turbulence, a bird flying into the engine, a loose wire and we'd drop on them.

All it takes is one moment to change everything.

One moment.

A misfiled paper.

A flicked switch.

One moment can create scars that take eons to erode.

Geological time. Deep time.

Aberdeen,
July 6th 1988

'You're sure Mr and Mrs Galloway don't mind?' Kim rubbed more suntan lotion into her slender legs, peeling off a piece of grass pasted to her thigh. Top notes of coconut and a hydrocarbon base took me back to a beach in Italy the summer before, Etna tenting the sky and Sicilian boys frolicking for attention, competing unfavourably with James Gleick's book on chaos theory. The Summer of Chaos, Dad called it. Italian trains. Roman roads all leading to traffic jams, gesticulating drivers and the über-stylish. Not our scene, me and Dad, St Mark's Square and espressos. This year it would be Iceland. Active volcanoes, desolate landscapes and deep faults – much more us. Iceland with Dad, Portugal with Mum the week after.

Holidays with Mum were fractal, each trip a replica of the one before. Cafés and pools, seafood restaurants and tan lines. Mum worked hard and holidays were for unspooling. Dad worked hard too but he said his holidays were for living. We hadn't been abroad as a trio since Japan.

The vicious Mediterranean sun could be a sister to the pale lemon slice warming Aberdeen. Distance from the source alters the impact. The hottest part of the flame is the blue zone. I followed the smoke from the barbecue as it drifted over the fence and into the Galloways' washing. There was music, but not too loud; people, but not too many; laughing and talking but not too much swearing. A party, but within the rules laid out by Mum and the Galloways. The Johnstones on the other side were in Spain. For the moment I could relax, let responsibility and anxiety and a never-ending list of 'what ifs' simmer.

'No, they're fine. But we can't be out here after nine.' It was only two. Twenty-two thousand two hundred seconds to go, roughly. Mark was DJing. The Stereo Nazi we called him because he wouldn't let anyone else near the hi-fi, strict fascist control and ghetto-like segregation between acceptable and unacceptable bands. He'd got the record player and tape decks set up so he could switch between tracks like a professional, he thought. I didn't care that much about music but Mark thought it was the most important thing in the world so I had to pretend, at least a little. The music was what couples did, compromised for the sake of peace. It was something with screeching guitars and he and Neil and Kevin were playing air guitar and moshing on the patio. How would they compare if the Sicilian beach boys were there? I knew which ones Kim and Lesley would choose.

'Boys,' said Kim, lying back on the tartan blanket. She 'schlepped' – her word, brought back like a souvenir – to Florida every summer and returned teak. This year she wanted to get a tan before she got there. 'It's so embarrassing,' she said as we were changing into our bikinis. 'For the first week I'm so pale and sick I look like a corpse or something while everyone else is bronzed and gorgeous.'

The granite sparkled in the sunlight. Aberdeen had a magic quality on days like that, grey transmogrifying alchemically into silver, twinkling like Tinkerbell had scattered fairy dust over the city. Really it was quartz, feldspars and micas. Muscovite gave it the silver twinkle. No less magic, and more satisfying to know. The slate roof tiles baking reminded me of the *okonomiyaki* restaurant we went to in Japan, the hot plate at the table we cooked our Japanese pancakes on. A bee bumbled over us, blithely ignoring Kim's scream. It was the third day of the school holidays but it felt like the first because it was the first day with no parents. Dad was offshore and Mum was at some conference in Bristol, had left first thing that morning.

'Now you have the number of my hotel but only use it in an emergency, okay?'

'Okay.'

'Seriously, Caroline, if I come back from a long boring meeting to a message to "call my daughter immediately" and it's because you want to know where the popcorn is, this will be the first and last time we leave you alone overnight.'

'Yes, Mum.'

'And you know the rules of the barbecue. Finish at nine o'clock and everyone goes home. Kim and Lesley can stay over. No one else. No one. Do you understand me?'

'Yes, Mum.'

'And by no one I specifically mean Mark.'

'Mum, I'm sixteen. I'll be fine.'

'What has sixteen got to do with anything? I can quite easily cancel if I think for one second you're going to break any of the rules.'

'Mum, I meant I'm sixteen, I'm not stupid.'

'I know. You're clever. That's what worries me.'

She went in the end, a taxi to the station, leaving me in charge. What had I done in my life so far to make her think an orgy was the first thing I'd plan once her back was turned? When Dad got picked up for work on Monday all he'd said was 'have fun'. She was so frustrating, like she'd got this imaginary daughter who looked like me but couldn't be trusted. The wind slid gently over the church and down into our garden, circulating lazily through the flowers, mixing scents like a casual perfumer. If it wasn't for the music and the fact that this lot were my responsibility I could have drifted off. Some peace and quiet. I shouldn't have let Kim talk me into the barbecue. Just the three of us dozing, inhaling the summer and exhaling a termload of stress, that's what I needed. Too late now.

I was cooking, my body a fatty slab of white meat grilling. Kim, and Lesley on the far side of her, loved sunbathing. They could both lie happily for hours in the sun, turning over occasionally, sizzling like eggs. The lying, the napping, I liked that bit, but the burning? Dad took me fossil hunting to Colorado a couple of years before. The ground, the rocks desiccated and baked by the sun. I pictured my skin like that, cracking like a terracotta dish, ravines opening, desperate for moisture, a lizard hotfooting across the desert of my flesh. Turned to dust, dissolved into constituent chemicals, seeping into the ground, flitting on the wind, rejoining the cycle and subducting. My atoms in a magma river circling the world, seeking release through volcanic fire, my elements in Pele's domain.

I needed to cool off.

'How's the barbecue coming?' Graeme loved barbecues. Anything outdoorsy. He went camping and hillwalking with his family every summer. Dad and I bumped into his family last Easter at Loch Morlich and we all spent the evening on the beach with a bonfire and marshmallows. Our parents talked about house prices, the downturn in the oil industry, the layoffs. Graeme and I gossiped about school, books, plans for the future. He was going to be a lawyer. When I thought of him on the sand, lit by the fire's glow, the ragged Cairngorms behind him, his muscles carved out of oak, I couldn't imagine him in a courtroom.

'Almost there. Hungry?'

'Starving.'

Julie was helping him, cutting rolls, vegetables, opening packs of paper plates, her long curly blonde hair pulled back into a loose ponytail, spirals spilling out. I couldn't think of anything to say around Julie. She and Graeme were a couple.

I went in through the kitchen and upstairs to my room, checking everything was intact as I went, straightening Mum's framed Renoir print, smoothing the one-sixteenth size kimono on its stand. My shoulders were tingling and I was already pink. That was the other thing I didn't like about sunbathing – I didn't tan. I burned. Vanilla white – lobster red – vanilla white. Even fake tan somehow didn't work and I ended up looking like an Oompa-Loompa with a liver complaint.

The safe silence of my room. My books, my pictures, the glow-in-the-dark constellations on the ceiling, my fossil collection, my suitcase open, ready for Iceland. On my windowsill a row of rocks. I rubbed my fingers over the glass-smooth moss agate, felt the tension drawn out. I shouldn't have invited everyone. Too much could go wrong. I pulled on a white T-shirt and my denim cut-off shorts. The door opened behind me just as I was doing up the buttons.

'Why are you covering up?' Mark's shaved head appeared round the door, a wispy caterpillar on his upper lip.

'Because I'm melting faster than a marshmallow in a star.'

'Yeah, but you looked good.'

'You mean I don't now?'

He put his arms around my waist and I linked my hands behind his neck the way I'd seen everyone else do when they kissed. We'd been going out for three weeks and this bit still felt awkward. Were my hands in the right place? Was I doing the right thing with my tongue? I needed to keep my eyes closed because if I opened them it wasn't sexy and I could see his skin from a centimetre away and I started thinking about cells and pores and shaving and I forgot to keep kissing. I was still waiting for sparks, for love, for something. Kissing was just this mechanical act, quite disgusting when you thought about what was actually happening. In the movies women melted when kissed. Maybe I was doing it wrong. He tried to push me back towards the bed. Off balance I took a step, slipped under his arm.

'Carrie, come on?'

'No. Not with my house full of people.'

'Later then, when they've gone.' His ears pricked up like a sheepdog. 'Fucking hell.'

He was out the door and down the stairs three at a time. Kylie hadn't even finished the first chorus of *I Should Be So Lucky* before the needle scratched across her grooves. I was going to have to think of something to put him off. He'd been hinting since the last day of term. He was getting pretty insistent. Maybe I should just let him. Kim said I should. She did it with Robert in sixth year at Hogmanay, said it wasn't that scary and only a little bit painful at first. Lesley didn't say anything. I knew she hadn't done it but she worried about whether Kim thought she was cool. I knew Kim didn't think I was cool so I didn't need to worry about it. Kim was the cool one. I was the smart one. Lesley was the one we wanted to protect. It was all so much hassle. When I was in Iceland, in a tent surrounded by volcanoes I wouldn't have to worry about that crap. I fought the urge to begin packing and returned to my post, hostess and enforcer.

The sausages and burgers were already burning. The perfect smell of summer, memories of Dad and I outside the tent sitting on folding chairs or blankets on the ground, Dad's beer and my juice in a bag in the stream to keep cool, mountain bikes chained to a nearby tree and covered in tarpaulin for when it rained, green coils of totally ineffective midge repellent, Dad putting way too much butter on the rolls, the little paint-stained portable radio playing Radio 1 or Radio 2 depending on who got to the dial first, evening drinks in a local hotel bar, lying reading while the rain battered the canvas.

Graeme handed me a roll with two sausages on a paper plate, I added some HP sauce and some tomatoes, a handful of lettuce.

'Taadaa!' Mark pulled two Co-op bags out of his rucksack and emptied their contents onto the picnic table. Three bottles of cider, twelve cans of lager and three bottles of Vodka. I checked but the shed roof hid the table from the Galloways' garden.

'Mark. Be careful.'

'Don't worry, babe, I'll take the empties with me. No one will ever know.'

Even from the far end of the garden people had noticed what was going on and gathered round, drawn by the drink. In the Easter holidays I went to a party at Ed's house when his parents were away. People were vomiting in the garden, Mark got his head shaved in the kitchen then someone spilt cider on the floor and it stuck the hair to the tiles. The music eventually brought the police and we all had to jump over the back fence and run for it. I had to take control now. My house. My rules.

'Okay. You drink from paper cups. All bottles and cans in the kitchen. I don't want a single can outside where next door can see it. And keep the noise down. If you're going to be sick, do it in the toilet but don't pass out with the door locked. And don't break anything.'

They laughed but they knew me. Mark looked relieved I hadn't thrown him out or poured his booze down the sink. He blew me a kiss and poured me a cup of cider. 'In the kitchen,' I pointed.

'Don't worry,' said Graeme, still at his post with tongs raised. 'Mark will be unconscious by dinner time. For all his bravado, he's a lightweight.'

'I shouldn't worry about him drinking himself unconscious?'

'Mark unconscious is a lot less to worry about than Mark conscious.'

I wanted to ask Graeme what he was implying, but Mark was back already. 'Cheers.' Mark sipped while watching me over the rim. I drank. His eyes smiled and he took a big gulp, emptying the mug. 'Refill.'

I loved those summer nights where it hardly ever seemed to get dark.

As the alcohol disappeared they got louder, and I moved further up the garden, into the shadow of the church, the humid richness of the greenhouse seeping out into the relaxing air. The corner, now strawberries, used to be my practice trench. Dad would hide some piece of rubbish, chicken bones, old toys I threw out, anything really, it didn't matter, then I'd practise excavating them. My own trowels, brushes, pretending Sunday's chicken was a dinosaur, which it kind of was. I'd spend hours down in the mud, Indiana Jones, while my father sat in his deckchair reading some report from work with a beer or a gin. Mum would do yoga on the grass or join him with a gin and a journal article.

The music surged up. Mrs Galloway was taking in her washing. She looked over the fence and made a face. 'Sorry, I'll turn it down.' She nodded, gestured at her watch, kind enough but I couldn't trust them not to tell my parents. I took a deep breath and plunged back in. Graeme, Tony, Julie and Kevin were standing around the still-smouldering barbecue, smoking, using a paper cup as an ashtray. Graeme had an arm around Julie, her head on his shoulder, hair hanging soft down his chest. She had a thumb tucked under his waistband at the hip. His hand on her waist, his long climber's fingers spread on her flat stomach.

I didn't have to worry too much about what was happening outside as long as Graeme was there. Inside was less controlled, bodies everywhere. Gleick said order could arise from chaos but I didn't see it. Order had to be imposed. I leaned over the sofa and turned down the stereo. Something tickled the inside of my thigh making me jump, nearly over the back of the sofa. Mark. He had a cigarette paper stuck to his forehead. It said *Kylie*. He went to kiss me but the sofa tipped and I pushed him away. 'Hey!' he said.

'Hey nothing. Why have you got *Kylie* written on your forehead?'

A bray of complaint from the rest of the room. They all had Rizlas on their foreheads.

'Why did you tell him? He'd never have got it.'

'It's a game.' Lesley had *Morrissey* on hers. 'We have to ask questions and work out who we are.'

'Can't you just ask *who am I*?'

'No, it's yes or no.' Lesley was a bit tipsy. I was surprised but saw Kim was drinking. That explained it. 'Do you want to play?'

'No, I—'

'Yeah, play!' A chorus from the circle.

'I'll do it.' Mark hauled himself off the sofa and lunged at the Rizla, 'I'll give her one.'

Laughter from the boys. I blushed. Mark slobbered all over the paper and pasted it like wallpaper to my forehead.

'Oh, that's cruel.' Neil was holding Kim's hand.

'But fair.' Kim was pretending she hadn't noticed. I'd better keep an eye on them. I didn't want them disappearing into my room. Or my parents' room.

'Quite a good match, I think.' Mark had that smug expression he reserved for when he got something right in class.

Cruel but fair? A musician, no doubt. Someone he thought I should know but didn't. He crashed down next to me, arm around my shoulder. I leaned forward, breaking out of his grip under the pretence of seeing the other names. Tom Cruise, Tiffany, Rick Astley. Neil was John Major. I couldn't quite hide my laugh. I bet Kim gave him that one. Few would have believed it to look at her, but she took a big interest in politics. The questions went round. Some got theirs easily, others, like me, struggled. Neil worked out he was a politician. He didn't know any politicians. When Kim explained who John Major was, Neil realised he had no chance with her. I was stumped. I wasn't a musician, an actor, an artist or a scientist – not that Mark knew any scientists. I should have given him Dian Fossey. I was a woman, middle-aged and British.

'Am I Margaret Thatcher?' The cheer told me I was right. 'Apt?' I looked at Mark. 'Fair?' At Kim.

'The Iron Lady.' Kim raised her cup at me. I pulled the cigarette paper off my head, scrunched it up and threw it at Mark. He caught it in his mouth and swallowed. That smug look again.

Nine swirled by. The smokers joined us in the living room. The heat was taken out of the party, folk drifted home. That suited me fine. There were dishes to do and I'd need to hoover. The chat went round. I let it wash over me. I'd only had that one cup of cider but I was tired, the sun had boiled all the energy out of me, evaporated my desire for fun and company.

Kim stretched out on the sofa, her head on Lesley's lap. 'I feel like the cinema tomorrow.'

Julie was cross-legged between the sofa and the armchair rolling cigarettes for later. 'Has anyone seen *Coming To America* yet?'

'No! I really want to see that. Eddie Murphy is brilliant,' said Kevin.

Neil was on the armchair, one leg over the side. 'Anyone fancy going to the beach?'

'To the beach or to Codonas?' Julie was taking the piss. Neil threw up once after being on the roller coaster and he'd never been allowed to forget it.

'We could go to Café Continental,' I said.

'Hot chocolates!' Kim cried. It was our favourite thing to do as a threesome.

Lesley pushed Kim's head aside and rubbed the muscle. 'Let's watch a film now.'

Mark rolled his eyes. 'That'll really kill the party. Carrie's practically asleep as it is.'

'I'm not. I'm fine.'

Kim and Lesley called out together, '*Heathers*!' We watched it whenever they stayed over, could recite all the lines.

The party split in two: the smokers – Graeme, Julie, Kevin and Tony – in the kitchen, close to the back door; Lesley, Kim and Neil in the living room. I dotted back and forth between them, checking everything was okay, making sure no one was doing anything they shouldn't. I quickly washed some glasses, put all the boozy paper cups in a plastic bag so Mum wouldn't find them in the bin. Mark followed me from room to room. I handed him a towel to dry but he played with it, a pirate, a turban, a bandit.

Maybe Graeme could take Mark home, they lived a couple of streets apart. It was still warm, still light.

'We're keeping our voices down.' Graeme was raking the charcoal in the barbecue. Julie dropped her cigarette in an overflowing paper cup ashtray.

Their hands on each other. 'Where are you going this year?' I asked him.

'We're going to France to climb Mont Blanc.'

'Really? No fair. The closest I've been is when we went skiing at Chamonix. I got some gorgeous photos.'

'I'm going there in November,' he said. 'Amateur Championships.'

'Snowboarding?'

'Yeah. When are you off to Iceland?' Graeme offered his cigarettes around.

'Next week. Dad's offshore until the end of the week.' There were more than a hundred volcanoes in Iceland. It was my present for my O-Grade results.

'Why is he offshore? I thought he worked in the office.'

'I'm not sure. He has to go off from time to time. This is one of those times.' Apart from Neil, whose dad worked at the Grammar School, all of our dads worked in the oil industry. Fathers disappearing for weeks was the norm. My dad was a geologist so occasionally he had to go out to where the rocks and oil and gas were. A 'rock sniffer' they called him.

'Are you going into oil?' Graeme tapped Mark on the head. He seemed to have fallen asleep on my shoulder.

'What?'

'The oil industry? You?'

'Sure. Not much else around here to choose from.'

'You don't have to stay in Aberdeen.' Julie wanted to move to London. She wanted to do something in theatre.

'Why would I leave? My family is here. My friends are here. The Dons are here. My girl is here.'

'You're not staying, are you?' Graeme raised an eyebrow at me.

'I might. Aberdeen is one of the best for geology.'

'But you're going to apply to others?'

'Edinburgh. Durham. I don't know. It's two years away. You're going to Glasgow?'

'That's the plan.'

'I can't imagine you as a lawyer,' said Julie.

'Me neither,' he replied.

'Hey, it's summer,' Mark had got his third or fourth wind, 'and a party. Fuck the future. Come on,' he clutched my arm tight, 'I've got something for you.'

His pestering abilities were well-known. It was that non-stop pestering that made me eventually agree to go out with him. After a while it had just seemed easier to say yes. Not having a boyfriend, not ever having had a boyfriend, was starting to become an issue. Going out with Mark would at least stop speculation. Lesley had asked me about it once. I didn't know what to say. I didn't know myself.

To save my shoulder from being yanked out I gave in and followed him. He pulled me into the house like a stubborn dog on a lead, through the kitchen and up the stairs into my bedroom.

'Mark—'

'I wanted to show you this.' He pushed me against the back of the closed door and kissed me too hard, his teeth crashing into mine. He tasted of stale beer and barbecued meat, his wet tongue wriggling in my mouth like a snake in a sack. I tried to push him back a little, get my breath, but his whole weight was pushing me into the door. It was only thin plywood and it might break. I might break. His hands were at work.

'Mark.'

He shoved my right hand down, rubbed himself still holding my wrist, a growl.

'Mark. No.'

He got my T-shirt up.

'Mark, ow. Stop.'

His weight on me, I couldn't move. I wriggled, made a bit of space, got my knees up and pushed with everything I had. He staggered back, his jeans down around his knees, and crashed into the wall, knocking my fossil display case. It shattered on the floor, rocks and glass and trilobites everywhere. All that deep history lying smashed on the floor.

'Fuck sake, bitch.'

'Mark, I said stop.'

'You said "later". You've been walking around like that all day. You're a fucking prick-tease. You should finish what you started.'

'I didn't say later. You did. I don't want—'

The door opened and Graeme walked in. 'Everything all right?'

'Fuck off, this is none of your business, get the fuck out.'

'It is my business. Carrie, do you want him gone?' I nodded. 'Then it's time to go.'

'You gonna make me?'

Graeme shrugged, stepped forward and smashed Mark hard and fast in the face. He fell to the floor, blood flowing between his fingers. 'Carrie, go into the bathroom and sort yourself out. I'll make sure he's gone.'

I locked the door, sat on the edge of the bath, numb. I shut my eyes and the strongest memory hit me. I was lying on the floor of the cave in Japan looking down into the magma chamber and above me Pele rose. Her heat came again, as strong as it did eight years ago, the fire rousing my blood, baking my bones. I pushed the heel of my palms deeper into my eye sockets, saw red mist, saw Pele, her face ambivalent, a mixture of rage and sympathy. Below me the magma came to the boil, bubbles of escaping gasses umbrellaed the surface, charcoal and sulphur filled my senses. I launched to my feet, ripped the door open.

Lesley and Kim were there, huddled, deciding whether to knock. 'Are you okay?'

I pushed by them, looking for Mark. I was going to blow up, I was going to explode. He wasn't in the house, the front door was open, Graeme was sitting on the wall, smoking. 'He's gone. I doubt he'll be back but I'll wait here a while.'

The cool summer breeze, Graeme's calm words. There was no one else on the street. Everyone was at my door looking out. They'd want to know details.

'Thanks Graeme. How's your hand?' He showed me a cut in his knuckles.

Teeth marks. 'Thank you. I don't—'

'Don't worry about it,' he looked closely at my face. 'He did this, not you.'

'Aye.'

Everyone in my doorway. People crowded round me, hugged, touching my shoulder. I pushed through into the kitchen, lifted the vodka and swigged straight from the bottle. It scorched my throat on the way down, again when I coughed, but it was good, cauterising. I took another swig.

'Here,' Graeme handed me a spliff, 'this is less harsh.'

We went outside, lit, drew, coughed, drew again. He was right, my head disengaged, my muscles untensed, unreeling like a fishing line. I walked over to the lawn, lay back on the soft, scented grass. Another draw. The stars spun, the washing line quivered. Voices receded. I tried to say something but nothing came. It didn't matter. I drifted. The last thing I saw was Pele watching me from the stars.

I woke with a start, a helicopter chopping overhead, sat up and watched it land at the hospital. Alone in the garden, the house was silent, the lights off. I stood, unsteady, remembered. The bottle and the roach weren't there. The helicopter lifted again, headed off across the city towards the coast. Was it picking up or dropping off? The hypnotic beat of the rotors through the silent sky. My mind flickering pictures of Mark in my room. Tears came again. Maybe Mark was right and I was a prick-tease. I didn't want to be. What did I say when he said 'later'? I knew I hadn't said yes, but I couldn't remember if I said no. Thank God Graeme was there. I saw Mark's nose buckle. School was going to be hell. An endless summer, that's all I wanted.

'Caroline? Are you okay?'

'Mr Galloway, you startled me.'

The fence was low enough that he could rest his arms on it. His white hair was mussed from sleeping and it looked like he was in his pyjamas. Mr Galloway used to work for the same company as my dad but had retired. They had a big garden party and went on a cruise.

'*You* startled *me*. I got up for the bathroom and I heard a helicopter coming in so I looked out of the window and saw someone sitting on your lawn. Are you sure you're okay?'

'I'm fine, thanks. I heard the helicopter as well. It landed and took off again really quickly.'

'Unusual at this time of night. That's why I switched the telly on. Have you seen the news?'

'No? Why?'

'There's been some kind of accident offshore. Caroline, which platform is your father on?'

'What kind of accident?'

'The news isn't clear. A fire on Piper Alpha.'

Mr Galloway was speaking from somewhere on the moon, a woozy bass that I could feel more than hear, like when the batteries went in my Walkman and the audiobook fell into a black hole, stretched and deepened.

'Caroline?'

'Yes.'

'Are you alone?'

'I…I don't know.'

'Do you have a number for your mother?'

'Inside.'

'Go inside. Elaine and I will be over in a minute.' I looked at him. Saw him. Did he just speak?

Kim and Lesley were still up, under a double duvet at either end of the couch watching *The Breakfast Club*. It was the final scene, detention over, the cast walked out into Saturday sunshine, their lives ahead of them. Simple Minds kicked in, *Don't You (Forget About Me)*. The rest of the house was empty, throbbing with it. The party long over, Mark's echo stalking the stairs. I flicked through all four channels. Nothing. Nothing. No fire. No accident offshore. Mr Galloway was a dream and nothing more, the helicopter nothing to do with me.

Doorbell.

'What's going on?' Kim was almost asleep, wriggled upright.

'Did you get cold? Kim wanted to wake you but Graeme said to let you sleep it off. Was that right?'

What was she talking about? I flicked channels again. Nothing. The doorbell.

Mr and Mrs Galloway came in. No one locked the door. Or they had a key. I couldn't remember. He was properly dressed now. She'd got trousers on and a coat but I could see her nightie underneath. It was blue with yellow flowers. Kim and Lesley glanced around the room for anything incriminating.

'Hi girls,' said Mrs Galloway. 'Is there anyone else in the house?'

'No.'

'There's nothing on TV,' I said. 'Are you sure?'

'There are bulletins through the night. It's nearly half twelve. You should sit down.'

'I'll get the kettle on.' Mrs Galloway went into the kitchen. I didn't think to check on the way through if there was any drink left. I ran, beat her to it, pushing by her. But it was okay, there were no cans, no bottles. A smell of cigarettes from the bin, that was it. I stood in the kitchen. I didn't know what to do. None of this made sense. I must still be dreaming, out on the lawn.

'Caroline, it's on.'

'Go on through, I'll make a pot of tea.'

Grampian TV said Mr Galloway was telling the truth. A fire offshore. A rescue operation underway. The helicopter we'd heard was taking doctors to the *Tharos*, a semi-submersible platform nearby. As we listened another helicopter buzzed overhead. Mr Galloway pulled the curtains back and looked.

'Coming in.'

'Survivors will be taken to Aberdeen Royal Infirmary by helicopter,' said the TV. They had no film, just old photos of Piper Alpha. It looked fine. A bright, clear day out at sea. Maybe he was on that helicopter, maybe he was already at the hospital and no one there to meet him. Maybe he was coming on the next one and I still had time, it only took five or ten minutes to walk to A&E from here. Maybe he wasn't on the helicopter. Maybe he wouldn't be on any.

'We need to call your mother.' Mr Galloway switched the TV off. 'Where's the number?'

It was by the phone. I unfroze, adrenaline peaking. I needed to call her. I needed to do it. These people were neighbours, this was my house. They didn't belong there. I did. I was in charge. I needed to do something, something to regain control. This was something I could do.

'Carrie, is that where your dad is?' I'd forgotten Kim and Lesley were even there. I couldn't look at them. Their faces, scared, small and frightened, like children. There couldn't be fear. I couldn't be small. In control. In control.

I dialled.

It rang. It rang.

A voice, male and full of sleep, 'Yes, Frank Carpenter, what is it?'

'Oh, I'm sorry, I must have dialled the wrong number. I was

looking for Doctor Hannah Fraser.'

'Shit. Hang on.'

Mumblings. Rumblings. Scratching on the phone. What kind of hotel was this?

'Caroline, what the hell are you doing? Do you know what time it is?'

'Mum, there's...' I couldn't say it. There were no words, nothing there.

'Caroline?'

I was sitting on the floor looking at the phone. Where were the words? I was in control so why wasn't my body doing what I told it?

Mr Galloway took the phone from me. 'Hannah? It's Doug Galloway... No, everything here is fine but... No, it's not about Caroline or anything with the party. I'm sorry, Hannah, will you please listen to me? There's been an accident offshore. Marcus is on Piper Alpha, isn't he?... No, we don't know. The TV says a rescue operation is under way. I thought you should know right away...yes, we'll take care of her until you can get back...yes, if we hear anything before then. It's no problem, see you soon.' He hung up. 'She'll get the first train back in the morning.'

'Come on, Caroline,' Mrs Galloway had the tea things on a tray. 'You can't sit there.'

She wasn't at a hotel. She was in bed with whoever Frank Carpenter was.

When two tectonic plates meet, one of them is forced under the other. It's called subduction. One rises and becomes mountains. The other sinks into the earth. This causes earthquakes, tsunamis and volcanic activity. One plate must win out over the other.

I grabbed my jacket.

'I'm going to find my dad.'

Outside in the fresh night air, alone on the street with wind and muffled starlight, summer scent from the gardens, from Westburn Park. Deep breath. I was back in control. Minds are just machines, organic machines, thoughts controlled by electricity and proteins and pathways and can therefore be rerouted, diverted, pushed into sidings. Control. Deep breath. There were two halves of my brain. The half that was emotional and terrified and crying *Daddy Daddy Daddy*. The half that was rational and scientific and controlling my heart rate and my left right left right walking and organising those thoughts. Would I be a gibbering wreck or a rational being? All those nights lying listening to them argue, trying to block it out, trying not to think of words like 'divorce', 'separation', 'estranged', 'dysfunctional'. You could use physical distractors like audiobooks which cut out sound and engaged the intellect. I didn't have my Walkman with me. So how else could you escape the present? With memories and dreams, Christmases past and future, holidays and university. It was kind of like what Buddhists do, we learned in RE, with meditation. You let the mind drift, find its own equilibrium. Except without surrendering control. Buddhists floated on water letting the currents take them. My technique was more like cycling downhill; the momentum of the bike and the laws of physics dictated the speed and direction but I still had my hands on the handlebars, fingering the brakes in case I needed to swerve. Or stop. To retain rational control of an animalistic brain, you distracted the panicky pup with warm and cuddly memories and shiny, shiny hopes. Deep breath.

I turned onto Westburn Road, the solid, reliable granite and fragile-looking modern metal and plastic hybrid of Aberdeen Royal Infirmary. Foresterhill, where I was born, where I went with a broken arm, another time with broken fingers and most recently with a broken rib. The arm and the fingers I was vaguely proud of, the former done while skiing, the latter while abseiling. The rib was thoroughly embarrassing. Kim, Lesley and I were walking down Union Street one weekend on our way shopping. We were messing about, dancing around, pushing each other into passing boys. I tried a *Singing in the Rain* style jump onto the steps of the Music Hall and missed, cracked my rib on the top step. I thought it was just bruised and we went to the cinema but all the way through I couldn't laugh or eat popcorn or, by the end, stand up without help, because of this excruciating pierce in my chest. Dad picked us up and Mum said I was exaggerating.

ARI, where Mum worked. Having a mother who was a doctor was a blessing and a curse. Those times in A&E, she was a huge help, explaining things to me and scaring the crap out of the nurses so I got seen quickly. No waiting time when a surgeon's daughter is in the house. But that was only when she accepted I had broken bones. With my rib, she refused point blank to believe I'd broken it. Same with the arm. Take a couple of aspirin and it'll be better in the morning. Except the pain was so bad I couldn't sleep. All kids of medics go through this; everyone has similar stories. Our parents see so much worse every day that our aches and pains get minimalised. It's not deliberate, it's not cruel, it's kind of understandable. A matter of scale. Heart surgeons crack ribs all day long, it's how you get into the heart. You can't touch someone's heart without breaking bones.

Who was Frank Carpenter?

That song was going round and round my head, I knew all the words from start to finish, the amount of times we'd watched *The Breakfast Club*. Detention was never like that film. Apart from the start where everyone was bored, maybe. You just sat there doing your homework until even the teacher had had enough and let you go. Pretty much what you'd do after school anyway, just still in uniform. I got detention before the end of term for telling Mr Mitchell that he was wrong. We were reviewing photosynthesis and he wrote the basic formula on the board $6CO_2 + 6H_2O \rightarrow C_6H_{12}O_6 + 6O_2$ only he missed the 1 in H_{12} making it H_2 which was obviously wrong. Only Mr Mitchell didn't like being told he was wrong.

I crossed the road and stepped over the low wall that separated the hospital from the pavement. The grass was dry and soft, freshly cut. Grass was like home to me. All the trips we went on,

Colorado, Sicily, Sakurajima, Spain, Greece, they were all dusty landscapes, scrub bushes, grass that cut your feet, or sand and rock from horizon to horizon. When I came home, when we came in over the coast to land in Aberdeen, the full frequency range of greens on display was like a welcome mat laid out for me. In the window seat peering down I could already feel the spongy give, smell the tangy crispness.

I paused to breathe deep the lawn, the memories.

There were people, reporters I assumed, around the helipad. Maybe some relatives. It was the middle of the night, how many were awake, watching the news? How many were sleeping soundly, wrapped in comforting ignorance of whatever was going on a hundred odd miles from here?

I'd no idea how many people were even on a platform at any one time.

Dozens? Hundreds? Thousands?

Velcro grass, my feet fixed. Walking in the dark it was easy to lose myself in memories and futures. I was about to step inside the hospital where reality was splashed on the floor, echoed around the corridors, carried through the ventilation. Hospitals were where the truth of our weakness was laid bare. Meatbags rotting, fragile machines falling apart. Hospitals were the front line in the fight against entropy, where the laws of the universe were challenged. Where we lost the battle.

I bypassed the reporters and followed the road from the helipad to A&E, a shortcut through Foresterhill I took whenever I went to Lesley's house. There were people outside A&E, relatives it looked like, smoking. Clusters of sleep hair and thrown together clothes, hands on shoulders, heads bowed under weight, heads raised to the purple summer night, ears pricked for rotors. Eyes ran over me, assessed me for news, passed on. Through the ominous yellow entrance and it was chaos, proper Gleick chaos, ordered disorder, like it was on *Casualty*, people everywhere, doctors, nurses, patients, more relatives. It didn't seem real. Maybe they were all actors. At school we learned that in 1938 Orson Welles broadcast *The War of the Worlds* on radio and the listeners thought it was the news. They panicked, ran from their homes, blocked the highways.

I went up to the counter.

'Yes?' The nurse barely looked up, that voice of exasperation – couldn't I see she was run off her feet? She was overweight and the tiredness made her look older than she really was. She looked like she hadn't had a holiday in years, skin pale with teabag blotches. I reached in for my mother's voice, the voice of authority. To be in control you had to convince others that you were in control. Teachers, doctors, politicians, they have that voice. A flash of Mark's smug face: the Iron Lady. So be it.

'My name is Caroline Fraser. My mother is Doctor Hannah Fraser, she works here. My father is on Piper Alpha. I want to know what's happening.'

The exasperation still there but it softened. 'Doesn't your mother know?'

'She's at a conference.' *Yes, this is Frank Carpenter. What is it?*

'Are you here alone? How old are you?'

'Sixteen. Will you tell me what's happening?'

'The relatives are all in a waiting room. You should go there. When we have news you'll be told in there.'

'You don't know anything?'

'Cathy, would you show this girl where the relatives are?'

Cathy was small and quite young. Mousy, her glasses had a turquoise tint. She smiled sympathetically and held out a hand like she was directing traffic. 'What's your name?'

'Caroline. Carrie.'

'Nice to meet you. Are you here by yourself?'

'My mum's in Bristol at…she's in Bristol. My dad's…'

'Your grandparents?'

'My mum's parents retired to France. Dad's are dead.'

She showed me into a full waiting room. When the door opened every face turned to us. The expressions, the exhaustion, the tears, that was a room waiting for horror. I turned back to Cathy but she was quietly easing the door closed.

Silence. Then noise hit me like an eruption. There were

about forty people in the room, including some young children. Questions overwhelmed, smothering me like ash.

'What did they tell you?'

'What news is there?'

'Did they give you any names?'

I shook my head. They turned back into their groups and held each other. There were no empty seats so I slid down the wall and sat on the floor. This room reflected me, uncovered what I was trying to hide. I looked at the space between my feet.

A man came in holding up his hands. His kindly smile showed a man barely above water. 'I'm sorry, I have no more news. This room is a little cramped, isn't it? Why don't we all move to the chapel? There's more space there and we've set up some tea and biscuits for you. So, if you'd all like to follow me...'

There were no more memories, no more hopes, just one, just the one.

Come back to me.

I let myself be led.

We traipsed after him.

We sat down.

Some of the kids got a biscuit.

There was a window overlooking the helipad.

We sat.

Others came in.

No news.

A minister came.

No news.

Just a comforting word and a hand on the shoulder.

We sat.

There must have been near two hundred people.

Mothers.

Wives.

Children.

Brothers.

Fathers.

No news.

'Are you here by yourself, love?' The woman next to me had a baby asleep in her arms. Soft fuzzy head, rolls of puppy fat like sleeves on a puffer jacket. 'It's your dad on the Piper?'

I nodded.

'Same as this one. He's due back tomorrow. Needs to finish the painting. You should see the house, the state of it. Masking tape everywhere, everything under sheets. We moved in six months ago. A fixer-upper, lovely wee cottage out towards Ellon. He's from Ellon, see? But with him being offshore that much and me with this one to look after, there's never enough time to get it finished, never enough in the day. I told him we could get someone in, a professional like, and just get it over and done with but you know what they're like up here, why pay for something you can do yourself? He's a painter himself after all which is part of the problem. If you spend your days painting an oil rig the last thing you want to do on your time off is more painting. He'd much rather spend it on his arse in front of the golf or in the pub. He's due home tomorrow.'

Someone brought in a TV.

We sat.

I took a look out the window. Next to me, an elderly man, about the age of Mr Galloway, leaned against the frame absentmindedly picking a whorl in the wood, his eyes fixed on the helipad.

'This city's seen some tragedies over the years, lassie. Now it's oil but before that it was the fishing. There's a decent living to be made out of the North Sea, God saw sure it was well stocked with things we'd find useful, but by Christ He made the cost too high. A fair few I grew up with never came back. Most folks my age'll tell you the same. But youth can't be told. My son thinks the ocean is a playground for him to muck about in, as if it's not dangerous enough without strapping your air to your back and going hundreds of feet under it. Tried to get me out there once, a birthday present he called it but I've no death wish. You'll never catch me scuba diving. I'm a fishmonger, my brother was a fisherman. He'd catch them, I'd sell them. Made a decent living at it but the industry's on its back now. Never did recover from the Cod Wars and those thieving Icelandic bastards. And to think I was thankful he never went into the fishing.'

We sat. No names.

People were talking. The sound of your voice drowned the sound of your thoughts. The prosaic. The everyday. No one asked questions. We were radios, broadcasting only. We were not set to receive, not that night. Only me. I needed their voices to drown out mine. *Who is Frank Carpenter?* They were my talking books, my stories. I didn't need to prompt.

'Not a single representative here, no one with any information. Hiding away in their offices behind locked doors and security, probably all on their way to the airport non-stop for LA in private jets while my husband is out there in God knows what kind of misery. He said it would happen. They all said it would happen, didn't they, Maggie? After the fire in eighty-four. All the cutbacks, cutting corners and scrimping on safety. Easy to cut a safety budget when the most dangerous thing you have to face is Great Northern Road on your way to the office and your comfy desk, easy to cut other people's safety when you don't have to stand face-to-face with the men you put in danger. He said this would happen, didn't he, Maggie? He said it was a death trap.'

It was 2:30.

No names.

Helicopter ETA 3:30.

Estimated Time of Arrival.

We sat.

No names.

The Dutch boy who stuck his finger in the dyke, if he ever existed, must have had doubts. There was a point when, finger aching, arm rigid, back stiff, he realised he couldn't do this forever. The sea would win eventually. What was natural was necessarily more patient than the man made. No amount of fingers would hold back the flood.

Maybe he was already dead.

My dad, the man who taught me to play tennis against the garage wall, who first called me Carrie, who introduced me to the deep history of time, the sculpting processes of the earth, to creatures who swam in the warm oceans, who first made me an ice cream float, took me to see *ET*, shared a private world of gestures, looks and smiles. My dad who was burning covered in oil, his flesh melting off him like he had opened the Arc of the Covenant, a campfire marshmallow black and bubbling, a witch, a Joan of Arc burnt alive, an offering to Pele. My dad who was floating in the North Sea, face down, sucking in water, a lifejacket that broke his neck as he hit the water at terminal velocity leaping a hundred and eighty feet out of the frying pan, his corpse drifting with the current, oil industry jetsam, a bottled up message circling the planet in a decaying orbit until the weight of continued existence dragged him to the bottom, Davy Jones' locker, an unmarked grave. My dad who was fighting for survival in a dingy, on a rescue boat, on the *Tharos*, on a helicopter, burns wrapped in silver, broken bones splinted with salvaged wood, dehydration fought with drips, slipping in and out of consciousness, mumbling words to himself, my name maybe, wondering if he'll see his wife again who at that moment was kissing Frank Carpenter goodbye as the taxi driver put her suitcase in the boot and yawned, and my finger broke, the ocean burst through the wall and I heard this voice that was distantly connected to me wail out, I felt my face melt too, tears and snot and all my hope dribbling down my face and there was an arm around me, *poor lassie here all by herself*, and another of the endless supply of tissues and I cried and cried and cried because he was gone, he was alive, he was dead, he would be there soon and if I never ever saw him again what would I do? How would I survive in a world without my dad? I couldn't say goodbye. I couldn't say I love you. I couldn't say sorry. I couldn't say thank you. I couldn't say how much I was looking forward to going to Iceland with him. How much I wished it was her. I couldn't say how much I hated myself for thinking that and how much I hated myself because I knew it was true because if he was gone and she had Frank Carpenter who did I have? I was empty, all cried out, a vacuum, and Pele moved into the space bringing her fire, her heat, and I was all magma and seismic quakes and I wanted to smash something, crush something, I wanted to smash her, crush her because she wasn't there and if by some miracle he was on a helicopter she wouldn't be there for that either and all he had was me and all I had was him and for all I knew all I had was nothing, no one, because he was ash, he was fish food, he was vaporised in the hottest part of the flame, the blue zone, his atoms dispersed into the air following the laws of quantum mechanics, fluid dynamics, at the mercy of meteorology, precipitation, the nitrogen cycle, photosynthesis, subduction, thermodynamics, and I was alone, outside nature looking in with my microscope and magnifying glass and archaeologist's brush and chisel and I would live my life wondering if the carbon or nitrogen or hydrogen or oxygen I was testing was once part of my dad, his blue eyes maybe, or a piece of his stubble. A clipped finger nail. The hard skin on his feet. The scar tissue on his chest from the motorbike crash when he was nineteen.

And then we heard it. Thrum. Beat. Rotors. A crush to the window, a dive to the door, we ran, pushing the backs of those in front, little steps in a crowded space. Through A&E and out, spread around the entrance, lining the road like a parade was coming. It was still dark, the helicopter's lights fearsomely bright, a UFO coming down for us, nose raised, a yellow Sea King whipping up a tempest. Around the helipad ambulances and reporters, their puny flashes batted away by those fierce landing lights. A door burst open, nurses and paramedics darted forward with stretchers and blankets. One man on a stretcher, burn foil glinting in the camera flashes, another man holding his drip, into an ambulance and they drove the short road to us. We parted, a Red Sea of hope, we needed faces, we needed names. The stretcher rushed past, the face covered. The other man walked by, head down, he wouldn't meet our eyes. He didn't have anything for us.

There were more emotions here than there were words. We were causing a jam, crushed faces, eyes on the sky, there must be more helicopters, more survivors. Ushered inside, back to the chapel past the whiteboard, 3.30 erased, 3.40 drawn in, more were coming. We fought for window space. No one spoke now. Some cried silently. My hands were clammy, nail marks in the palm, blood drawn on a chewed lip.

The first helicopter left.

The next landed. Seven men, all on stretchers. Another charge, but some of us stayed. In A&E there was a woman with a list of names. They would come and get us. They couldn't all be in that one helicopter. But I needed news. I needed names. A&E looked like something out of *M*A*S*H*. The man who walked off the first helicopter holding the drip was on the phone. His wife, I guessed. She'd be at home, not in Bristol with Frank Carpenter.

We waited.

I moved between the chapel and A&E. There was no place for me.

No one from the company came. We had a minister and the Head of Public Relations for the hospital. No one from the company.

More helicopters. Walking wounded. The worst came first. The survivors. They kept using that word. If some were called survivors then some weren't. The worst came first. The dead last. The longer we waited.

Names on the list. She gave each man an identity bracelet.

A woman shouted that she could see her husband, rushed from the chapel. I followed her to A&E.

It wasn't him.

She broke down, there on the floor of A&E.

As the men came in they glanced at our faces. Then they looked away.

What had they seen?

We sat.

No names.

No news.

Five helicopters.

Six.

Seven.

Eight.

Nine.

Ten.

Out on the road. The crowd must have been five hundred, relatives, press. The eleventh helicopter landed. I couldn't see anything. The ambulance sirens parted us. Then he was there. I saw him step from the ambulance, a blanket around him. The plug blew and the lava poured out, I screamed '*Dad*', elbowed people out of the way, crashed into him and nearly knocked him off his feet. A nurse tried to part us but I found his hand and squeezed with everything I had. He put his arm around me and we went inside. We didn't speak. He answered the questions, got his bracelet. They tried to separate us again so they could check him but neither of us would let go, so they gave in. He had burns on his hands but that was it. They bandaged him up and let us go.

'Let's go home.' He kissed me on the head and I started crying again. 'Did you speak to your mother?'

'Yes, I...' His face, his eyes. 'Mr Galloway spoke to her. She's getting the first train back.'

'How was the party?'

'What party?'

'We can talk later. Let's get out of here.'

'Excuse me, Mr...' Someone from the hospital.

'Fraser, Marcus Fraser.'

'If you would accompany me, any survivors who haven't been admitted to hospital are being taken to the Skean Dhu hotel. The police need statements from you all.'

'Now? I'd really like to go home with my daughter.'

'I'm sorry, sir.'

'How long will it take?'

'I don't know, sir. But there are showers and a change of

clothes. You and the other survivors will be made very comfortable.'

Dad paused for a moment, looked around him like he'd just woken up. 'Survivors? How many?'

'Sir...'

'How many?'

'I don't have exact figures. About sixty, I think.'

'Sixty? Out of how many?'

'Two hundred and twenty-seven.'

He sagged, near enough collapsed. The man caught him, sat him down.

'Dad,' I rubbed his arm, 'you go to the hotel. The sooner you go, the sooner you can come home. I'll get everything ready. A warm bath, some food, okay?' He looked at me, and it was like seeing him as a child. 'Okay, Dad?'

He nodded. The man took him out to a minibus and away.

The whiteboard said 'Next helicopter ETA'. There was no time written. In the chapel the minister was speaking.

'There will be no more helicopters.'

Aberdeen,
June 2013

Marcus looked out at the two-thirds empty lecture hall. It was his third year of part-time teaching at the University of Aberdeen and even he'd grown bored with the sound of his own voice. The clock at the back of the hall showed 11:33. Twenty-seven minutes to go and he was done for the day, done for the week. Paperwork – check. Calls returned to Total and Shell – check. Inbox clear of anything important – check. Confirmation of attendance at next week's Geological & Earth Sciences Conference...

Silence in the room. He'd lost his place, stopped speaking for long enough that everyone was staring at him. These were summer school students, keen to learn, paying attention.

'Any questions so far?' He turned to the next page and started from the top. It was turgid. Marcus usually ran two classes. The class on Health, Safety and Risk Ethics was one: with the discussions, the arguments, the implications. Profit versus risk, health and safety regulation versus on-the-job common sense. Responsibility. In the event of an accident, in the event of a disaster, who was responsible?

Then there was this class, which he was delivering verbatim even though it was advertised as a one-off to attract this international crowd, all future high-flyers. Oil Field Redevelopment. What do you do when all the oil and gas is gone? Do you pack up and fuck off or are there options? These questions would become real in their working lifetimes, though with a bit of luck he'd be dead by then. He'd lived through enough oil slumps, had seen the damage a drop in price could inflict on Aberdeen. God only knew what a full-scale withdrawal by the industry would do to the city. But North Sea oil was running out, they said. Although that was probably just scare tactics ahead of the referendum.

11:47. Thirteen minutes. He had everything with him, didn't

even need to swing back to the office, just straight to the Machar for a pint of Guinness and maybe some scran. He could already taste the creaminess, the richness sliding down his throat, the alcohol flicking his switches, bringing him to life. But he had thirteen more minutes to work first. That was the deal that got him this job in the first place. The deal with Isobel that meant they could be together. The deal with Dr Shaw. Weekends only. Nothing during the week. Not anymore. At 12:00 it was officially the weekend. He'd kept his side of the deal for another week. His liver was his own until Monday morning.

Monday morning. 10:00. MacRobert lecture hall, *Geothermal Energy Extraction and Collateral Seismic Events* by Professor Caroline Fraser. Professor at her age. They'd have to start inventing positions just so they could promote her. Surely she'd win the Vetlesen Prize at some point, the Nobel for geologists.

'Any questions?'

No. Out the door before the students realised he was done, into the car park between the Meston and Fraser Noble buildings, the new library all glitter and glass in the autumn sunshine, turned right across Elphinstone Road and down the alley to the smell of fresh pies, left onto the High Street and its treacherous picturesque cobbles, a spring in his step, marching through such a beautiful campus on such a beautiful day to such a beautiful goal, the little cottages, the idiosyncratic ancient walls and modern geometrical granite buildings, just a few steps beyond the bank and in through the black door.

He still missed the smell of smoke that used to envelop old bars like this. You could fit the Machar into a railway carriage. Seats and tables along the left wall, bar along the right, toilets and dartboard at the back. His corner was free, back to the wall, cash on the counter, 'the usual Marcus?' from Duncan the barman, big of heart and big of gut, University Rugby Club shirt and a mug of tea in his special mug, the white one with the black handle and U N T in black, the handle making the C. Pint handed over, correctly settled, head an exact three quarters of an inch, no fucking stupid harp etched onto the top. Quality craftsmanship. Almost seemed a shame to ruin the effect. Almost. The chill of the glass, the familiar curves spooned by the scars on his palms.

He drank.

Tomorrow they'd go out to Bennachie, him and Isobel. Part of the deal. She'd do the driving if he got some exercise. A decent walk, a pub lunch in Kemnay, back into town for whatever fun the evening held. They did that every weekend, a different walk but the same routine. Loch of Skene, Findhorn, Scolty sometimes, out to Braemar, Ballatar. Some proper hills, not that he could climb them, not with his hip, but the view was enough. Lochnagar. Loch Muick. He liked Loch Muick best. There was a bench there dedicated to a good friend from his oil days, a helicopter pilot. He liked to sit on the bench and have a tot from the flask. Remember Mike, toast him.

Should auld acquaintance be forgot.

She might be in the city already, getting a taxi from the airport to some hotel. A hotel in her hometown. He didn't know. Didn't know she was coming until he'd seen the conference schedule, seen her name.

He nodded at Duncan. He'd reached the level where the glass narrowed. If Duncan began pouring now it would be settled and ready just as the last mouthful trickled down his gullet, tickling his tonsils according to the laws of fluid dynamics. He wanted a fag but it would mean going outside and he couldn't take his pint with him. Three pints. Piss then fag. Repeat. Repeat again with variation, usually a whisky chaser or a G&T to freshen the palate.

How he missed the peaks. Nobody to blame but himself and it could be a hell of a lot worse. He looked his age, he knew, if not more. Taka had come out from Japan last year, the first time they'd met up in ages. Bloody Japanese genes, Taka looked about fifty. Lost all the weight, gym twice a week, tennis, golf. Still liked a drink though. Still couldn't handle it. He'd joined them on one of their weekend walks, they'd stopped at the Huntly Arms Hotel in Aboyne for lunch and Marcus had ended up getting thrown out. The barman took one look at Taka and switched the TV from some game show to the History Channel, a programme about the Bataan Death March. Marcus asked him to change it. He wouldn't. Marcus told him to change it. He said no. Marcus was warned. Marcus tried to rip the TV off its bracket. Marcus was thrown out. He felt justified. Racist bastards. He'd never drink there again.

One o'clock. He was the only adult in the bar, the rest were students, postgrads by the look. Did Carrie drink here when she was an undergrad? She'd had her heart set on Edinburgh, he knew that, knew she hadn't applied. The scars on his palms twitched. She'd stayed to look after him.

He finished his third, went for a piss, out for a fag in the street. She did well here, Carrie. First Class Honours, won prizes, had her pick of postgrad courses. Did she spend much time in Blackwell's, browsing the shelves? Lunch in the refectory or a sandwich from the bakery? Sitting alone with a textbook or in a group on the grass, heads on legs, all talk and jokes and plans for later that night, that term, that year?

His pride was muddied with guilt. How little he knew of his daughter's life, even when she lived at home. A shared house only in fact. Those years when she should have been out having fun, making mistakes, drinking, sleeping around, cramming for exams, those years he had stolen from her, Hannah had stolen from her. Then she left. Standing in the doorway watching her load her bags into the taxi. Eleven in the morning and he wasn't safe to drive, not by a long way.

A toot from the cab. Time to go.

'All right, Marcus?'

He jumped, a hand on his shoulder. Done it again, lost in memories, living in the past. He stubbed the fag out, turning from Harry to wipe his eyes. Harry wouldn't say anything. Harry understood.

'You coming in? It's nippy out of the sun.'

Marcus's next pint was waiting for him, Duncan pumped the IPA when he saw Harry, placed it down. Marcus beat Harry with the tenner. 'So you got away?'

'Yes, done all I can for the moment. You know what it's like, send out queries, ask people to do things and then you can't do anything until they get back, until they do their job. So I thought I'd come and seek you here in this den of iniquity.'

Harry Boyle was from Donegal originally, by way of Trinity College, Dublin and Oxford. As a lecturer he'd favoured cords and woolly jumpers, a flat cap when outside, big hiking boots whether he was in the classroom or out in the field. Once he moved into management, started making his way up the ladder to Head of Department and found himself with little time for teaching or research, he edged into shirts and ties.

'Off out tramping the countryside tomorrow?' Harry asked. 'Where is it this week?'

'Bennachie.'

'You'll have the weather for it.' There must be some problems with the conference – Harry's pint was disappearing faster than normal. 'I might take the mutt for a leg-stretching along the beach.'

'Just down here?' Marcus pointed beyond the edge of campus, over the golf course where the North Sea started.

'Just down here. The mutt prefers Balmedie but have you been up there since they let that arse Trump build his eighteen holes? Ruined it. That's your SNP for you.'

Harry was hoping for an argument. Marcus waved at Duncan.

'I'll get these,' said Harry, draining his pint.

'So what's up?'

'Oh, nothing. Usual fuck-ups, double bookings, confusion. You'd think Aberdeen was on the moon the way some of these arseholes are behaving. No doubt we'll get a week of Americans saying "why couldn't we have it in America?". The English complaining about the cold, the French complaining about the food, the Germans complaining about things not being well organised and the Japanese pissing off every five minutes to play golf.'

'Any more stereotypes you want to roll out?'

Harry laughed. Marcus let him rattle on, getting it all off his chest. Some people liked to talk their stress out, others nursed it to keep it warm like Tam O'Shanter's wife and her wrath. Marcus had been the latter. Still was, to a certain extent. Harry would have two pints and a bit of a rant, then he'd be purged.

'Well,' he said when he was done, draining his glass. 'Back to the grindstone. You'll be here later?'

'Chances are.'

'Cheers Duncan.'

'Harry...'

Harry stopped at the door, turned back towards him. Marcus couldn't speak. He wanted to ask, wanted to say something but he couldn't, the words were blocked.

'Marcus?'

'Nothing. I...' Harry came back over, put his hand on Marcus's shoulder.

Marcus flinched at the touch. 'Nothing, Harry. It's fine. Forget about it.'

'Malmaison.'

'Malmaison?'

'On Queen's Road. Booked in from tomorrow.'

'How did you...?'

'How long have we known each other, Marcus?' Marcus looked down, to the side, anywhere to avoid making eye contact. He pulled his lighter and fags out, slid off the stool.

Harry stepped back. 'Two things. Go and see her. At the hotel. Don't see her for the first time in years just before she delivers her paper. Secondly, do it sober. For fuck sake be sober when you see her. Now, give us one of those sticks. I'd better be getting back.'

Harry took a fag, Marcus followed him outside and sparked his own, the smell of hydrocarbons and smoke around him.

Piper Alpha,
July 6th 1988

You, Marcus, you're there in the cinema watching *Caddyshack*. You've seen it before but what else is there? Go for a walk? On an oil rig at night you're taking your life into your hands, wandering about. Get in someone's way, slip on something, and before you can say 'oops' you're in the North Sea with a broken spine. Back in a cramped room with a good book and a bunkmate snoring? No, there's fuck all to do offshore when you're only there for a few days, don't know anyone and no one wants to know you. A few frames of snooker? Everyone's suddenly busy. You're management. You're an unknown risk. You could try explaining your job has nothing to do with theirs but they won't believe you. Too much ill-feeling. You're a geologist, but out here you represent every desk onshore. So you sit in the dark of the cinema listening to the roar of the gas flare and watch Bill Murray fight with a gopher.

You hate golf. A good way to ruin a nice walk. Take that course down at the beach in Aberdeen, out the back of Pittodrie. A long, beautiful stretch of coastline fenced off and turned into a playground for wankers who count their handicaps. Nature divided into fairways, greens and bunkers.

You could do with a shot, a beer, a bottle of something. Life is dry offshore. Rodney Dangerfield downswings and this scream like a Stuka raining down on Guernica drills through the platform. Underneath it a death rattle. You're shaken to your feet, the platform jerking like a rodeo bull, lights flickering, and the screen crumples to the floor like a poleaxed drunk. You look around, you know the safety procedure, remember it from your younger days when offshore was part of your routine, and you remember it from the refresher when you arrived. You don't know this platform that well but the men do. Muster in the galley or your lifeboat station and await instructions.

A space filled with darkness and smoke, flickering lights, shouts, tears, even jokes, black humour in the blackest of times. You run through smoke, the heels of the men in front of you, your jumper pulled up over your mouth and nose.

In the galley now, walls heating, floors heating, the platform is ablaze, explosions tilting the world. You're waiting for someone to come and tell you what to do but no one comes. Some leave, alone and in groups, to find their own way out. One lad is crying in the corner. You dip towels in the fish tank, the cold water soothing for a second or two, then you're dry and parched again. The fish swim in ever decreasing circles. Throw them over the side, let them escape. Would they survive the fall? Tomatoes smashed onto the face, the juice dripping. You wonder about the sprinklers, why there's nothing coming out of them. You wonder if this is cutbacks. People are trying doors but everywhere there's smoke and flame. Black pouring in through the galley, through the roof space. You look around like it's freeze-framed, like everything is frozen in time, and it's then that you realise you're going to die.

You're going to die.

You look at the men on the floor, the men sitting in groups, looking lost, waiting. And you say, 'we've got to get out of here.'
    'They'll send choppers in.'
    'They can't land, the helideck's burning.'
    'We've done our muster. We wait here for instructions.'
    'There are no instructions coming. We have to get out. Get off.'
    And you join the men opening and closing doors, smoke everywhere. You dip your towel in the fish tank again, wrap it round your head.
    'I'm getting out. Who's with me?'
    'We're to wait here for instructions.' But you can't wait. You leave.
    In the corridor there are bodies.

You crawl over them, find the stairs, crawl down. Bodies. Five. Ten.

You can't see if anyone followed you. There's too much smoke.

Each breath hurts.

Each breath hurts. You're going to die.

Carrie's at home.

Alone.

Each breath hurts. You're going to die.

But you can't.

You crawl over the bodies.

Explosions.

You get to the drill floor. You can stand up now. The floor is melting. The handrails molten.

You keep going down.

You pass men going in different directions. Some have lifejackets. Some don't. You don't.

At the edge you look down. Sixty-eight feet. Too high.

You look along and there's a hose. Someone's tied a hose and men are going down it. About thirty feet above the water it hangs, they hang, then drop. There's a zodiac zipping around the legs. The sea is on fire. The platform is on fire from the bottom to the top. You get in line. Your boots are melting into the deck. It's your turn. Your hands are burnt but you grip the hose. You slip. Slip down faster and faster until there's no more hose and you're falling. You try to remember your training, legs straight, toes pointed, arse clenched, hand over nose and mouth then you batter through the surface.

Kick up. Kick away. The current will pull you under but arms under yours and you're pulled into the zodiac.

'Are you hurt?'

You shake your head. Cough. No. You don't know. You're alive.

A bigger rescue boat. You climb up the side netting, are pulled onto the deck. Blankets. Cigarettes. Someone takes your name, adds it to a list. A short list. You're alive.

And there is Piper Alpha, from sea level to helideck an inferno, a vent into hell opened in the North Sea, all that rage flaming out, gas from the risers still burning, burning, more and more explosions. There are men still on it, men still in the water. Men jumping from the helideck a hundred and eighty feet up. Hundreds of men fighting for life. You're alive.

The boat circles. More men are pulled on. The deck is strewn with survivors. The worst injured are taken inside. *Tharos* sprays water over the platform but it's like hoping to stop a train with a breath. It's as bright as day. You're alive.

It falls apart. Melted metal buckling, dropping into the sea. It would hiss if you could hear over the roar of a thousand jet engines. You watch the accommodation block. The galley. All those men you left in there. You watch from the boat as it tilts, it slides into the sea and is gone.

Were they still alive when it hit the water?

What killed them?

Smoke.

Fire.

Water.

You.

You're alive.

You're alive.

You left them.

The sun rises.

You're alive.

Piper Alpha is a stump.

You left them.

You're alive.

A helicopter winches you up.

You're alive.

You're alive.

Aberdeen,
June 2013

'A bit Third World, isn't it?'

'*Less Developed* World. What is?' said Ash.

'The infrastructure. No rail link between the city and the airport. Swap the miserable taxi drivers for shouting tuk tuk drivers, crank the temperature up another twenty degrees, sprinkle liberally with dust and we could be in Southeast Asia.'

'Glad to be home? Do you know what Third World actually means?'

'Does it come after Middle Earth?'

'It's a Cold War term. The First World was the US and all those countries aligned with it. The Second World was the Soviet Union, the Eastern Bloc, China, all the Communist countries.'

'And the Third World was everyone else?'

The front of Aberdeen Airport was boarded up. A refit underway, a sprucing up, but it made the place feel closed for business. We joined the taxi queue and before too long our turn came. Ash climbed into the back and I made a half-hearted attempt to help the driver with the bags.

'You're fine,' he said. 'Get in oot fae the cauld.'

I was drained, dirty. We'd had a four hour wait in Schiphol for the first morning flight. I watched the sun rise across the runway while dropping in and out of sleep. Ash, full of energy after sleeping through most of Eurasia, toured the shops, coming back to me with a bag of cheese, a wooden tulip and a bundle of newspapers. I drank coffee after coffee hoping the caffeine would wake me up and dislodge the blockage in my guts. Whether airline food or stress was the cause, I felt bloated and nauseous. I just wanted to get to the hotel.

'Far aboots?'

Ash looked at me, baffled.

'Into town. Malmaison Hotel. Queen's Road.'

'First time in Aiberdeen?'

'Born and bred.'

'Aye? Ye dinnae sound it.'

'Been away a while.'

I never did sound it, not like he did. I knew he was putting it on a bit. The airport drivers loved confusing tourists, particularly Americans and the English, by speaking the broadest Doric they could manage, but I'd never sounded particularly local. With Dad being from Perthshire and Hannah from Bath it wasn't like much Doric was spoken at home. Still, I was as Aberdonian as he was and he wasn't going to have fun at my expense.

All the way through Bucksburn along Great Northern Road, sitting for ages at the Haudagain Roundabout, heart of Aberdeen's mismanaged road network, and up North Anderson Drive, the driver moaned about the traffic, about people parking at the side of the dual carriageway, about the wrong vehicles using the bus lanes and idiots who didn't know how roundabouts worked. I stared out of the window at the familiar and the changed. This was the main route out to the Highlands and I'd come this way so often with Dad, stopped at that bakery for camping treats, the Danestone Tesco for supplies. His Saab had once had a blowout just after the Haudagain Roundabout and he'd jacked it up and changed it in front of what was now some MSP's constituency office.

'Is it how you remember it?' Ash asked.

'Yes and no. It's like visiting a film set. In a way it's hard to believe it's not plywood and paint.'

'Have you ever been on a movie set?'

'No. But you know what I mean.'

'Strange to be home.'

There was something in her voice, a little catch. When I looked over she was looking out the window. Ash was from North Carolina, hadn't been home since she was seventeen. I'd never see where she came from, never meet her family. She'd left – or they'd thrown her out – when she came out. Lived her final year of high school with an aunt then moved to New York. Few coming-outs are easy – mine wasn't – but Ash's was worse than most. I laid my hand on hers and squeezed, rejoiced in the pressure I received back. Ten years together and she could still give me that rush I never got from anyone else.

I kept an eye on the road in case the driver tried to pull a fast one, taking the long way round. As we turned left off Anderson Drive I made the connections, twigged the route he was taking. The traffic on the Drive was clogging up so he was going to cut through by the hospital, over Midstocket and King's Gate. He was going to take me right through my own neighbourhood, maybe even right by my old house.

'Are you okay?' Ash squeezed again.

'Yeah.'

'Memories?'

'Yeah.'

'We'll check in, run a hot bath and order room service. You've nothing on your schedule the rest of the day?'

'I'll email Harry Boyle, let him know I've arrived.'

'Try and think of it as just another conference. You've done hundreds of them.'

'It's not though, is it?'

Slowly down the hill, the taxi stopped at the crossing by the hospital entrance. Visitors coming, visitors going. Patients checking out, walking out. The lucky ones. Arms around shoulders, hunched in jackets, tentative steps. My father had walked out, into the minibus and away to the Skean Dhu where he and the others had been debriefed, cleaned up, given fresh clothes, transport money and a few stiff drinks. I remembered like it was a film, like I was watching myself walk down this road in the early morning light with all my thoughts numb, my emotions spent, an automaton making its way across the lights and down Westburn Road, back home where Mr and Mrs Galloway waited. Kim and Lesley's parents had picked them up. Mrs Galloway ran a bath for me and then we all waited, watching the news, footage coming in of that burnt, twisted stump protruding above the North Sea like the top of Hell's tallest tower, gas and oil pumping out, burning, flaming, inferno. We waited, watching. Couldn't look away until Hannah came home.

National tragedy. Domestic disaster.

Hannah flustered and blustered, tried to take control. Like she was in charge.

Like she had any right to be.

It was mid-afternoon before Dad came home, ringing the doorbell because his keys were at the bottom of the sea.

He hugged his wife. She hugged him back.

He drew me into the embrace.

I hugged him, elbowed Hannah out of the way.

The Galloways went home, left us to our misery, our relief.

Straight across at the lights, left past the Atholl, right onto Forest Road, right onto Queen's Road. I saw none of it. Ash paid the taxi. Bags on the side. I stood washed in the silvery light of the granite, the pink blush. Huge bay windows, rows of chimneys like apothecary jars, black spiked railings and the trees preparing for autumn. I was home.

Ash gave me a tissue and led me inside.

I leaned back in the bath and sipped my green tea. The bath, a deep free- standing tub strangely in the main room and not the bathroom, a set-up that meant we had to wait for room service to leave before getting in. Ash sat on the edge of the bed with her G&T. She'd tried to get me to have a drink, as she did, playfully, every so often, but I refused. I'd drawn the curtains, the triangular peaks of the buildings across the road flashing like neon signs saying HOME HOME HOME. It was too much. Drink would make it worse.

'Pass me my phone.'

I tapped out a quick email to Harry Boyle and hit send, tossed the phone back to Ash.

'Does your family have a tartan?' she asked. The carpet and most of the decor were variations on the theme.

'Fraser of Lovat. It's green, red and purple. We'll get you fitted up before we leave.'

'I thought kilts were for men.'

'There are female ones. No one wears them though. At least not to weddings or anything. For Scottish country dancing. But we can add to your collection of national dress.'

'I have a couple of kimonos, that's all.'

'And that Chinese dress. And the Mets shirt you wear in bed.'

'That's not national dress.'

'We should fly home via Germany, get you some *Lederhosen*.'

'You'd like that, would you? Leather shorts?'

'Are you getting in here?'

'Thought you'd never ask.'

With Ash's flight from Hawaii to Japan, and then the long haul via Seoul and Amsterdam, we'd both been inside for what felt like weeks. Even so, I wasn't too keen to get outside and go 'on safari' as Ash liked to call it. Whenever we went anywhere new, the first day we'd spend wandering, poking our fingers and noses into street snacks and shops and whatever nooks and niches presented themselves. Ash loved people watching and inventing stories about their lives. She claimed it was her creativity bursting out while I maintained, about ninety percent tongue-in-cheek, that it was her lawyer's instincts, making up convincing narratives to explain the most circumstantial evidence.

'Come on, get dressed and let's go on safari. I want to see your roots.'

'Roots are usually hidden in the dirt.' I pulled the curtains back. I'd lost the knack of Aberdeen weather. It looked sunny and warm, but that could mean anything. Union Street would be a wind tunnel and the second the sun disappeared we'd freeze. I tipped my backpack out onto the bed and began repacking it, adding jumpers.

'I didn't mean we should really go on safari.'

'We'll need warmer clothes later. I'll put in a bottle of water. Do you want one? And some tissues.'

'Yes, Mom.'

I sounded like Hannah. I could hear the voice, see her in

Japan, in that hotel in Kagoshima packing the bag with rolls of toilet paper, tied up plastic bags just in case. In disgust I threw the bag back on the bed, then thought better of it. We really would be cold later on.

'Which way?' We were out on the street, the sunshine was warm and the wind gentle.

'Do you want to see the city centre, the beach or some greenery?'

'You have beaches here?'

'Not like at home, but yeah, sand, water. The usual.'

'City centre. Some window shopping. Find a café, watch the world go by.' I shook the dust off my internal map, ran through images of cafés and bars, restaurants and shops I'd known as a kid and a student. Were any of them still there? 'The best cafe was Café 52 but it's down on The Green. Not an ideal place to watch the world go by, unless you have a thing about drunk old men pissing in doorways.'

'Don't be so down on the place. This is gorgeous. Big trees, wide streets and these solid, stern buildings. It's all a bit like you, really.'

'Like me?'

'Solid, stern with hints of red. You really need to get your roots done.'

'I thought you wanted to see my roots. Are you okay to walk or should we jump in a cab?'

'Walking's good. To be honest I wouldn't mind a run.'

'Me too. Maybe later.'

'No, first thing tomorrow. I had that gin, remember?'

'And you're planning on having another.' There was something in my tone, something that slipped past my censor.

'You don't mind, do you?'

'Sorry. No, you know I don't. It's just...being here.'

When we turned onto Union Street, I expected something, a grand reveal like in a gallery, where you turn a corner and there are Van Gogh's *Sunflowers* or the *Mona Lisa*. Instead Union

Street was a warp hole, a rip in the fabric of time and space. Memories were trickling into my consciousness, images, sounds, smells. Like a drowning person grabbing at passing debris, I took hold of one memory, a good one, hoping it would keep me afloat. 'Aberdeen University does a thing called the Torcher, it's a charity fundraising parade every year. Each student group gets a flatbed truck and turns it into a parade float. Usually themed on what the society does.'

'The music club plays music, the hockey club have a hockey theme.'

'Exactly. I was in the Geology Society.'

'Nerd.'

'Pretty much. We went on field trips, fossil hunts. Mostly it was just a way to make friends who liked the same stuff.'

'Other nerds.'

'Sex, drugs and rock and coal.'

'That's bad.'

'Anyway, the year I was president—'

'Chief Nerd—'

'We made a volcano on the back of the truck. It erupted and everything. A combination of food dyes, water and washing up liquid. It looked really cool when we left campus. But we were just turning onto Union Street when the rain started. It mixed with the detergent and food dye and—'

'Your volcano properly erupted?'

'Overflowing, over the truck, over us and over the sides onto the street. This dirty red froth trailed us all the way around the city. Dyed my legs red for most of the next week.'

I could see them all, the GeoSoc: me, Calum, Anthony, Mel, Stuart and Nicola, the core of the group, knee-deep in rusty bubbles, laughing. If I could hang onto positive memories, maybe the others would stream by like a river around a rock.

Every paving slab, every streetlight evoked something, drew out a strand of me at a time, unravelling me like a knitted jumper. Indian restaurants, charity shops, an ATM I'd used, The College bar where we celebrated Anthony's birthday,

Josephine's pizza restaurant where I went with Mel. But so much had changed. Maybe it was just my own negativity but I didn't remember it being so dilapidated. Empty stores, boarded shops, To Let signs, business after business closed and replaced by yet another charity shop or chain store. In some ways I was relieved to see the faded front of The Balmoral pub, unchanged for centuries it seemed. We turned into Belmont Street, the heart of the student world, all the bars and fast-food shops I'd known were still there, with maybe a lick of paint or a new name. One Up, the independent record store, had gone. No one had any money for music. Businesses went under but pubs and betting shops thrived. I pined for our home in Hawaii with its views of the sea to one side and the forest and mountains on the other. In every direction a scene that would pick me up. Hawaii renewed itself; Aberdeen aged, withered.

Ash was taking photos. I looked up. I'd been so drawn into the darkness at street level that I'd forgotten the glory of the Aberdeen skyline. Church spires and townhouse gables, bay windows jutting out of slate roofs, the sun glinting off the granite.

The Wild Boar, one of my favourite student lunch spots, was still there. I led Ash inside, took a table as far at the back as I could, away from the window and its bright view into my past. When the waitress came over Ash took control, ordered some food, a fruit juice for me and a glass of *Mâcon-villages*. The waitress repeated the order back.

'No,' I said. 'No fruit juice. Make it a bottle. Two glasses.'

Aberdeen,
October 1988

Dad was in the garden, digging. He had started in the corner where I used to pretend I was Indiana Jones. Before dawn he was out there, shush, whack, shush, whack, the spade chunking into the ground, the dirt landing in a pile behind him. I peeked through my curtains and watched him in his tracksuit bottoms and his painting jumper, strawberry plant roots hanging from the shovel like melted cheese from a pizza slice. I watched him stick it in, foot on the top, force it down, lever it back, up and over his shoulder. I watched him for twenty minutes kneeling on my bed before I realised Hannah was below me, standing one step outside the house in her dressing gown and slippers, a cup of camomile held in both hands. Her hair was starting to turn, even from up there I could see a sliver or two of silver. She plucked them when she found them, stuck them to the bathroom mirror like a hunter mounting trophies on the wall, sometimes forgot to clean them up again. I found them there, four, five in a row. Dad was making good progress, the hole deep enough that I couldn't see his knees.

It was the weekend, Saturday morning. I had a little bit of homework I hadn't finished last night. Before the summer I'd have gone down in my pyjamas, made a hot chocolate and done it at the kitchen table, Dad pottering like this in the garden, Hannah out for a run if she wasn't working, hoovering, reading the paper with a mug of tea. Often it was just me and Dad, the radio on. He'd take a week's worth of stress out on the weeds and slugs. After lunch we'd head out on the bikes maybe, saving the hills for Sunday when we'd have the whole day free, an early start and we could be up Lochnagar before most people had switched on the cartoons.

Before summer.

I sat at my desk, opened my maths book. Shush, whack, shush, whack. The problems were easy but I'd left them for today because last night I couldn't concentrate. Since school started back I'd been making mistakes, simple, stupid mistakes, things I knew but I couldn't concentrate, in class, at home, I couldn't focus. Last night I wrote *d* instead of *b* three times in the equation so I packed it in and went to bed. I couldn't take another day of Miss Brown looking at me with that sympathetic chubby face when she gave me my work back with a B on it, that look. That look, nothing but that look from teachers and my friends. Pity. Shush, whack, shush, whack.

So I left my homework for the morning thinking I'd be able to concentrate then. Fat chance. My fossils lay in a line on the desk, their smashed display case thrown out but not replaced. My rocks on the windowsill. Milky quartz, the light glinting off the violet amethyst, black pockmarked basalt from Sakurajima like something from another planet, thousands of holes, bubbles made by heat and pressure, made by Pele.

It's not a priority right now, Caroline.

No. Obviously.

The priority is Dad, shush, whack. We needed all our time, all our patience, all our understanding for him. He refused help. Refused treatment. *Fucking shrinks*, he called them. *Why can't they just leave me alone, leave us alone. I just want to forget but they want me to go over it again and again. Group sessions, sitting in front of complete strangers crying and talking about your dreams? Californian bullshit. Tell me about your mother. And how does that make you feel? Why don't they just watch fucking North Tonight, there's never anything else fucking on.* Standing in front of the TV with a glass of whisky. Always standing. He couldn't sit, couldn't stay still for a moment. But that was okay, the shouting at the TV. He'd done that before anyway. Not as much, and not so sweary, but he'd always liked heckling politicians, newsreaders, anyone who annoyed him. So that was fine. It was the nights. Every night. Last night.

The nightmares. The screaming.

In Japan the walls were paper-thin, I remember putting my hand through one and thinking how thick our granite walls were. We couldn't hear the Galloways. But even granite isn't soundproof. My audiobooks didn't work, didn't keep the sounds out. Nothing did. Nothing. None of us got much sleep, it was no wonder I couldn't concentrate, couldn't tell the difference between *b* and *d* anymore.

Most nights. Most days. Something. Flashbacks. Dreams. Panic attacks. Drunk. Three months of understanding. He wouldn't get help and it wasn't getting better. So this was how we lived now, everyone on edge, waiting for the next alarm.

At least the phone had stopped ringing. The doorbell. Reporters. Journalists. The house under siege over the summer, friends, neighbours, well-meaning well-wishers, pot of tea after pot of tea in the living room with all the *thank Gods* and the *you always think it'll happen to someone elses* and the *you're looking well, considerings*.

He'd gone back to work after two weeks, though how he managed in his office I had no idea. They told him to take all the time he needed. But he went back.

I triple-checked my working and put the maths away, got my essay out, my notepad for the rough draft. Essays for English were so much harder than science reports. In science the conclusion was straightforward. This is what happened. This is what I learned. Direct. Clear. Unambiguous. In English the conclusion was a wrapping up of everything already said. What was the point of that? I'd already said it so why say it again? If it wasn't clear the first time, I could make it clearer. I wished they'd let me drop those stupid arts subjects. Biology, chemistry, physics and maths. I could fill my day with those. How would *King Lear* help me get into a good Earth Science department?

Hoops to jump through, things you had to do even if you didn't want to. *That's what being an adult means, Caroline.* Unless that something was getting treatment, unless that something was not drinking. Unless that something was not screwing Frank Carpenter. Sometimes the phone rang and it wasn't a reporter or a well-wisher. Sometimes Hannah answered it and her voice changed. Sometimes it was him.

Some things never changed.

School was far from a refuge. I'd pushed the party out of my mind, pushed Mark to one side. He'd spent the rest of the summer inventing stories.

Frigid. Whore. Bitch. Slut.

Liar.

There'd been fights. Graeme, Neil, groups of boys in the playground, in the streets. During sports, crunching tackles, dirty play in scrums. Some girls too. Laughter, names. Silence fell when I went into the toilet, my ears burning.

Pity in the classroom. Hatred in the corridors.

Half the year against me, the teachers thinking I was some kind of jelly, and Dad out the back, shush, whack, shush, whack. I wished I was like one of those TV prodigy kids and I could go to university two years early, pack up and go, leave them to it.

'Marcus.' I could hear Hannah through the glass, through the half-closed curtains.

Shush, whack, shush, whack. 'Marcus. Please stop.' Shush, whack, shush, whack.

'What are you doing? Trying to reach New Zealand?' Shush, whack, shush, whack.

Some of the survivors were interviewed on the news. Some of the families. The way they talked about it like they couldn't keep any of it in for a second longer, the stories coming out. Where they were when it started, the first explosion. Where they went. Who they saw. How they got off. How they felt when the boat picked them up, the helicopter, seeing their family at the hospital, all of it pouring out.

The exhaustion in them. Haunted. The smiles, their arms around wives and girlfriends, sons and daughters. Happy to be home. Glad to be alive. Counting blessings, thanking lucky stars.

Dad never said a word. He was debriefed at the Skean Dhu and that was it. Clammed up. No interviews. No fucking shrinks. He hadn't even told me anything. His burns healed but there was scarring. He'd run his fingers over the scars on his palms, tracing something, following canals in his flesh, remembering, the flashbacks coming. He'd be there, back on the platform, screaming at night, during the day, at any time they might come, *we have to get out of here, we have to go, we're going to die.* He couldn't see us, thought we were there with him, thought we were part of the crew. *He's reliving it,* Hannah said, *it's like a sleepwalker, don't interrupt, the effect could be damaging.* Did she know this? Did cardiac surgeons study psychology?

Surely you didn't just leave him to it?

I'd been reading about trauma, sitting in the library. I didn't take the books out in case he found them in the house. 'Bomb happy' the soldiers called it. After trauma like that it was very difficult to readjust to normality. He needed help but wouldn't even consider the idea. They tried, professionals, charities, knocking on the door, calling. He would have none of it.

The disaster hung over the city. I'd followed a lot of the investigation into Piper Alpha, the programmes, articles. It wasn't just Dad. Aberdeen changed that day. Oil was no longer something over the horizon that jacked up house prices and flooded the city with Americans.

His memories overwhelmed him when they were triggered by something. Usually it was a flickering light. He had a flashback one day in the Co-op when one of the strip lights was about to go. He stood stock-still for a few seconds then broke into a run, a burst of speed up and down the aisles, shouting that we had to get out.

Did he have them at work?

When he was driving?

Would he get better with time? 'Marcus. Marcus look at me.'

He was waist-deep in the hole, a mound behind him like Mount Fuji for moles. How far down would he go? Soon enough there'd be nothing left a shovel could shift. You couldn't get to the other side of the world with a spade. His back was to the house so I couldn't see his face, couldn't see if this was relaxing him, if this was some form of physical therapy or if he had that look, the manic look before he'd run out of the house, get into the Saab and race off for hours, for a night, for a day or two. But this was new, this digging.

Hannah was halfway up the lawn, still in her gown and slippers, minus the tea. The Galloways were in their garden, Mr Johnstone on the other side, watching the show. My Crazy Dad, like it was some sitcom and I was watching too, the TV frame of the window, the curtains like it was a theatre, a soap opera. Down there the cheating wife and the alcoholic father, act one, scene one.

She crossed the grass. A step at a time. Slowly. You don't interrupt them. It could be dangerous. 'Marcus. Please. Speak to me. Please stop.' She was crying, trying to control it, her voice. She cried in her room. Kept it to herself but I could hear her. I wondered when she would leave. When the calls would stop. When she would choose.

She reached him. He hadn't stopped. It looked like he didn't even know she was there, his back to her, arms going shush, whack, shush, whack. She reached out. A hand. 'Marcus.'

He turned. Took one hand off the spade. His face. Empty. Drawn. Then he moved, jumped out of the hole and grabbed her. She screamed. He pushed her, pulled her into the hole, down onto her back. 'Marcus, stop, stop it.' He held her down, shovelled dirt back into the hole, on top of her. She wriggled, fought, coughed. He couldn't hold her with one hand and shovel with the other. He dropped the shovel, slapped her hard, pushed her back down, began shovelling again. Mr Galloway ran into the house. Mr Johnstone climbed over the fence into our garden, dragged Dad off Hannah. Dad swung at him but Mr Johnstone was fit, fast, and ducked it. Mr Galloway burst out of our kitchen and together they got Dad on the ground, held him down.

'Marcus, calm the fuck down, okay?' said Mr Galloway. 'We've got you. You have to calm down.'

Mrs Galloway ran through, helped Hannah to stand and brushed the worst of the dirt off, held her. Dad was writhing but slowly he calmed, stopped fighting them. He lay there on the grass, on his back, a neighbour on each side, a knee on each shoulder.

'Is she okay?' Mr Galloway called over to his wife.

'Of course she's not okay.'

'I mean is she hurt? Do we need to take her to casualty?'

Hannah shook her head, dirt rising from her like smoke, like ash, a hand to her cheek, coughing. Then Dad was up and running, free from them and into the house, leaving them all standing, out the other side I heard the Saab rev, screech out of the drive. Below me in the garden Hannah looked up, saw me watching. For a moment we stared at each other, me kneeling on my bed, her in the garden covered in dirt.

I pulled the curtains closed.

Aberdeen,
Summer 1990

In the summer between school and university I got a job at the
Beach Leisure Centre. Every day when my shift finished I spent
an hour or two on the climbing wall. I was climbing six-a/b
routes, taking it in turns with Roddy, who worked there full-
time. I was trying for a hold just beyond my reach, made a lunge
for it and missed. Roddy lowered me to the ground, laughing.
'What was that?'

'You saw.'

'It looked like you were trying to high-five the wall, not grab
a hold.'

'You've got these holds set up for people your own height.
You're discriminating against the shorter climber.'

'Did you not see the other hold?' This third voice made us
both turn. Graeme and Tony, geared up for their climb. Graeme
pointed. 'Straight up instead of across. You get your left hand onto
that, shift your right foot from there to there, and you're home.'

'You climb six-b?' I asked.

'In fourth year,' Tony snorted.

'You go first,' Graeme said to him.

Roddy and I were done but I decided to stay for a bit and
watch. Graeme had been climbing for years and I was curious to
see how good he was. Roddy set to cleaning chalk off the holds.
Tony, all tied up, took his position at the start of the seven-a
route, Graeme holding his rope.

'Do you climb the same?' I asked him.

'First climb, to warm up. I'm trying seven-c. Haven't managed
it yet. You see up there, the reach from underneath the ledge?
Tricky.'

It looked nigh impossible. 'Do you climb every day?' I hadn't
seen him around. Things had been weird with Graeme for the
past couple of years. I'd been clearing a space around me,
shedding friends, focussed only on Dad and getting into university.

I didn't have time for all that social bullshit.

'No. Tony's working for the council cutting grass so we come down whenever he's free. You work here, don't you?'

I blushed. That meant he'd seen me in my uniform. 'Yeah, just for the summer.'

'Nice. You get to use the wall for free?'

'Yeah. I could...I mean...' What was wrong with me? 'I climb after work every day. If you want to. I mean, if Tony's busy.'

'Cool. Tomorrow?'

So we started climbing together. He was a good teacher, patient but firm. I moved up the grades, pushing myself, pushing my body. I could feel a hardening, a new kind of strength. I took to working out in the gym, lifting weights, circuits. I was burning, packed with potential energy. I'd started running seriously after Piper Alpha. Ran until I was so empty I couldn't feel. This was different, fulfilling rather than draining.

It didn't take long before I started looking forward to those climbs and on the days Graeme didn't come, Roddy would take the piss. 'Just because your boyfriend's not here, that's no reason to throw yourself off the top.' I knew Graeme had split up with Julie, that she was off to drama school in London. There was chemistry between us, something about the stretch of his neck when he reached for a hold, the tightness of his calves. I knew I was bisexual, had made my peace with the fact even though I hadn't come out to anyone – no one asked, convinced I was as frigid as Mark had claimed. But I hadn't been attracted to a man in a long time. So what were these feelings for Graeme? I put it down to loneliness, warm memories, shared interests. Whatever. He was leaving at the end of the summer and I had an unconditional from Aberdeen. With Dad as he was, relationships weren't an option.

The summer passed in a cycle of sun and rain, temperatures rising and falling like an EKG, the usual for Aberdeen. I worked, I climbed with Graeme, I looked after the house, paid the bills, made sure Dad had clean, ironed shirts for work, woke him in the morning, took the empties to the recycling bins, and read in my room while he raged. I'd discovered a memoir, *Dislodging Fossils* by Kiana Lau, a Hawaiian geologist and feminist. She wrote about her childhood, a horrific past, her parents killed when Mauna Loa erupted in 1950. It was heart-breaking, her memories of the heat and loss intertwined. But she had strength. Life moved on. In a lively, sardonic style she wrote about her experiences as a woman in science, the sexism and sexual harassment, but also the discoveries, the theories, the work she did. I was captivated by the book, by the woman, the personality that spoke to me through those pages. I imagined the volcanoes of Hawaii, the islands, the sea. I'd go there one day, I decided. Go to Pele's home. Kiana Lau's home. When I left Aberdeen. When I could leave.

It was our last climb. It was Wednesday and as of Friday I would be an unemployed student. When I came out of the changing room afterwards, Graeme was waiting for me, sitting legs stretched out, one over the other, a spiral notebook open in his lap, mouthing something.

'First sign of madness, talking to yourself,' I said.

'Not running today?'

'I'll go later. I fancy a hot chocolate. You?' I must have paused too long. 'If, you know, you're not busy or anything.' This confident, cool boy was shy.

'Sounds good.' I unchained my bike and wheeled it along the beachfront to the café, locking it up again. Café Continental served their hot chocolates in tall glasses with marshmallows and whipped cream. I'd loved them since I was a kid and Kim, Lesley and I used to come down regularly. I hadn't seen either of them since the end of school.

'So when does term start?' Graeme asked after the waiter brought out drinks.

'Next week. Well, matriculation and all that stuff is next week. Classes are the week after. How about you? Glasgow's later isn't it?'

'I'm not going.'

I nearly knocked my glass over. 'Not going? Why?'

'Don't want to.' The way he said it, it sounded almost petulant, like a small boy. He was looking at the table, tapping his long teaspoon so the handle rose up and tapped back onto the wood.

'But your dad? He must be—'

'Then he can fucking go to Glasgow. Shit. Sorry Carrie. You know my dad, you can guess how he took it. It hasn't been fun at home, he's been raging since…Jesus, look who I'm saying this to. I didn't mean…sorry.'

'It's okay. Start again. Why don't you want to go? Is it Glasgow? Law? Do you want to do something else?'

'I…' he laughed, a self-deprecating mock laugh. 'I want to be a professional snowboarder.' He looked straight at me.

'Are you good enough?' I didn't mean it to come out like that, but I'd never seen him on a board. He spent every winter on the slopes, had even been to New Zealand in our summer to get his fix, but so did a lot of people. How many were good enough to turn pro?

'You know I won that competition?' I shook my head. That was news to me. He looked surprised, hurt. 'Last January, in Switzerland?'

'Sorry. Yes.' I tried to keep the cold out of my voice but couldn't quite.

He was silent for a moment, in thought. 'January. Yes. Sorry. Your mother.'

'You won a competition?'

'Yeah, the European Amateur Snowboarding Championship. I won the Halfpipe.'

'Congratulations.'

He laughed. 'Thanks. Well, afterwards I got offered sponsorship. It's impossible to get sponsorship. I mean, nobody gets sponsorship. And they offered me.'

'So they'd pay you?'

'Yeah, I'd use their gear and they pay for me to travel around the world competing in all the pro games.'

'And your father says no, go to law school.'

'He says to get the law degree first so I'll have that to fall back on. He doesn't get that by then it'll be too late. I can't put it on hold for four years and come back.'

I stirred my marshmallows around the glass, pink and white whales chasing each other. 'If you get sponsorship you don't need your father's money?'

'No.'

'And you're old enough that you don't need his permission.'

'Yes.'

'And you've made up your mind.'

'Yes.'

'But you're scared that if you go against your father's wishes, he'll never forgive you.'

His face, open. 'Yes.'

I looked at the clock. 17:43. Dad would be in Under The Hammer, probably on his second pint. He'd stagger home at about half twelve, sleep fully clothed on the sofa with the TV and the stereo on. In Edinburgh and Durham students were moving into halls, unpacking bags, meeting new friends, going out to explore their new homes. 'You've got to do what you want. If you wait until it suits him, it'll be too late.'

'He should be happy for me. No one gets sponsorship. No one.'

'At least he gives enough of a fuck to be angry.'

I left him on the front, my legs pumping the pedals up Beach Boulevard, sweat breaking out on my head, on my back, tears pricking my eyes. Graeme had to get out. Had to follow his dreams. He had to. It was all so unfair.

Aberdeen,
December 25th 1990

Whether anyone was dreaming of it or not, we had a white Christmas. The garden under snow like Atlantis under the waves, the corner of the barbecue prodded through black, the shed roof a miniature ski run, but the heating was on high and the oven was helping, keeping everything warm for Christmas lunch. The table was set, same as every year: crackers from Marks and Spencer, red and green napkins, all the good cutlery and dishes, coasters and hot plates ready for the veg, the turkey and trimmings, the sausages wrapped in bacon. The radio on, festive cheer from the BBC. Wine glasses. Wine. Waiting for a family.

In the living room, the tree was felled, the framed Monet over the fireplace smashed, whisky sticky on the wall and mantelpiece. I'd just closed the door.

I had my fleece and my slippers on, so I was toasty. I refilled the teapot, added a couple of fresh bags and returned to the dining room, pushed the crackers aside, opened my binder.

Another memorable Christmas then. Christmas last year. 1989. It was like some soap opera through there. Hannah rattling pots and pans, slamming drawers and attacking parsnips with one of the knives Dad sharpened the night before, standing in the garden with the steel refining each blade until it drew blood. Him out there, in the garage, the pieces of his mountain bike spread around him on newspaper and rags, the latest thing he had dismantled. The fight. The shouting.

This year, 1990, the silence.

Focus on your books, Carrie. Focus.

First Year Geology wasn't that tricky. All the books I'd read, the field trips Dad took me on. No one really studied geology at school so the lecturers assumed a starting knowledge of zero. Not that I was being complacent.

I turned page after page, searching for something, anything I hadn't learned properly.

Our first Christmas since she left. Ten months since she moved to Bristol to be with Frank Carpenter. I should have known he couldn't take it. That he would run off. I should have known, but I hoped.

All I seemed to do, hope.

I thought about phoning someone; phoning Graeme but he was in Austria, celebrating a silver in his first competition as a professional; phoning Kim or Lesley but they were both at their grandparents'. Someone from uni, Calum, Mel, Nicola, but I didn't know their home numbers and no one stayed in Aberdeen over the holidays. Why would they? Christmas is for families but what did you do if your mother walked out and your father hadn't been home since yesterday morning and the car was gone and the living rooms trashed?

You cooked Christmas lunch and studied for your exams.

He always came home in the end.

I wiped my eyes on the red Christmas napkin, dabbed at my notes trying not to smudge them anymore. The paper ripped. Pushing down the urge to tear the page out, crumple and throw it, I clicked up the lever so the arches opened and gently lifted it out. The sheet below was a little damp but nothing to worry about. I found the next empty page in my pad and copied my notes afresh. I only needed to glance at the original. It was all memorised, it was all in there, layers and layers of knowledge, strata pushing down, compressing whatever else might be in there. Fossilising things best forgotten.

Oven off. The state he'd be in when he eventually rolled up, he'd be lucky to keep down cheese on toast let alone a turkey dinner. I'd lost my appetite too. I packed up my notes. As I passed the front door to go upstairs I pulled the curtains back and looked out at the bright white world. Fallen snow had covered the tracks his car made out of the drive. If he came home now he'd never get it back in.

The phone shrilled into the empty house. It'd be her. Hannah. She still called once a month or so when the guilt got to her. I watched until it stopped, grabbed my ski jacket and gloves from the hall cupboard and stepped into the bitter wind.

In the garage I stretched out my muscles, calves and hamstrings, touched my toes, rolled my shoulders, my neck, made my arms supple and strong. The urge to run was explosive but I wouldn't reach the street before falling. I took the shovel and rammed it into the snow, the gravelly scrape as the blade raked along the driveway. There was nowhere to put the snow but onto the laden lawn. I flung it feeling the strain of my muscles. Bent again, another load, another.

The heat. I was putting too much into it but the energy had to go somewhere. Dig. Throw. Dig. Throw. Memories threw themselves at me.

Dad in the kitchen, a knife stabbed into the wooden chopping board. Another heap of snow on the pile.

Dad on the hall floor, face down, a crystal whisky tumbler smashed, blood leaking from his hand into the carpet.

Another shovel load, the scratch of metal on stone.

Half of the driveway was clear, but flakes were drifting down again. Sisyphus.

Dad gone for days, somewhere north, drunk on the roads, driving at full speed. Each time reminding me of the first time I didn't know if he was coming home, and each time I hated him for making me hate him.

I leaned on the shovel, out of breath, hot.

More images. Hannah this time, her face changing, hardening, she'd already left him for Frank Carpenter in her heart but Dad made it so much easier for her to walk out. Why did she wait so long to leave?

I kept her secret, thinking there would be a better time to tell him. Memories.

He was away. Hannah's Merc was in the driveway, February 1990, not even a year ago. Her boot open, suitcases, boxes, bags.

'So you're leaving us.'

She had the decency to be crying. 'Caroline.'

'Don't call me that.'

'Carrie. I can't stay. I can't do it anymore.'

'Has the commute to Bristol finally got you down?'

'It's not like that—'

'You're not going to Bristol?'

'I am but…he's not the man I married, Carrie. He's changed. He…he scares me. Since Piper Alpha—'

'Don't you dare blame him for that. Blame that for this. You were with *him* that day. While Dad was fighting for his life you were flat on your back with Frank fucking Carpenter.'

She flinched. We'd never spoken about it. What was there to say?

'It's hard to understand, I know. We're your parents so you can't view it objectively. Our marriage has been over for a long time. We've both…strayed. Him much more than me, not that that excuses me, I know. The truth is, Carrie, we only stayed together for you. If you hadn't…we'd never…'

Something in me froze, crystallised. I could feel myself frosting over, arms folded rigid across my chest. 'Go then. We'll be fine without you.'

'Caroline, Carrie, he needs help. Professional help. What's wrong with him, it's a mental illness. Without help he could…'

'What?'

'You finish school in a few months. Then you'll be away to university. I was going to wait until then but I can't take it. Even those few months… I'm sorry Carrie. I can't do it anymore.'

'And what happens to him?'

'Maybe my leaving will shock him into getting help.'

'And if it doesn't?'

She shut the boot. 'I'm sorry.'

'That makes it all right then.'

'Carrie—'

'Go.'

I continued beyond the driveway and cleared the pavement outside our house, shifted a path from the road, a valley between two hills of dirty snow and sand ploughed up in the gutter. I could have kept going along the pavement, round onto Midstocket, up onto the Drive and out of the city, gone forever.

Scottish Highlands,
December 25th 1990

A car horn blasted over the desolate landscape and it took Marcus a moment to realise it was him doing it. He let his arm go slack and it fell from the steering wheel into his lap. The vision of Piper Alpha blazing in the night gave way to the morning sun. There was a bottle of Laphroaig on the passenger seat, about two inches left. He took a swig, the burn of it confirming he was alive, he was awake. Merry Christmas. Marcus Fraser, still alive. Survivor.

Where the fuck was he?

The Saab was parked on a patch of grass at the side of a single-track road. He clambered out into the bitter bracing air and fumbled for a cigarette. The hills were covered in snow, dirty off-white patches, a mottled effect of dark brush, bare rock, puddles and bogs. About twenty metres ahead the road curved to the right, the hill blocking his view of what might be lurking. The road back wriggled like an uncoiled intestine along the shore of a smallish loch before disappearing behind another hill. It looked familiar but most of the roads in the Highlands were familiar. How had he got there? Shards of memory. Christmas Eve in Under The Hammer. Mistletoe, a kiss from that solicitor, Isobel. No taxis to be had. Icy roads home.

There was something about the Christmas tree. The twinkling lights.

Driving into the Highlands. If this was the west coast then that was about four hours of driving.

A wave battered him and he threw up in the ditch next to the car. He wiped his mouth on the sleeve of his fleece and rooted around in the boot amongst the camping gear that lived there, found his emergency kit – a bottle of water and some peanuts. Washed his mouth out. Left the nuts. Didn't think he could manage them. A tot of whisky. Dug some Aspirin out the first aid kit. Just gone half six. He should find somewhere less conspicuous to park the car. He pissed into the ditch, his urine the colour of rust, the colour of whisky, like it had just passed straight through him. Probably could get pissed off it. Can it, call it lager, nice froth on it. Make a fortune.

On the back seat he noticed his kitbag, the one he'd used whenever he went offshore. He hadn't touched it since. He picked it up and it tinkled happily. Felt like he had emptied the drinks cabinet into it. Good man, Marcus, planning ahead.

The engine caught and he eased her onto the road. She was an old lady, Ruby, the Saab, but he could still rely on her. They'd been through a lot together, her red paintwork and leather interior racing up the A96 and into the Highlands every chance he got. She knew the roads herself, could find her way even without him at the wheel. Never let him down.

As soon as he was round the corner, he knew where he was. The Ullapool road. Of course it was, fucking autopilot. Like a homing pigeon, he kept coming back here. He couldn't think of anywhere better to go than onwards.

He braked milliseconds before a corner, dropped two gears, was already accelerating again and back up to top before the car was straight. This was driving. Him and this car, they'd had some fun. He turned off the main road, gunning the engine. He hit a humpback bridge and almost took off. He raked in the glove box and pulled out some tapes, Frank Zappa, Genesis – Peter Gabriel era of course – yes, there it was, Pink Floyd. He popped out the tape already in the machine. The Corries? He must've been in quite the melancholy mood last night. He banged in *The Piper at the Gates of Dawn* and cranked it up, welcomed the morning as he broached a hill and saw the Atlantic below.

About twenty miles up the coast there was a little dirt road you'd miss if you didn't know it was there. He swung in, the Saab jumping as he dragged the back wheel over a rock. Sorry old girl, won't happen again.

The road dipped down, turned to the right and ended at a stone dyke. No one could see him from the road and the farmhouse was two fields away. No one would know he was there unless they deliberately came and found him.

He took the tent, sleeping bag and blankets, the mat, and climbed down onto the sand. It was a small beach, beautiful white sand, the bay that jutted out farther on the northern side, just now it was an island but when the tide went out, it exposed a rocky causeway. It would be easier to set up at the southern side, near the car, but he knew from experience there was no shelter there. At the north end there was more protection from the wind, an almost cave, dry and peaceful. That was where Hannah and he had first camped.

Tent up, ropes weighted by stones. If anyone could see him they'd think he was mad. Suicidal. Maybe he was. Like it mattered. He'd camped in colder conditions than this, up mountains, in the Arctic circle. No such thing as bad weather, just bad clothes. If people could survive on the top of Everest, he could survive winter in Scotland. He scratched out a fireplace, lined it with rocks, big enough to provide heat, small enough to escape notice. He finished the Laphroaig, rattled through the kitbag and pulled out half a Caol Ila.

Last night, memories like fireworks. No taxis. A kiss under the mistletoe from Isobel.

He went down, landed hard on his arse outside the Spar. Up again, arm around a lamppost, tried to light a fag.

He huddled closer into his jacket, the hood up over his hat, trying to remember.

The snow on the lawn up over his boots, dragging his feet through it. The curtains in the living room still open, the Christmas tree lights still on, blinking.

Blinking.

The key circling the lock like water around a drain, eventually slipping in, then he couldn't get it back out again, tripped over the step. But home. Made it.

He went to the drinks cabinet, poured himself a nightcap, a decent slug of Laphroaig in the crystal tumbler they got as a wedding present. The last one standing.

He put some music on.

On the sofa. Boots dripping onto the carpet. Glass in his gloved hand. Merry Christmas.

Carrie upstairs. He couldn't face her in that state, the look she'd give him.

Couldn't meet her eye.

Merry Christmas.

Above him, there on the west coast, a gull scooted by, the wind carrying it. It arced down and round, landed on the sand in the lee of a rock and watched him. He watched it.

He must have dozed off on the sofa. The lights. Blinking.

Blinking. Flashing. Each light a face. Faces, blinking. Faces without names.

Flashing lights. Sirens. In the darkness with flashing lights. You were back. You were there. A space filled with darkness and smoke, flickering lights, shouts.

The glass, smashed into the picture frame over the fireplace. Shards.

Whisky.

The blinking. The tree.

Needles catching in your clothes. The tree was down, baubles bouncing across the carpet. You yanked the lights from the wall, the wire coming out the plug, shorn.

Darkness. The blinking gone. The faces still there.

You left.

Got in the car and drove.

Aberdeen,
June 2013

'Let's see some greenery.'

We'd finished the wine and I was feeling a bit spacey. I ran through a mental picture of Aberdeen. There were gaps I couldn't immediately recall, like those old maps that just had blank spaces and *here be dragons*. 'There's Union Terrace Gardens. A bit small and boring but in the centre. Westburn, but that's...' too close to home, I didn't say. 'Hazelhead Park isn't far from here. It's nice.'

'Done.'

It was only when the taxi dropped us at the entrance that I made the connection. Something in me had chosen this particular park. We passed by families with young children playing on the grass, teenagers sitting on benches, lounging like gangsters, staring at us. Dogs fetching sticks, frisbees. The maze was dilapidated, the building at the entrance boarded up, a window on the second floor smashed. The hedges hadn't been trimmed for a long time. The ice cream stall closed.

I took Ash down the path opposite the maze and through the trees. I'd only been here once, in 1994 just before going to Durham. Dad had refused to go to any of the services, had refused to come to the unveiling of the memorial in 1991. 'I don't belong there,' he'd said. 'I wasn't part of the crew. I was just there for a day or two.'

On top of a granite plinth three bronze figures, their backs to each other like three corners of a triangle, looking into the distance. A roustabout, a man in a survival suit, a man holding a pool of oil in his hand, symbolic figures, symbolic poses.

Ash read out, 'Dedicated to the memory of the one hundred and sixty-seven men who lost their lives in the Piper Alpha oil platform disaster. 6th July 1988.' Around the plinth, gold lettering on the granite, were the names. 'This was the one your dad...?'

'Yeah. It should be one hundred and sixty-eight. One of the survivors killed himself.'

'Post-traumatic stress?'

That was why we came, finally, in 1994. 'When the *Press & Journal* ran the article, Dad went to pieces, disappeared for three days. When he came back he sat opposite me in the kitchen, my suitcases open upstairs, my train tickets to Durham booked. I thought I'd have to cancel them. What happened, the survivor's guilt, that was Dad. We both saw that article and knew that...that it could be him. I called a taxi and we came here. He didn't argue, followed me like a child. I sat over there. He walked round and round it, reading the names, looking at the figures, letting himself remember. Either this would shock him into getting help or... He sat next to me on the bench and cried and cried.'

'Did it help?'

'Enough to make me believe it was safe to go to Durham.'

Durham,
January 1999

'Doctor Caroline Fraser.'

'You can stop saying that, Dad.'

'I'll never get tired of saying that. Doctor Caroline Fraser BSc, MSc, PhD, Volcanologist. Like Spock.'

'He was a Vulcan.'

'You don't have the ears for that. But live long and prosper.'

We were in a restaurant overlooking the River Wear. It used to be a brewery pub but about eighteen months ago friends of my girlfriend, Anna, had taken it over and converted it into a restaurant and art space. When Hannah heard I knew the people running it she had insisted on making a reservation for my graduation dinner. She'd been trying to get back into my life and, tired of it all, in the flush of post-PhD completion I relented, let her invite herself up. And the problem with divorced parents is you can't favour one over the other, so Dad came too.

While Hannah was in the toilet, Dad ordered another bottle of Pinot. I wasn't drinking. Hannah was drinking the Chablis recommended with the sea bass.

'I saw that Graeme Anderson the other day,' Dad said. 'Did I tell you?'

'He's back in Aberdeen? Did they have a parade?'

Graeme had won bronze in the Halfpipe at the Winter Olympics in Japan the year before. I'd watched all the heats with Anna, both of us cheering him on.

'Just visiting. He was having a drink in Under The Hammer with his father. Said to say hi.'

Hannah returned, face suitably powdered. They'd both been on their best behaviour so far, but an increase in wine meant all bets were off. I'd kept them apart last night, dinner with Hannah, leading Dad on something of a pub crawl around the real ale haunts. At breakfast they'd been civil. So civil in fact that I worried Dad had started early. In the cathedral they both reverted to public roles. Dad, the proud ebullient father, that's my daughter you know, the PhD. That was when I spotted the hip flask being slipped back into the sporran as he came out from behind a pillar. At least he was trying to be subtle.

'Say hi back.'

'Hi to who?' said Hannah.

'You remember Graeme Anderson? My year at school?'

'The snowboarder.'

'I'm surprised you know that, Hannah,' said Dad. 'Doesn't strike me as your kind of sport.'

'Jonathan, Frank's son, is the fan. I heard about Graeme during the Olympics. They kept mentioning Aberdeen. He's very handsome. Were you two friends?'

'Yeah,' I said. 'We used to climb together.'

'And he's trying to get back in touch?'

I could see what she was thinking. Hannah was the mother trying not to be the mother, straight back and shoulders, dress cut a little bit too young for a woman with a PhD daughter, gratified when Anna – introduced as a friend of course – exclaimed, 'You can't possibly be old enough to be Carrie's mother.' But she couldn't help herself. Some part of her wanted to be a grandmother and I was the only chance she had.

There would be no grandkids for Hannah. My sexuality didn't preclude it but my upbringing did. Bringing someone into the world with the chance they could have the kind of childhood I had? Fighting, affairs, divorce, recriminations. A child of mine hiding in their room drowning out reality with audiobooks? The risk was too great.

'Dad just bumped into him and he said hi.'

'He seemed quite keen,' said Dad. 'Kept asking about where you were and what you were doing. He gave me his email address to pass on to you.' He patted down his pockets before remembering he was in a kilt. 'Back at the hotel.'

The waitress cleared the plates away, the sea bass and Dad's lamb reduced to smears and flakes, my stuffed mushrooms half-eaten.

'Anyone for dessert?' Hannah asked. I shook my head. 'Go on, Caroline, it's your day, treat yourself. Why don't you order the pecan pie and if you don't want it all, I can help.'

'If you want the pecan pie, order it yourself. I'm full.'

'Stuffed with stuffed mushrooms. So there isn't much room.'

'Thanks, Dad, now I do feel sick.'

'How about an aperitif. A liqueur? Hannah you were always a fan of the rusty nail. Can I tempt you with one now? Carrie? Baileys?'

'No. Thanks. So, Caroline.'

'Yes, Hannah?'

'I wish you'd stop calling me that.'

'Ditto.'

'You can call me Al.'

'Helpful, Dad. Hannah, you were saying?'

'What's next? You've got your PhD.'

'A job,' said Dad. 'You'll have your pick, all those publications under your belt.'

'You've been published?' Hannah emailed me regularly, in love with the technology since it was harder for me to dodge than a phone call, but if I replied at all it was short, lacking in information.

'A few papers.' Dad smiled smugly.

'So what were you thinking?' Hannah sipped her wine. 'Is there anything here in Durham? It's nice, the castle and the cathedral.'

'There's a position going but I'm not sure. The pay's not great and I've been here for four years.' Anna was leaving for a job in Norway, so there was no point staying. She was out with her own parents. We hadn't spoken about it yet but it was over. We both had futures and they didn't involve each other. 'Did I tell you Harry Boyle's at Aberdeen now?' said Dad. 'Maybe he could get you something.'

'She's not moving back to Aberdeen.'

'Nothing wrong with Aberdeen.'

'Do you want the list or the highlights? Anyway, it would be a backwards step. How about Bristol? They've got a top-class geology department, or so I'm told.'

'Bristol?' said Dad, dismissing the whole city with a wave. 'How about Oxford? Cambridge? Edinburgh? Get into one of those institutions and you're set for life. Who you know, you know?' He was slurring, not noticeably but enough for me. 'But Hannah's right, don't come back to Aberdeen. It's going downhill. Overrun by students and house prices are insane.'

'Well I haven't decided anything yet. There are a lot of things to weigh up.'

'Are you going to take a holiday?' said Hannah. 'When was the last time you went away?'

'I went to Tenerife last spring.'

'Tenerife? Really? Wasn't that a bit...cheap?'

'Teide?' said Dad.

'What's Teide? Oh don't tell me. I didn't mean a field trip, I meant a holiday.'

Anna came with me. 'It was relaxing. I can take a month or so off, depending on what job I take.'

'Take? So you've had offers?' said Hannah.

'A few.'

'That's great, where?'

That Chablis looked really good. 'New Zealand. Washington.' I'd hoped for a job in Hawaii but nothing came up. Professor Kiana Lau was still there. I reread *Dislodging Fossils* at least once a year.

'DC?' said Dad.

'State.'

'But they're both the other side of the world,' said Hannah.

'That's who offered.'

Hannah's face soured, drew into that lemon-sucking pout that meant she was upset but didn't want to be the one to say it. Did she think a PhD would give us a new relationship? We're both called doctor, so what?

'Probably just as well.' Dad waved at the waitress with his empty glass, the bottle finished already.

'And why would that be?' said Hannah, cut-glass tone.

'Nowhere to stay if you came back to Aberdeen. I sold the house.'

Into the silence came the waitress with Dad's glass. He sipped. 'Just delightful.' He eyed her over the rim of the glass and watched her bare legs, her arse in the tight black skirt, move back to the bar.

'You've sold the house?' said Hannah. 'Why?'

'Seemed like a good idea. It's mine now after all.' He had bought her out a year after she left.

'Yours in keeping for Caroline.'

'And she can have half now.' He reached behind him to his jacket, his elbow knocking his wine glass. I lurched and caught it, practised, only a drop or two splashed out, blood-red on the tablecloth. He twisted back round, oblivious, and handed me something. A cheque. 'There you go. Start a new life with that. You can go wherever you want, do anything you want. You have the cash and you have the qualifications. Despite it all, we've done our duty as parents, Hannah. She's grown up, educated, rich, not a junkie, not pregnant and not married to some wee shite. I think we can pat ourselves on the back.' He leaned over to pat her back.

'You think you've got anything to be proud of?'

'Hannah. Volume,' I snapped. 'Dad, this is generous and thoughtful. But why did you sell the house? Where are you living?'

'I got a flat on George Street. There's only me now. Stupid to have a house like that.'

'There's no garage on George Street. Are you really going to park your beloved Saab out in the street?' Hannah's voice was like the whistle from a pressure cooker.

'Sold that too.'

'Ruby?'

'No point having a car. Always pissed,' he laughed. 'Cheers!'

'But how will you get to work?' I said, this feeling, this knowledge.

'Doesn't really matter, does it. They let me go. SERVICE!' he bellowed, silencing the restaurant, turning heads. The waitress came, wary. 'Ah there you are, my lovely. Liqueurs. A rusty nail. A Baileys. A brandy. And something for yourself. Add it to the bill.'

'Marcus,' said Hannah, a venomous hiss.

'We're celebrating.' He was fighting it now. For all his bluster the terror and the anger were still there, in his eyes. I wanted to hold him and I wanted to punch him.

'Hannah,' I hissed back, turning on her. 'Not the time, not the place.' The waitress was still there, unsure. 'Please bring the drinks. He'll be quieter now. Won't you, Dad?'

'As long as you're happy, I'm happy,' he slurred.

'You got fired? I knew it, I—'

'Hannah. I'm warning you. Let's just finish our drinks and leave.'

If only nature were as predictably explosive as the Frasers. The drinks came. Hannah and I drank ours as fast as we could, barely touching the sides, the ice rattling into my teeth. Dad savoured his, finishing the wine before moving on to the brandy. Hannah was ready to blow and I just wanted out. That cheque in my pocket. Half a semi-detached two-bedroomed house at current Aberdeen prices. I'd give it back. I had a job, two to choose from. He'd lost his. I was amazed it had taken this long. Sympathy and loyalty only get you so far. But the house was gone. The last relic of our family, sold. My surname the only tangible souvenir. The thick Baileys coated my stomach like oil. I felt sick. The waitress was talking to one of the owners and pointing at our table. I made the universal symbol for the bill.

'I'll get this,' said Hannah.

'It's on me,' said Dad.

'I've just come into some money,' I said, 'it's my treat.' I thrust my card at the waitress, 'please.' She understood the pleading tone in my voice, took the card. I pulled my coat on, my faculty scarf.

'Carrie, it's your day, here take this.' Hannah waved notes at me.

'Look, if you pay, he'll be upset. If he pays, you'll be upset. If I pay none of us will be happy. That's the fairest way. The Fraser way. Equal pain for all.' As I walked by her towards the door I felt her stuff the notes in my pocket. I changed direction, pulled them out without looking and handed them to the waitress. 'Sorry about that. Divorced parents. Can't take them anywhere.'

Outside, Hannah looked shocked. 'Do you know how much that was? Jesus, Carrie.'

'She deserved it. You're very quiet,' I said to Dad.

'Seemed safest.'

'Your job, Marcus? The house? Your car?' Hannah said.

'The oil industry giveth and the oil industry taketh away.'

'You're going to kill yourself, Marcus. Look at me. I know you don't want to hear it, least of all from me, but if you don't stop you're going to die. Who knows what state your liver and kidneys are in? You need to get help.'

He looked at her, and it was like all support had been taken from him. His face sagged, shoulders hunched, his body a strange mix of bloated fat and malnourished hollows. 'Not. Your. Fucking. Problem.'

'Dad...'

'Carrie. I'm sorry. We've ruined your day. We've ruined everything. By Christ that Larkin was right. You enjoy the night. If her and I stay around each other much longer... I need a pub. Hannah, congratulations. Don't worry about me. I'm a survivor, remember?'

'Dad, wait,' I followed him for a few steps, stopped. Watched him go.

I turned back to Hannah standing under the streetlight, hands in her pockets. 'What did he mean, congratulations?'

'We can talk about it tomorrow. You should go after him.'

'There's a pub around the corner. He'll be fine in there.'

'He won't be fine.'

Something snapped. 'You think I don't know that? You think I haven't known that for ten years?' I could hear my voice echoing back in the narrow street, shrill, just like hers. 'What do you want me to do?'

For a minute we stared at each other in the hellish glow under the lamppost, then she stepped forward and hugged me, crying, her head on my shoulder. I clenched all my muscles, blocked the tears, bottled the emotion. I wouldn't cry. Not with her.

'I know, Carrie. You think I don't know what I did? A mother wants to protect her children and I couldn't protect you from any of this. It was too big. It still is.'

A distant ambulance siren. Laughter from inside the restaurant. 'Congratulations for what?'

She wiped her eyes, folded the tissue and replaced it in her pocket. 'Frank and I are getting married.'

Aberdeen,
January 1999

For Marcus, January was the best time to drink in Under The Hammer. The weeks after Hogmanay were miserable, rain or snow, freezing winds whipping off the North Sea, low skies and short days. Where better to hibernate than in a basement? Once you were down the stairs and into the warm, candlelit room beneath the auction house the climate could do what it liked. The pub itself in January felt like a battlefield recovering from December wars, the last Friday before Christmas, the worst night to be in a pub, all those work nights out. No idea of bar etiquette, waving tenners, tapping coins on the counter. But they were all gone and the place could get back to normal.

Under The Hammer was in the centre of Aberdeen but just far enough from Union Street and Belmont Street to be left alone by the passing cattle. Surrounded by offices, legal firms and oil companies, the main clientele were those who went straight from work to the bar, students of a more sophisticated taste, and artists. Marcus had ensconced himself in the corner by the bar, back against the wall, with the other regulars, all men in their late forties or fifties who drank there every day. Some were married, most for the second or third time. Some had little to go home to. Women occasionally joined the group, girlfriends or colleagues, but none had the commitment of these men. Isobel was, a solicitor with an office off Golden Square, and Marcus was hoping she'd be in later.

They'd first met on Christmas Eve eight years ago, her Shetland accent catching his ear. They had kissed under the mistletoe before he'd taken his impromptu camping trip on the west coast. He shook his head remembering that, wrapped up in a sleeping bag, a whisky haar, listening to the wind batter the canvas. He'd stay over at hers tonight, listen to Miles Davis and fuck the stress away.

He called the new girl, Siobhan, over, got a round in, handed

Keith his pint. 'Cheers,' said Keith. 'When did you get back?'

'This morning, first train.' He'd stayed out in Durham until five, some casino he'd never be able to find again, then gone back to the hotel for his bags. His hangover kicked in around Edinburgh. The look on the trolley woman's face when he ordered alcohol.

'How was it?'

'You know these things, robes and all that shite, fucking Latin fest. In Durham Cathedral though. Beautiful building that. A thousand years old.'

'When a thousand years old, look so good you will not.'

'How's work?'

'Accountancy is as accountancy does.' Keith came from somewhere in Wales originally. Marcus had asked but hadn't bothered. His accent was warped after decades in Aberdeen but you could still hear it around the vowels. He was bald apart from a horseshoe of thin dark hair. He should shave it off, Marcus thought, and accept his disability, but Keith claimed it made him look like Julius Caesar.

'Boring as fuck then?'

Bill came back from the toilet, reached between them for his pint. 'Cheers. Is this right, Marcus? Keith was saying you've lost your job?'

'Told them where to stick it.'

Bill worked for Shell and there were no secrets in the oil industry. He'd know the whole story. Marcus had been keeping it as quiet as he could, but word always got out. Most had the courtesy to keep their noses out of it. He knew they gossiped about him behind his back, a bunch of old women, the lot of them, but Bill had never learned any tact or diplomacy. Think it, say it, was his motto. 'You're better off. What are your plans?'

'Take a fucking holiday for a start. I fancy getting into the mountains, maybe lie on a beach.' With the house and car sold, the flat on George Street paid outright, the savings and shares that had survived Hannah's divorce lawyer, he didn't have to worry about money for a while.

'The mountains in January?' Keith lit a cigarette. 'Doesn't sound like fun.'

'That's when it's the most fun. Me against nature.'

'Well watch nature doesn't kick your teeth in.'

'You looking for another job?' Bill glanced around for a spare stool.

'No rush. Why, you got anything?'

'You could try consulting. You know Barry McLean? He's setting up a consultancy. Contract stuff, so you can pick your hours. Wish I could just pack it in,' said Bill. 'Tell the boss to shove it.'

'What would you do with yourself?' Keith swirled his pint around the glass, washing off the foamy residue. 'Retirement sounds great every Monday morning, but I'd need something to do otherwise I'd just sit in here from opening time to chucking out time.'

'You do that anyway.'

In the opposite corner, beside the door, the bar manager Simon was moving tables and chairs out of the way, making an open space.

'What's going on there?' said Marcus.

'Open mic night.'

'Fuck. Thought that was last night. Thought I'd missed it.'

The open mic night was a new invention concocted by the bar staff, all of whom were arts students of one stripe or another. Simon was a performance poet, whatever the fuck that was, and had convinced the owner to let him and his hippy friends hold this event once a month on a quiet evening. The regulars resented it at first and still pretended to, although they had to admit it livened up their evening. Every week would be too much, but once a month was okay. Besides, which of them would honestly say they'd rather all these nineteen, twenty, twenty-one-year-old girls didn't come into the bar? It was all right as long as the music outweighed the poetry. There's a time and a place for poetry, Marcus had said to Simon, and it's the past. Some of the regulars even got up and did a turn. Bill did

Lou Reed's *Walk on the Wild Side* every time without fail.

Marcus had thrown up when he got back to the flat from Durham, then slept until three. He was feeling good now though, the Guinness sitting well. His nose was twitching as if it could already smell the Bunnahabhain he'd have in two pints' time. When would Isobel get here? He could phone her but he didn't want to come across as needy. He'd tried to sound casual the week before when he told her about going down to Durham, about seeing Hannah again, but he figured she wasn't fooled. The parts of his story he hadn't told her she'd have got from the gossips in the bar. He had no idea what she saw in him. While he was still technically employed, if pushed sideways and surviving on the understanding of old friendships, he thought he could fool her: just another heavy drinker in the oil industry. Aberdeen had more of those than seagulls. But now he was an unemployed drunk, albeit a financially comfortable one, what would she do?

The pub was filling up and Simon had to leave the setting up to a friend in order to help Siobhan behind the bar. From his perch in the corner Marcus got a good view of her arse every time she bent over the sink to rinse a glass. It did nothing for him. What had happened? He was getting old. Ten years earlier he'd have been flirting with her, trying to see down her top. He might think about her while having a wank but it would be without passion. Age. He was falling apart. Was this all that was left? This, until death?

The PA was tested, one, two, and an acoustic guitar tuned. Marcus stretched to see over the people at the bar. 'It's that lad, Kenny is it?'

'Aye,' Simon pulled a pint of Red Cuillin next to them.

'He's good. Is he going to do *Baba O'Reilly*?'

'No idea. Do you want me to ask him?'

'Please. And a whisky when you've got a minute.'

'Coming up.'

Kenny started. He had a loop pedal so his songs always took a minute to get going as he sampled riffs and rhythms, building up a band just by himself. The first time he'd played Marcus had his back to him and assumed it was three or four guys. When Kenny did The Who, managing both Pete Townshend and Roger Daltrey's parts, Marcus became a fan. It had been a long time since new music had made any kind of an impression on him. Maybe that's something he could do with his time. Rediscover rock music. All his favourite albums were ones he'd bought as a teenager. Surely something not shite had been made since then.

During Kenny's first song, he saw Isobel coming down the stairs. 'Simon, large glass of red.' She made her way over to him, weaving around tables and students, greeting people she knew. He watched her, feeling like a teenager himself. She had short hair, thick and black, that reminded him of a female rock star though he'd never worked out who. She was from Shetland originally but had been in Aberdeen since university, married twice. The first had been violent, the second ran off with her best friend. She fitted in well.

She took off her coat and hung it up on the wall on top of Marcus's. He gave up his stool for her. 'Cheers,' she took a sip of her wine.

'How are you?'

'Good. I got loads done today. I need this. You? How was it?'

'Yeah, you know.'

'That good?'

The chat swirled around, people coming and going, the fluidity of social interaction, the grease of alcohol.

'So you've got some time on your hands?' Isobel padded an eyelash off his cheek.

He studied her expression hoping for a clue. Was this a test? Was she gearing up to chuck him? 'Aye. Bill mentioned some work that might be going. Contract stuff. But I was thinking about a holiday. Getting up into the mountains. Or maybe a beach.'

'I've got a better idea.'

'Oh aye?'

'Aye. Have you ever been to Up Helly Aa?'

'Is that the Viking festival in Shetland? They burn a Viking longship and get hammered.'

'There's more to it than that, but generally, yes. I haven't been home since my mum passed away. I thought I could get a week or so off work and we could head off together.'

He couldn't stop grinning. 'Guinness, please, Simon, and a wine, and a Bunnahabhain, a pint for Bill, one for Keith, Matthew? One for yourself and for Siobhan. No bother.'

The music was good, the warmth of the people around him. He could feel himself reviving. A plan. The love of a good woman. Love. The word stopped him. Eight years since they'd first met, a growing closeness over the years, nights together, weekends away, definite affection, concrete feelings. And she was a good woman, too good for the likes of him. But love? He'd thought he was done with that.

Seeing Hannah again. First time for four years, since Carrie graduated from Aberdeen. When would be the next time he'd have to see her? Carrie's wedding? He couldn't imagine Carrie having a big do, white dress and speeches. No doubt he'd get a phone call one day telling him she was married to some academic, a registry office job, two co-workers as witnesses and back to work. Well, good on her. Marcus and Hannah had done the traditional, kilts and meringues, dancing and throwing bouquets, and look where that had got them. He couldn't blame Piper Alpha for that. Not really. She was fucking Frank Carpenter, Marcus was balls-deep by the first night of every business trip, and there'd been a lot of business trips back then, a lot of hotel bars. The best thing Carrie could do was stay single.

'You okay?'

'Sorry, out of it.'

He necked his whisky, waved the glass at Siobhan. 'Something for yourself.'

There it was, the intro to *Baba O'Reilly* looped, the bar chords ringing out. He'd seen The Who back in the day, touring *Who's Next*. 1971 it must have been, maybe 1972, the year

Carrie was born. His last gig before becoming a father. This song, it was his song of freedom. He felt the adrenaline surge those chords always gave him. They'd gone to that gig together, him and Hannah. She might have been pregnant already, but he didn't know it, didn't know the changes coming, just a young couple with ringing ears having sweaty sex in the back of his car in a lay-by on the way home.

He leaned over to Isobel, whispered in her ear, 'Take me home tonight.' She smiled at him, gave him a quick kiss on the lips. He got another Guinness, a gin and tonic to chase it down, he'd missed dinner so got some dry-roasted peanuts and crisps, ripped open the bags on the bar so anyone could help themselves.

The door opened and a group of lads came in, not regulars, not the usual kind of customer. Lads. Five of them. Shoes. Trousers. Club clothes, bouncer-compliant. Laughing, shouting. They were midway towards the bar when the one at the front noticed everyone staring at them.

'Fuck's going on here?'

'Open mic night,' said Simon.

'Aye? Gies us a song? Do you know *Wonderwall*? Five pints of Stella and five tequilas.'

'No tequila,' said Simon, starting the pints.

'Jesus, what kind of bar has no tequila? Sambuca then.'

'No Sambuca either.'

'Fuck sake. We want to do shots. What've you got?'

'Brandy. Whisky. Gin. Baileys.'

'Drambuie?'

'Yeah.'

'Five Drambuies.'

The regulars' corner was full of muttering. Kenny played on but no one was listening now. At the other end of the bar they set the Drambuies on fire, hands over the glass to kill the flame and on the count of three they downed them. Flame shot out of one of the boys and everyone jumped back, the top of the bar on fire, ashtray and peanut packets. Simon, the fastest to react, dipped a towel in the sink and smothered it. Siobhan looked shaken.

'Fuck sake, Ryan, what the fuck was that?' Ryan was coughing, bent over. 'You're supposed to put the fucking fire out, you fuckwit.'

Marcus saw the flames, the rush of it, the flash, and was over before Isobel noticed he'd moved, had the boy by the collar, marching him across the pub, opening the door and pushing him up the stairs. 'Come on, you're fucking out of here.' The lad's mates saw what was going on and rushed after them, the regulars right behind. Out in the street a melee of pushing, Marcus and Ryan grappling, a punch, another, two groups squaring up between the railings and the parked cars.

'Fucking come on.'

'Why don't you piss off boys, it's way past your bedtimes.' Keith tried to get in between them. 'Easy boys, come on now.' Ryan landed a punch, another, and Marcus went back, lost his footing on the top step and went down like a sack of tatties a step at a time, on that hard perpendicular granite. He lay at the bottom, not moving.

The lads ran, Isobel crouched next to Marcus, someone's jacket under his head, his leg at a strange angle, everyone else on the stairs, a fug of adrenaline in the air. Simon phoned an ambulance then his boss while Kenny and his pals tidied up. The night was over. After a minute or two Marcus came round.

'How do you feel?' asked Isobel, stroking his head.

'I can't feel my leg. What's wrong with it?'

'It looks fucked,' said Bill.

'Ambulance is coming.'

'Where's my whisky?' said Marcus. Isobel shook her head at the spectators.

A siren echoing around the streets. The paramedics came and struggled in the narrow stairwell to get him on the stretcher, watched by a crowd clutching glasses and exchanging stories and advice, a bar full of amateur doctors each with a diagnosis, a prognosis, none of them good. Isobel collected their coats and followed him into the ambulance.

'Is his leg broken?' she asked the paramedic.

'His hip, I'd say. But we won't know until he's had an X-ray. You look like you've been in the wars, mate.'

So exhausted, the weight on him. He lay watching the roof of the ambulance sway as they changed lanes, took the corners up to Foresterhill.

Four weeks in that bed. Four weeks. Orthopaedics. Not a drink in Orthopaedics. Not a drop. A desert. Fuck, he'd kill for a drink. Anything. Campari. Cinzano Bianco. Anything. Maybe not McEwan's Export. He had some standards.

No, he didn't. He had no standards and it only took three days to prove it. The DTs. Shakes. Hallucinations. They'd had to sedate him, heavily at first so he wouldn't do himself any more damage, then bringing the doses down, light sedation, just enough Diazepam to keep him groggy. After two weeks the physiotherapy started, but they kept the drugs in him, the Diazepam, the painkillers, huge doses of vitamins. The cravings were awful, the anger. He was thankful for the drugs. Under sedation he didn't dream.

Isobel came every day after work, after lunch on the weekends. Up Helly Aa had been and gone without either of them there. She'd chuck him now for sure, now she'd seen it, what was inside of him. But she came back every day.

In the last week a psychologist, Dr Shaw, appeared. He sent her away again.

The next day, Isobel. She had a different face on. Not the bedside face, not the visitor's face. He guessed it was her work face, her solicitor's face. They spoke.

The day after, Dr Shaw came back. Isobel came back. They worked out a deal.

'You're going home on Friday, Marcus,' said Dr Shaw, her red hair pulled into a ponytail, a thistle pin on her lapel. She sat on a plastic chair at the foot of his bed. Marcus was propped up, his physio done for the day. 'Your body has been pinned and fixed, to a point. But you can't continue like you have been. You're sick but we can fix that too.'

'You can make it all better?'

'We can make it more manageable.'

'I manage fine.'

Isobel, sat by his shoulder, put a hand on his arm.

'You have post-traumatic stress disorder, Marcus, which, with treatment, is manageable. You haven't received treatment. You've been self-medicating with alcohol but that doesn't solve the problem, it just puts it at arm's length. When you stop drinking, you're back where you started, yes?'

He hated her being inside his head, but he'd made a deal with Isobel. Treatment or she was gone. She hadn't worded it like that but that's what it amounted to.

'What are you going to do when you leave here on Friday and the sedation that's been keeping the dreams at bay stops?'

The dreams would come back. He didn't need her to tell him that. He knew it. Felt it. The dreams would come back.

'And you are going to drink again, aren't you?'

A Guinness, ice-cold, condensation beading the glass.

'Marcus, do you want to stop drinking?' It was Isobel, but Dr Shaw looked at him like they'd pre-agreed the question.

'You need to be truthful, Marcus. No one is judging you, but you need to be truthful.'

'No,' he said, the word bursting out from somewhere deep. 'No, I don't want to stop drinking. I like drinking. I love drinking. I don't want to stop.'

'Do you think you can reduce the amount you drink?' said Dr Shaw.

'What, aren't you going to tell me that I have to stop drinking?'

'Would there be any point? You've already planned your first drink, haven't you?'

He looked at them. Shaw with that endless patience, nothing to rail against. Isobel fiddling with her watch. He was lost. This wasn't going how he expected. 'So what are you saying? I can keep drinking?'

'I'm saying you're going to regardless of what I tell you, so let's try something else. Alcoholism is not your major problem.

It's a symptom. If you stop drinking you'll still have PTSD. You'll still have nightmares, flashbacks, mood swings, all the rest of it. Alcohol is a crutch. You don't take the crutch away until the leg is mended. What I propose is this: We treat the PTSD directly through counselling. At the same time we work together, all three of us, to reduce the amount of alcohol you consume. We do both in tandem, reduce your reliance on alcohol while treating the root cause of your need to drink.'

'I don't have to stop drinking?'

'You should stop. If you don't it'll kill you. But going cold turkey isn't going to work. What I'm proposing is common in these situations. It works.'

'How does that sound, Marcus?' Isobel asked. 'We can do this together.'

He walked with a cane, this horrible metal thing that looked like it came in a set with a bed pan and a kidney dish. His mobility would improve, slowly, but his days of munros and running were over. Walking. Soft inclines. That was his range now.

Checked out. Discharged. He thanked the nurses, the doctors. Dr Shaw came by again and they worked out a schedule and a plan for his sessions. Achievable goals were discussed and agreed. Number of units. Number of drinks.

Isobel waiting with a taxi, the crisp February air rushing into his lungs. He took a breath, another. Shuffled like an old man, angled his body into the back seat. Isobel patient, the meter running.

Just a month but the city looked new to him, down Westburn Road and Hutcheon Street, onto George Street. By his old home to his new home. His one-bedroom above the kebab shop. One, two, three, hup out and he fumbled for his keys as Isobel paid. He felt like crying and didn't know why. Key in, up the stairs to the first floor, a step at a time, rest. He had to get Isobel to push the door, the weight of junk mail behind it, he had no strength, no pivot to rely on. The flat was dark, stank like a crime scene.

'Jesus,' he said. 'Maybe you should come back when I've had a chance to clean up.'

'I'll help.'

The mail on the floor. That would take him a good ten minutes to pick up. 'I don't deserve you.'

'Let's get some air in here.' She opened the curtains, hoisted the windows up. The remnants of his life, still boxed, sat in the living room. He'd dumped most of the furniture, put Carrie's things in storage. He'd never found the energy to unpack. Temporary. Everything, temporary. He needed a drink.

Isobel pulled coffee and milk from her plastic bag. He followed her into the kitchen. The bin was rotten, the milk in the fridge now a fountain of life. He eased himself into one of the two kitchen chairs he'd kept. 'This is fucking depressing. Let's go out.'

'No. It just needs a bit of care.' She looked around the kitchen, opened a few cupboards and drawers, her lips moving as she totted something up. 'Right, you sit there. I'll be back in a minute.'

'Where are you going?'

'The corner shop. I'm not drinking out of those cups until they've been thoroughly scrubbed.'

A thought. He fought it. The words rose like vomit. 'Bring back a bottle of something.' He disgusted himself. She'd be out of the door and gone and he'd deserve that too.

'I'll think about it. You don't want to drink your entire ration before lunch.

Strip the sheets off your bed and put them in the machine.'

The tears came. 'I don't deserve you. This. I'm—'

'Strip the bed. In the machine. I'll be back in a minute.'

The click of the door. Stark. Stated like that. Life or death.

The bed, the original marital bed. Another fucking crime scene. He got the sheets in the machine, some clothes on the floor, the worst offenders he hooked with his stick, shoved them in too. Enough for at least two loads and no garden to dry them in. How many minutes was that? The remaining clothes he pushed into a pile, like a park keeper with leaves, added the two sets of pyjamas Isobel had bought him from Marks and Spencer.

Key in the lock. The relief, he thought he was going to cry again, skin hot, heart rising. She had three bags, all different.

The neck of a bottle sticking out. Just one. Maybe there were cans as well. 'Let me help you.'

'No, you sit down.'

He wanted that bottle. Who was she to keep it from him? She placed a cold palm on his cheek. 'It's going to be hard.'

The heat eased out of him. It was there. He could wait. Four weeks.

Another few minutes were okay.

'Right, Hop-along, you do the dishes, I'll deal with the rubbish and the washing.' She handed him a bottle of washing up liquid and some rubber gloves, propelled him gently to the sink. 'Let's get at least one room habitable.'

The first laundry load done, the second safely in the machine waiting for sufficient space to dry, the heating on, the windows wide. The wine stood unopened beside the microwave, a Kiwi Pinot Noir. They sat either side of the kitchen table, her back to the fridge, his to the door. Mugs half-empty, the room smelled of disinfectant and instant coffee.

'So,' she said. Hands flat on the table.

'So.'

'You need a hobby.'

'What?'

'Cooking.'

'You're going to teach me how to cook?'

'No, we're going to learn together.' She showed him a Thai cookbook. 'I got this as a present two years ago. There's not much point in cooking complicated recipes when you're eating alone.'

'No. Takeaways and tinned soup.'

'Well, I ate a bit better than that, but yes.' He helped her unpack the bags, put things in the fridge. It looked so much more colourful, the tomatoes and peppers, than the solitary carton of milk.

'What are we making?'

'I'm going to teach you to make green curry.'

'That smells delicious,' he said. They were sitting in the living room surrounded by boxes half-unpacked. 'Drink?'

'With dinner. Have you ever been to Thailand?'

'Twice, a long time ago.' He'd chopped vegetables while she read out the recipe and sorted spices and herbs. The bottle sat waiting, calling. He needed to keep busy so he'd started emptying boxes. The curry simmering, she came through to help, flattening cardboard and sliding it behind the sofa.

'Backpacking?'

'Business.'

'I can imagine.'

'Yeah. You?'

'No, never.'

'Where have you been?'

'Russia, Eastern Europe mostly. A lot of time in Germany.'

'Recently?'

'When I was younger.'

'Before the Wall came down?'

'I was there.'

'That's ten years ago. I vaguely remember seeing it on TV.'

'Vaguely?'

'1989 wasn't a good year.'

'No. For a lot of people.'

'Russia. Eastern Europe. You were a Communist?'

'Socialist.'

'A Socialist solicitor.'

'There are a few of us. The food should be ready.'

'Joan Jett. It just came to me. You look like Joan Jett.'

'Joan Jett's mother, maybe.'

'Sure. What?'

'You pick.'

They connected up the TV and video, cleared a space to see. Bowls of green curry, brown bread, a glass of wine each. *Some Like It Hot* playing.

'This is nice,' he said. The smell from the wine. Flowers. Warmth. He gulped, every taste bud shocked, every nerve tingling.

'Slow,' she said. 'That's all there is.'

'We can get more.'

'No.'

The curry. The video. Her, there. It felt like a home. 'No.'

He was drunk. The first time in a month. A lightweight. Wine and painkillers. He stumbled into the hallway wall, had left his cane by the sofa. The corner shop was two minutes away. Another bottle would be perfect. The taste of it, the thirst. Isobel sat on the edge of the bed watching him. He looked at her. At the door.

'It's your choice,' she said. 'You can come in here with me or you can go to the shop.'

'We can do both.'

'I won't be here when you get back.'

The door closed behind him. Standing on the stairs. What was he doing? The first step. The second. His hip ached. Was this the choice he was making? Really? The cold air in the stairwell. The rough chipped bannister under his hand. Stark. Stated like that. A choice. He turned painfully, second step, first. Key in the lock.

She had her coat on.

'I need help.'

'I know. But will you accept help?'

'Will you help me?'

'Yes.'

'Why?'

'Because somewhere in the years we've known each other, I fell in love.' She took her coat off. He closed the door.

She put him to bed and cleaned the rest of the flat, finished off the last of her glass while watching him sleep. There was a good man in there, she knew. For eight years they'd known each other, becoming closer over that time, sex, weekends away, restaurants and long walks up at Balmedie. He'd been there for her while she extracted herself from her marriage to Calvin. Marcus, the drunken jester holding court in Under The Hammer, making her smile after a long day in the office, after another call from Calvin's solicitor about money. Somewhere along the way she had fallen for him, despite everything, despite herself. Life had kicked lumps out of him, but the real Marcus was still in there. She'd decided in the back of the ambulance she couldn't just walk away. What kind of a woman ran out when things got tough? She rinsed the glass and got in beside him.

The sessions came and went. Isobel worked her schedule around his so she could drive him there and back. He stuck to his targets, more or less, his intake certainly down on what it had been. She didn't ask him about the sessions but she gathered it wasn't going well.

'I don't know how to talk,' he said as they sat on the sofa in the silence, the turntable arm clicking back into place. 'Most of the time we sit there. She asks me questions but I don't know how to answer.'

'Were you ever one for talking about feelings?'

'Not really. Hannah and I never talked. Fought, yes, but never talked.'

'So why not try something else. How about writing it down?'

'Doctor Shaw suggested that. A way around the blockage. Like a diary.'

'Do you want to give it a go?'

The next morning, Saturday, it began. Isobel picked up a folding card table from her flat, bought an A4 notebook and an expensive fountain pen. She set him up in the living room surrounded by damp clothes then went to Safeway. He made a coffee. Sat down. Stood up again and checked if any of the clothes were dry. He sat again. Stood up and looked at his shelves. He could organise his LPs alphabetically, by genre, by release date. Listen to everything. A bit of Genesis, maybe, *Nursery Cryme*. He sat again. Wrote the date. Drank some coffee. Went over to the window and looked out onto George Street.

The charity shops. The halal butcher's. The betting shop. He sat again, wrote *I was born Marcus Edward Fraser in the year of our Lord* and scribbled it out. He closed his eyes. He could smell the wine, sitting in the kitchen, the ruby bouquet. Ruby, his Saab. He picked up the pen again, wrote *I wasn't part of the Piper Alpha crew. I was only there for a couple of days.* The memories came back, a flood of them, a tide battering into him. He stood up too fast, pain shooting through his hip, knocked the coffee over. He couldn't do this. He couldn't go there. That door needed to be closed. No words, no wine. He got a cloth, mopped up the coffee.

Key in the lock. Arms full of shopping. 'Here, let me help you.'

'How's it going?'

'Not great.'

'Show me what you've done.'

'Do you want to see the two sentences or the coffee stain?'

'Two sentences is good.'

'No, it's not.'

'It's better than no sentences.' She switched the kettle on, rinsed his cup out.

'Only mathematically.'

'Did you think you were going to write an entire book in one morning?' He shrugged. 'Don't start with that night,' she said. 'You need a run-up to it. Start at the beginning.'

'I was born...'

'If you like. You maybe don't need to go that far back. Start with your job. When did you join the company? Why? Ease into it that way.' She kissed him, handed him a mug. 'Take this coffee, sit down and when you get to the end of the first page you can quit for the day.'

Sunday. He wrote. They went for a walk. Another bottle. Just the one. Monday she went to work, came round after with a bottle. He'd made a noodle salad. She brought a bottle.

He filled pages. Went back, started again, said it better, clearer. They worked through the recipe book. Walked further

as his hip strengthened. Each day another bottle. Just the one.
She read what he wrote. He wanted her to. Needed her to.

'I won't be over tomorrow,' she said. 'I have to go to Edinburgh.'
   'But I was going to try the peanut sauce.'
   'The day after. It's only for one night.'
   'Business?'
   'Of course. You'll be okay?'
   'It's just one night.'

I was in the cinema, he wrote, *when the first explosion came.*

He stirred the sauce, unseeing. It was all down on paper, the
galley, the heat of it. The water, the chill of it. He was going to
die, there on the rig. He'd never see Carrie again. He'd survived
but had lost Carrie anyway.

Isobel found him the next morning on the kitchen floor. Three
empty bottles of wine. A bottle of whisky. All of his painkillers.
The stink in the flat. He'd be fine, the paramedics said on the
way to the hospital, must have thrown it all up. She took a taxi
back to his flat, cleaned. Opened his notebook and read.

University of Otago, Dunedin, New Zealand,
December 2000

You could pretend a letter hadn't arrived. Growing up in the UK, 'lost in the post' was rarely metaphorical. Email had no direct equivalent. Lost in the ether? Took a wrong turn on the information superhighway? All technology did was make it more difficult to avoid people. Avoiding people was what I did best.

In the past, when people fell out of favour with the royal court, with the Tudors or the Plantagenets or whoever, they took themselves off to their country estates and it was considered exile. I took myself to the other side of the planet. Literally, or near as dammit. The other side of the world from Dunedin would be off the north coast of Spain if you drilled right through. I escaped, exiled myself to the South Seas and then this happened. In amongst unread emails from Hannah and requests for papers, to attend conferences, I found this:

To: Dr Caroline Fraser From: Graeme Anderson Subject: New Zealand
   Hi Carrie, (this is you, isn't it?)
   Long time, no see. I heard you were in New Zealand and I got your email address from the website. I hope you don't mind. I'm going to be in New Zealand for a bit and I thought it would be nice to catch up.
   Cheers, Graeme.

Closing down the computer, I packed my desk into my khaki canvas bag, all my marking, papers I had to read, that book to review, all homework for the holidays. My nail caught on a loop of stitching, ripping the edge of the nail and drawing out more of the thread. Shit on both counts. I rummaged in my desk for the nail clippers but couldn't find them. In the stationery drawer I found a huge pair of paper scissors and snipped the offending snag. The nail now curled in like a bite had been taken from it.

That was going to hurt like hell when I went climbing later. Pulling on my jacket, I slung the backpack over my shoulder.

In the corridor, Jeannie Parker, palaeontologist and fellow immigrant, though only from Perth, the far side of Australia, was saying goodbye to Paul Harding, a senior lecturer in geology. Paul and I got on professionally but didn't socialise much outside the building. He liked bars and loud music, had little time for outdoors and exercise.

'Paul's off to India,' said Jeannie.

'The Deccan Traps?' Paul and I did have one thing in common – a love of those half-million square kilometre basalt steps in Western India, the result of a series of eruptions that many think played a part in the extinction of the dinosaurs.

'Yes, I'm taking the kids for the first time.'

'Enjoy it,' I said, locking my door. 'An Indian Christmas.'

'Turkey curry,' said Jeannie. 'Have a good trip.'

'You too.' He disappeared down the stairwell, heavy steps echoing.

'Finally done? I thought you'd still be here on Christmas Day.'

'Not done, Jeannie, just leaving.'

'It never gets done, does it?'

'When's your flight?' I asked on the stairs.

'Tomorrow afternoon. A few of us are going out for a drink later. Can I tempt you?'

'Looking for a designated driver?'

'Looking for your company.' Was there a hint of something there? 'It's just a quiet thing. That new Thai place on George Street. The Albar after. It won't be a late one. At least, it doesn't have to be.'

'Thanks, Jeannie, but I've got plans.'

'Actual plans or staying in with a book and a bath plans?'

'An old friend is in town.' Not strictly a lie.

'Bring her. Him? Or are these *plan* plans?'

'Nothing like that, just—'

'You're blushing.' Jeannie held the door open and as I passed I could smell the soap from the gym.

We sheltered under the roof of the bike garage and prepared for the weather. Two years and I still couldn't get my head around the climate. It was December so it should have been cold. But we were in the southern hemisphere so it should have been hot. But we were on the South Island, next stop Antarctica, so it should have been proper snowy December cold but actually it was just pissing with rain. You'd never have guessed the place was founded by Scots.

'Well, if you change your mind, you know where we'll be. If not, Merry Christmas, Happy New Year, all that crap.'

'You too. Enjoy the sun.' We connected an awkward hug, all arms and bags and jackets. I gave her a last wave, mounted the bike and rolled out into the rain. I dropped a couple of gears, stood on the peddles and rode as hard as I could down Leith Street, onto Union Street East and then Clyde Street, following the roads through the city, taking a winding route to avoid the traffic then along Portsmouth Drive, skirting the harbour, onto Portobello Road and into Waverley, where I lived.

The house was dark and quiet. I shared with Mike, who was doing his PhD in physiotherapy. He was from Christchurch and had gone home for the festive period. The house was a wooden villa with a tin roof, a deck and garden out the back where we could enjoy the sun. Mike's father was a property developer and owned it, so the rent was reasonable. Everything creaked and groaned in the wind that blustered from the harbour. Peeling off my soaking clothes and throwing them straight into the machine, I flicked the kettle on then had a shower. As easy to live with as Mike was – he was either studying, running or playing rugby – having the place to myself was bliss. The curtains all drawn, I could walk around in whatever state of undress I felt like. I'd never had my own place, so those moments I treasured, being truly alone, the rainy world shut out, the peace of nothing but my own breath and the clink of the lid on the teapot. It was like being high in the mountains but with five-star facilities. Well, maybe three-star.

I pulled on a T-shirt and tracksuit bottoms and settled into the couch with my camomile. So, Graeme was in New Zealand.

I hadn't seen him since that day in Café Continental but I'd followed his career. On his way to the Olympic bronze two years ago were a few golds in Aspen and a cupboard full of trophies. For ten years he'd been a mainstay at the top of his sport. But watching an old friend succeed from a distance and having him turn up unannounced on my doorstep? I put my misgivings aside. It would be nice to see him again.

I emailed him and agreed to meet for coffee the following day. My room was a mess of clothes as I tried to find the right balance of casual but not too casual, suitable for Dunedin's weather. What was wrong with me? I was a twenty-eight-year-old volcanologist, not a sixteen-year-old girl. I left my bike at home, took the number nineteen bus into town. How would he look? In my mind he was still somewhere between that hurt but determined boy in Café Continental and the gracious bronze medallist on the TV two years ago in his colourful gear, hat off, goggles up on his forehead spiking his hair like a pineapple.

It was summer in the Southern Hemisphere. What the hell was he doing in Dunedin?

He was in a dwam and didn't see me straight away. He hadn't changed, still the sharp cheekbones, the neck tendons standing out taut like they'd been carved from oak. His hair was thinning on the crown, receding from his forehead so he wore it shaved close, the tousled fresh-out-of-bed look gone. His clothes were expensive, factory-aged jeans, a tight checked shirt and a soft leather jacket. I dropped my bag and scarf on the chair opposite, startling him awake. 'Off in your own world?'

He stood and we shared a half-hug, half-peck on the cheek. 'Sorry,' he said, 'I was buffering. Still a bit jet lagged.'

'More coffee? Is that a long black?'

'I'll get it. What are you for?'

'Camomile. I can get it.'

'No, no, sit down.'

While he queued I sorted myself out. The coffee shop was quiet with most of the students gone for the holidays. His bag was hanging on his chair, the corner of the *New Zealand Lonely Planet* sticking out. When I moved over I bought a copy myself but since then a new edition had come out. I pointed to it as he sat back down. 'You're over on holiday then?'

He zipped up his bag before answering. 'Kind of. I've got a bit of time off.'

'You've been to New Zealand before, yeah?'

'Yeah, some competitions, a bit of climbing.'

'It's your kind of place. You still climb?'

'When I can. You're looking good.'

'Congratulations on the medal, by the way, that was amazing.'

'It's just a bronze.'

'It's an Olympic bronze.'

'I suppose. Gold would've been better.'

'Should we ask the guy who came fourth?'

'I suppose.'

'You can try again in two years. America, isn't it?'

'Salt Lake.' He fell silent while I sipped my tea. His coffee untouched. He looked tired, now I could see him closely, double bags under his eyes.

'Where did you fly in from?'

'New York,' he said, 'via…somewhere. San Francisco. Auckland.'

'That's a long way.'

'I've no idea what day it is. Is it Christmas yet?'

'Not quite.'

'I wasn't sure if you'd be here. I thought maybe you'd go home for Christmas.'

'That's a long way, too.'

'Too long.'

I caught his eye, the smoky blue, the pupil dilated and behind it, around it, an exhaustion that went beyond time zones.

'This place is surreal.' We were standing in the middle of the

122

Octagon, a pedestrianised plaza in the centre of town, looking at a statue of Robert Burns, taking advantage of a break in the rain to have a walk around. Two years I'd been in Dunedin and I'd never quite got used to the Edinburgh street names, the overwhelming Scottishness of it all. When I applied for the job at Otago University I knew nothing about Dunedin. Once I started researching I couldn't believe it.

'The Edinburgh of the South, the Lonely Planet calls it,' he said.

'And Edinburgh is the Athens of the North.'

'What does that make Athens? Did you know the Lonely Planet calls Aberdeen a "symphony in grey"?'

'Can't say I've ever looked. Dunedin comes from the Gaelic Dùn Èideann.'

'What does that mean?'

'Edinburgh. It was founded and designed by Scots.'

'Only Scots would choose the cold, rainy South Island over the hot, sunny North.'

'Most of them probably didn't want to leave Scotland in the first place. Only natural to make it more familiar.'

'Exiles rather than expats.'

'Which are we?'

'Can you be an exile through choice?'

'If you have a good enough reason for not going back. Anyway, I don't like that expression.'

'Expat? Why?'

'It's racist. Only white people who have moved to another country get called expats. Non-white people are called migrants.'

The rain had returned and, feeling peckish, I took him to Plato's down near the harbour. From outside it wasn't much, housed in an old seaman's mission by a flyover, but the food was outstanding.

'So, what are your plans?'

The waiter placed my blue cod, and Graeme's squid in garlic and chilli, and took away our unused and unwanted wine glasses.

'This evening?' he asked.

'This trip. I mean, you didn't come from New York just to eat seafood with me.'

'Maybe I did.' He sipped his water. 'No plans really. I just felt like a change of scenery.'

'New York got too boring?'

'Just...you know.'

'Insightful. Well, you've missed the ski season, but I guess I don't have to tell you that. Don't you need to be training? No Winter X Games this year?'

'I felt like a break. If I miss one the world won't end.'

'Fair enough. So, are you going to travel around the country? There are some great bike trails, and the national parks are just beautiful.'

'I haven't decided. How about you? You must be on vacation.'

'No classes but lots of work. Students get in the way of my research, so now they've all sodded off I can concentrate on the important stuff.'

'What are you researching?'

'You want to know? I'm studying something called magma evolution and storage, basically what is going on day-to-day inside a volcano, trying to understand the processes that govern stability versus volatility in volcanoes.'

'Predicting eruptions?'

'That's what everyone's working towards.'

'Cool.'

'Important, but I wouldn't call it cool.'

'Hey, I slide down mountains for a living, but I have no idea what's going on inside them. If you can tell a village that the volcano it's built on is about to blow, I'd say that qualifies as cool. What are you doing for Christmas?'

I lay in bed unable to sleep. Neither the biography of Arthur Eddington nor the book on volcano development I'd been asked to blurb could keep my attention for more than a few lines. In the darkness I stared at the ceiling.

When I lived in Aberdeen, my ceiling had been covered in glow-in-the-dark stars set out in various constellations. With

124

the light shade in centre, moving clockwise, you could travel a year in the Scottish sky, Gemini, Capella and Pleiades for spring; the summer triangle of Deneb, Vega and Altair; Pegasus as you moved into autumn and Orion bridging winter and spring. Astrophysics came a distant second to geology, but a passion nonetheless. I could still see them although the Kiwi sky was so alien. One thing Dunedin's founders couldn't make like home.

I'd made such deliberate efforts to leave Aberdeen behind. Four years in Durham, two in Dunedin, memories tightly packed away gathering dust and then Graeme lands, blasting cobwebs and picking locks.

Christmas was a day like any other. A Monday, in fact, and Monday was a day of work. I was sure Graeme would have been happy with me cooking him a turkey, but I was having none of that. If I was taking a day off I wasn't going to spend it in the house. Climbing seemed the obvious thing to do.

There were plenty of places to climb in Dunedin, but lacking a car limited our options. Mike had left his bike behind so once we'd fixed Graeme up with boots, we cycled away from Dunedin out to the Peninsula along Highcliff Road and down Sandymount to Lover's Leap, a crag facing out into the ocean. It was a beautiful day as we rode through the undulating green landscape, the sea iris blue between hills, the fields of sheep basking in the sun.

'It looks like Scotland,' said Graeme.

It was an outing in itself rather than a journey, and the roads that early were empty. We cycled side-by-side taking climbs in our stride, free-wheeled winding downhills, content with the chatter of lambs and the burr of wheels.

We carried the bikes down the gully and round to the crag. It stood perpendicular to the sea facing west, still in shade at that time of the day. I stretched and got everything ready, boots on and rope set. I usually went climbing at Long Beach. There was a cave with loads of bouldering lines, so I could go myself and didn't need to cart all the gear, but the climbing at Lover's Leap was great, basalt organ pipes meaning loads of long single-pitch routes. Getting started was tricky because of all the unclimbable choss but there were enough bolts and chains so that once you were over it, you were off. Occasionally it was better to be with someone.

Crimps and fingerlocks, highsteps and kneebars, there was nothing else in your mind but the rock, your position on it, where you were going next, next, next. Fingers rusty, I slipped and Graeme lowered me, we changed places, tried different lines, the sun at noon, warming the crags. We stopped for Christmas lunch on the grass, salad and leftovers, fruit juice and bottled water.

'I like this,' said Graeme. A chain of sea kayaks, violent orange against the bruise-dark sea, rounded the headland in caravan. 'I could stay here forever.'

'Three thousand years ago people set out across these waters, starting from Indonesia and spreading through the Polynesian islands, Fiji, Samoa, the Cooks and down here, up to Hawaii, right across to Easter Island. Almost all the way across the Pacific in canoes. They didn't even know if there was anything out there. They just got in their boats with some supplies and kicked off, knowing they'd never be back.' The hard curve of the horizon. 'Some stayed, made a home. Others kept going.'

'We're always searching for something. Some people never find it.'

'Like Bono.'

He laughed, threw a grape at me.

'How long are you staying? You didn't say,' I asked.

He finished his mango smoothie, waiting with the bottle upturned over his mouth for the pulp to drop out. He deliberately screwed the lid back on and put the empty into his bag. Got a tissue and dabbed at his mouth. 'No idea.' He wouldn't look at me.

'Are you going to tell me what's going on?'

'I don't know.' He must have noticed my increasing exasperation because he continued. 'I mean, I don't know because I haven't decided. I...I had to get away.'

'Are you in trouble?'

'No, nothing like that. I just...I don't know.'

'You're very happy to admit what you don't know. You'd make a good scientist.'

He laughed, but it was empty. 'I was supposed to be a lawyer, remember?

Lawyers always know everything.'

'Do you regret that? Not going to law school?'

'No, it was the right decision at the time. And thank you for that. Talking, that day in Café Continental. Your advice.'

'Yeah, I've always been good at what other people should be doing.'

'But Dad was right – I can't be a professional snowboarder my whole life.'

'So that's it? Career crisis?'

'Midlife crisis.'

'You're twenty-eight, you can't be having a midlife crisis.'

'Depends how old I am when I die.'

'God, you're cheery today.'

'Merry Christmas. Let's get back up there. Not thinking helps.'

'I'm not sure it does, but I know what you mean.'

Graeme was set on conquering a tricky line and I let him take a few runs at it. What do professional snowboarders do when they retire? Retiring at twenty-eight, the idea. I was just getting started on my career, still finding my feet in my first job. I was building a reputation, citations of my papers increasing. I had all these plans, the research I wanted to do, the papers I needed to write, the books. How lucky I'd been. Not everyone knew with complete certainty what they wanted to do with their lives. People drifted. Changed their minds. Tried different things. Took wrong turns. Hannah was like me, sure from a young age. Dad ended up in the oil industry because it came along when he was unsure. He'd have been happier as a field geologist than in an office making money for billionaires. The choices you made, they could take you by surprise.

We cycled home, silent, each with our thoughts, put the bikes in the garage. I wondered what to do about dinner, what to do with the evening. There'd be a restaurant open somewhere. Or we could eat in. Or we could go our separate ways. I felt like curling up on the couch with a film, maybe make a pizza. But it was Christmas. I had a depressed guest. Maybe he had some idea, knew his own mind. 'What do you want to do?'

'I need a shower.'

'Do you need to go back to your hotel?'

'Depends. I have clothes with me. Do you want to do something? Get some dinner?'

What a pair. 'Have a shower here and we can come up with a plan.' I wasn't used to being around one person this much, or having someone in my house. Apart from Mike, obviously, but Mike kept to himself. 'Shower's in there, towels in the cupboard, everything's self-explanatory.'

I straightened the place, made sure there were no stray items of underwear drying, opened the French windows to air the room. I turned on the TV so he'd have something to do while I showered. The news was full of the bombings in Indonesia, al-Qaeda, talking heads, carnage. Those families at home, in hospitals, waiting for news. Waiting to hear. I changed the channel, found *The Muppet Christmas Carol*. Graeme came out, fresh and damp, we swapped places. He fell asleep on the couch, Michael Caine and the Ghost of Christmas Present watching the Cratchits through the window.

Graeme slept for an hour while I prepared dinner. Homemade pizza and salad, ice cream for dessert. *Indiana Jones and the Last Crusade*. I'd had worse Christmases. The sun set, a chill wind off the sea rolled over the garden so I closed the doors, pulled the curtains.

'I should have got you a present,' he said. 'I never thought.'

'Don't be daft.' I was sitting on the floor, my back against the couch. He was above me, half lying, legs curled. I could feel his knee just behind my head.

'I wouldn't have known what to buy anyway. I usually give people bottles of stuff. Champagne. Wine. You don't drink.'

'It's a pain, isn't it?'

'You never did like making things easy.'

'I think I'm pretty straightforward.'

'Yeah, but in your own way. At school all the other girls were easy to work out. Kim, Lesley, Julie. You knew where you were with them. You were a whole different puzzle.'

'What do you mean?' Sean Connery had been shot. Harrison Ford was approaching the first test, the spinning blade that decapitated all but the penitent.

'You just always did your own thing.'

Ford was through and faced with the name of God.

'I seem to remember not having much choice with that.'

'Mark? Sure, there were dicks, but most of us were on your side. And then with your dad. We wanted to help but we...I...we couldn't find a way.'

Ford made it and now faced the final challenge. The leap from the lion's mouth. A test of faith. I remember the first time I watched this, Indiana Jones stepping off a cliff. I still held my breath.

'You know I really liked you?' he said.

'At school?'

'I had such a thing for you.'

'Shut up.'

'I did.'

I looked up at him. On the screen Indiana Jones found the knight, the room with the grail. 'You did?'

'I did. I do.' And he leaned over and kissed me.

And I kissed him back.

Findhorn,
May 2003

Findhorn is a coastal town a two-hour drive north from Aberdeen on the hellish A96. Famous for two things – a marina and the Findhorn Foundation, a community of hippies living in an ecovillage between the village proper and Kinloss RAF base. Marcus and Isobel set up the tent on a strip of grass separated from the road by a thick hedge, while *Tommy* by The Who played on the car stereo, windows down, earlier visits leaving them safe in the knowledge that no one would be organised enough to ask them for payment. Beyond the tents stood the static caravans and the toilet block. At the far end past the shop selling locally made jewellery and new age guidebooks were the ecohomes and holiday lets, the Universal Hall and the pottery. The community was a mix of retired middle-class couples and dropouts from society existing in an uneasy symbiosis with the rest of Findhorn. Marcus tended to ignore the weirdos, otherwise it was a good campground and the beaches, and the sea kayaking were fantastic.

There were only four other tents. Two were accompanied by expensive-looking road bikes chained to trees, German tourists cycling around the Highlands. Isobel had looked at them askance when they overtook her Alfa Romeo as they were stopping for lunch.

'Do those seats not hurt after a while?'

'Almost immediately.'

'So why do they do it?'

'To prove something.' Marcus had loved touring when he was younger. At university he and Taka had covered huge swathes of the country like that.

'Does it not hurt your balls?'

'Makes them go numb. I always used to have a wank afterwards to get the blood flowing again.'

'Any excuse.'

She'd turned back to the book. Isobel could read in the car without getting sick and over many road trips around the country they'd developed a routine where she would read aloud as he drove – always one way. Marcus never drove back.

His hip meant cycling was out. He missed it. Missed Ruby too. Isobel's car was nice but it wasn't a Saab, lacked those curves, the feel, the smell. He'd thought about getting his own car but his money wouldn't last forever.

She reparked the car so its body, the hedge and the tent formed a windbreak while Marcus filled the water bottle, unpacked mats and sleeping bags, stove and gas, sorted through the food, rearranged the coolbox. It was almost like a dance, they'd done this so often. They tried to get out of the city every weekend. Habits had to be broken and remade. The counselling continued, his drinking held steady at the compromise level but hanging around Aberdeen with nothing to do was asking for trouble. Loitering without intent, Isobel called it. From then on Marcus referred to their trips as 'loitering within tent'.

Three tartan blankets patchworked on the grass, shoes weighing the corners down, they stretched out, books, newspapers, wine in short glasses – stems were best avoided when camping – basking in the late summer sun. A Hercules took off from the base, a monstrous roar, a shadow cast like a dragon, the white wind turbine ticking round. Later they'd walk into town but for now they were content to be silent. Isobel on her back with the newspaper, holding it above her blocking the sun. Marcus lay on his front, a printout of his book, a red pen in his hand, the lid chewed between his lips like a Clint Eastwood cigar.

Dr Shaw had been right. Isobel had been right. Once he got out of hospital the second time he filled the notepad, filled another one, a total mess, a stream of thoughts, his entire life from birth to Isobel finding him on the kitchen floor, everything he could remember, everything he'd been told about his childhood. It all came out yet there was a hole in the centre of it, July 6th 1988. Slowly, painfully, never on days when Isobel was away, he filled it in, a word at a time, a sentence. A scene.

A memory. He worked his way through it, worked it out on lined foolscap, and once it was down there, once he had found the words, he could find them again with Dr Shaw, with Isobel. He could tell the story. His story. At times the nightmares increased, but gradually they receded, along with the flashbacks. Then the question – what was he going to do with himself now? What was he going to do with all of those notebooks?

It was Isobel who first suggested the book. It seemed Sisyphean but she pointed out that compared to what he'd just gone through, reorganising and rewriting was a doddle. So he got hold of a second-hand laptop and began wading through screeds of often incomprehensible nonsense. Monday to Friday, nine to five he worked, as Isobel did. In the evening they cooked, at the weekend they left the city to visit castles, lochs, gardens.

He topped up her glass, then his own. The salt in the air, the positive ions, he could already feel himself tingling, the sun on his skin, the tannins in his blood, the words passing in front of his eyes, his brain catching commas and typos. He'd have fish for dinner, maybe mussels. He could smell the garlic and butter already.

He'd gone to the Central Library, trawled through old newspapers, records, the Cullen inquiry. He got into Grampian TV through a friend and watched tapes from that night, from the weeks and months afterwards. He got Health and Safety reports, transcripts, minutes.

The book grew. So did his anger.

Anger is good. Anger is natural. When it's directed at the source, when it's directed, controlled, utilised, anger is one of the strongest motivations there is.

Anger is bad. Anger is destructive. When it flails around, splashing on everyone, when it's turned inwards anger poisons everything.

Dr Shaw talked him through the process, explained his emotions in clear, scientific terms. He'd never considered psychology a real science but everything she suggested worked.

Except one thing. One thing he wouldn't do. She wanted him to go to the Piper Alpha Families and Survivors Association and meet them. Meet the others. The survivors. The families.

He wouldn't. He couldn't.

But he kept on with the book. No one would ever see it but that was fine.

This was therapy. He'd show it to Isobel. Maybe Dr Shaw if she cared.

Carrie. Since she moved to New Zealand they'd so rarely spoken. Emails of two or three lines, ice age gaps between replies.

Would he send her a copy?

'Have you seen this?' Isobel tapped the newspaper.

'What is it?'

'There's going to be a meteor shower tonight. If the sky stays clear we should be able to see it.'

'Bonfire on the beach?'

'Definitely.'

They walked hand in hand along the side of the tree-lined road, a tunnel of green, the sea unseen a few metres away, passing houses with Gaelic names, a couple at first, then more until the road became a street and they were walking through the village, the greenery under control, tamed, the bay calm and grey, boats bobbing, the clang of wind through rigging. They took the left fork at the War Memorial, the road by the thin strip of beach and went into the Kimberley Inn. A proper pub. Wooden walls and floor, a big fireplace. Marcus got his mussels, Isobel opted for the sea bass.

'I forgot to tell you,' he said, a slice of chilli nipping his tongue. 'I heard back from Barry McLean.'

'The consultancy?'

'Yeah, he's invited me in on Wednesday.'

'A job interview? That's fantastic news.' She chewed a mouthful of fish, chased it with some Sauvignon Blanc.

'An exploratory chat, he called it, but yeah.'

'Do you think he knows everything about...everything?'

'Sure. He knows Bill well, they'll have had a talk. It's hardly a secret.'

'There are no secrets in Aberdeen.'

'All that money and it's still a village.'

'So he's willing to look beyond all that, do you think?'

'He's willing to meet. If he thought I was a liability he wouldn't have me anywhere near the office.'

'Well, make sure you're prepared. You've been out of the industry a long time.'

'You'll need to get me up to speed on Health and Safety legislation.'

'Can do. It would be great if he took you on.'

'No kidding. I'd be able to move out of that flat for a start.'

'Somewhere with a driveway.'

'Somewhere without a kebab shop.'

'A big kitchen. I've got us a new recipe book, Middle Eastern. Lots of lamb.'

'A big everything. A garden.'

'You got a lot done today?'

'One more chapter then you can see it.'

'Do you want dessert?'

'I want a smoke.'

'Beach?'

'Beach.'

The village of Findhorn faces the bay. Around the headland the beach widens into golden sand, dunes and scrub isolating it from any signs of civilisation. Along the way they collected driftwood, blown newspapers, anything that could make fire. The last of the dog walkers called 'Evening' to them. A sheltered spot on the edge of the dunes. The sun was setting as they constructed a pyre, got the flames going. He opened the wine, Isobel rolled a joint. He lay back in the sand, hands behind his head, waiting for the stars to come out. 'Doesn't get much better than this.'

Isobel inhaled deep, exhaled. 'Nope.'

He took the proffered joint, felt his muscles relax into the coast. She lay with him, her head on his shoulder. 'Did I tell you about Christmas nineteen ninety?'

'When we first met? A little. You went to the west coast.'

'Blind drunk in the middle of the night, I drove to Ullapool, camped on the beach for three nights. Minus fifteen it got to.'

'You must have had good equipment.'

'The best. I sat watching the sea for two days, drinking, hardly eating. I thought I might die there. I wanted to die there. Scottish beaches and me, we go way back.'

'We're an island people. You less than me. Shetland's a proper island.'

'You know the old joke? A wife says to her husband "When you die I'm going to dance on your grave." So her husband says, "Then I'm going to be buried at sea."'

'Wives used to be buried with their husbands. Burnt with them.'

'When I die I want to be scattered on a Scottish beach. Not cremated. Just scattered.'

'You're full of jokes tonight.'

'There's been too much seriousness recently.'

In silence they watched first one star, then four, then uncountable bright points pierce through the purple sky. They were alone in the world, a desert island, safe together, the shush of the sea, the whisper of the wind. Up above there were satellites, a space station; down here, out-at-sea ships and submarines and oil rigs, platforms of metal filled with men, the roar of the gas flare. Beyond them, Scandinavia, Iceland, the Arctic, keep going over the top and back down across the Pacific, as near as dammit on the International Date Line, catching the edge of Russia, through the islands, Kiribati, Tuvalu, Fiji and there was New Zealand, Carrie in Dunedin, the other side of the world and still a small piece of Scotland, all connected, all under the same sky but here, in the circle of light from the fire, just Marcus and Isobel.

The first meteor came. A ball of fire arcing across the sky. They couldn't believe it, had been expecting a shooting star but they were burning up right above them. Another like a crashing aeroplane or a spaceship, another, another, the sky alive with fire, streaked by flames, another, another, dozens of meteors burning up in the atmosphere above them.

Fewer and fewer, the spaces increasing. One last meteor and it was over.

Marcus kissed her forehead. She shifted her mouth to his.

'Isobel Mowat, will you marry me?'

Dunedin, New Zealand,
April 2003

'Where are you off to this time?'

'I told you a million times. Hawaii.'

My bags were open on the bed as I did my final check, scratching things off the list. The taxi was booked for three o'clock, in twenty minutes, and I couldn't concentrate.

'I could come over in a month or so.'

'No.'

'No? Just like that?'

'It's not a holiday. I'm going to be working all day, sleeping in a dorm, sometimes in a hut in the mountains. If you came over I wouldn't be able to spend any time with you.'

'You're working seven days?'

'Yes. Anyway you've got work to do.'

'Not much. Not until the ski season starts.'

'What about your designs? Did you get back to that company in Fife?'

'On the list for today.'

'You have an actual list?'

He tapped his head. 'All in here. I'm meeting Gabe later. We're going to talk about the shop. See if we can get something concrete.'

I went through the house checking the plugs, the windows and doors. Mike was in Auckland for a conference so I emptied the fridge into a plastic bag and handed it to Graeme. I'd been running the contents down for a week so there wasn't much: a pepper, some broccoli, pesto, cheese. My mobile rang. 'Shit, he's early. Move.' I pushed by him and closed up the bags, hoisted the suitcase and backpack to the door. 'Stand there and don't move.' A final check.

Graeme carried my bags to the taxi while I checked the garage.

Bags in the boot. 'Airport, please.'

'Forgetting something?' said Graeme.

'What?'

He held his arms out. Hug. Quick kiss.

'Take care, give me a call, have fun.'

'It's not a—'

'Yeah, yeah. Still, have fun. Love you.'

I got in the back, closed the door. 'See you,' through the window.

At the University of Hawaii a project researching issues around geothermal energy production was underway. As an expert in subterranean mapping, I'd been able to secure a research grant and a place on the study. I thought of myself as an anatomist of the planet. Blood circulation was a puzzle for thousands of years until the early anatomists from Galen to William Harvey got in there and demonstrated the network of veins, arteries and the role of the heart and lungs. I was trying to do the same with the planet, in a way.

My – everyone's – ultimate goal was eruption prediction but if I could help find a safe way to produce electricity through geothermal heating, that would be a hell of a contribution. To produce electricity you heat water, in this case by sending it into the earth to be boiled and turned into steam. Unfortunately, it could cause seismic events as a side effect. The project was trying to find a way to understand the process and then make it safe.

The flight to Auckland was just under two hours. Beth Osbourne, a seismologist at the University of Auckland was also joining the project. These trips could be intense, long hours and cramped conditions. Being able to get along with your colleagues was essential. Dressed in a long purple skirt, DM boots and a Guns N' Roses T-shirt, bottle-blonde hair with at least two inches of black roots showing, like the last ten years happened to other people, Beth and I had always got on fine, as long as we stayed away from politics.

'Carrie, how are you? Let's take a look at you? I wish I could be as thin but then I remember, I hate exercise and love chocolate. You've redyed your hair since last time. Is that purple?'

'Plum.'

'It suits you like that. I sometimes think about cutting my hair short too, it must be so much less hassle, but I don't think I ever could.'

She cleared some space for me next to her. Beth was a voracious reader. Newspapers, magazines and a fat fantasy novel cascaded over the two seats beside her.

'And how is that gorgeous snowboarder of yours?'

'Graeme's fine.' Beth had been down at Otago the year before for a conference and had taken a shine to Graeme. She'd been all but chasing him around Albar, flirting outrageously. 'How are things at Auckland?'

'Oh, God, don't ask. Jarvis is on a kick to improve teaching standards. As if we weren't busy enough. I've been looking forward to this trip for months. Have you been to Hawaii before?'

'No, Indonesia and Mexico. Merapi and Popocatépetl.'

'You're going to love it. It'll be a nice change for you after the South Island. It'll be a nice change for me too. My last trip was Erebus.'

'I can see Hawaii being more your style than Antarctica.'

The flight wasn't full so Beth shifted seats, blowing my chance of getting any work done. I didn't mind so much, Beth was a huge gossip and I usually ended up learning something interesting.

'Have you heard about Kevin Logan?'

'No.' Kevin was in Beth's department, a lecturer in geophysics. He'd written an interesting paper on geomagnetism and I'd been meaning to call him about it.

'Turns out he was having an affair with a student,' she hissed in a stage whisper trying to sledgehammer the drama through her voice. 'And the student has accused him of demanding sexual favours for grades.'

'Did he?'

'He denies it of course, but it's word against word. And what's worse, the student was male.'

I wasn't going to rise to it.

'What's going to happen to him?'

'Suspended pending an investigation. I imagine he'll move on and never darken our doors again.'

I let her witter on about who was sleeping with who and the internal politics of Auckland, idly wondering how she'd get on with Professor Lau, a feminist of Chinese heritage. This was, of course, my other big reason for being a stressy mess. My hero, Professor Lau, was still at Manoa and was, in part, overseeing everything I'd be doing. My copy of *Dislodging Fossils* nestled in my hand luggage.

It was good to get away from Dunedin for a while. I'd been there four and a half years, the longest I'd been anywhere since Aberdeen. I still loved working at the university but the town itself was getting old. Maybe when I went back I'd be refreshed. The ski season would have started by then and I could get out on the slopes and Graeme could do some work, get out from under my feet.

He retired. At twenty-eight? He retired and moved to Dunedin, got himself a flat. He made enough money as a pro to be comfortable for a while, taught during the season and had a design contract with a snowboard manufacturer back in Scotland. He was quite keen on that in the early days but recently...well recently he hadn't been doing much of anything, just surfing, skateboarding, climbing and getting stoned with guys he met at the skate park. And hanging around me.

Our food came and went, we exhausted departmental gossip and slowly descended into that numb silence only long-haul flights can elicit. Beth got her book out. I'd taken Richard Fortey's latest as well as *Dislodging Fossils* but I wasn't in the mood. I was tired. I'd been tired for some time. I closed my eyes and sank into the engine hum.

We were based at the University of Hawaii Manoa in Honolulu. In order to understand what's going on inside a volcano and move towards predicting eruptions, we need to be able to map the magma chamber and the plumbing system. What's happening in the top kilometre of the volcano conduit determines the size of the eruption, and whether it will be explosive or effusive. In this top kilometre the magma loses gases which control the fragmentation of magma. Degassing, particularly the rate, is very important. Beth and I were there to join a team imaging under the big island using seismic waves, electric conductivity, magnetism and a plethora of techniques. Some were long-term, others like the seismic tests were shorter. Putting together thousands of readings and collating them on the computer would build a three-dimensional picture of what was going on down there. Every day we would rise early, spread out around the island to set up equipment, conduct our experiments, take readings, usually not returning until nightfall. Those whose job it was to set off the blasts that sent seismic waves through the rock worked at night and we'd rotate this honour.

The project was managed by Professor Ben Seung, a Korean-American in his mid-forties. His paper on magma conductivity had been a huge influence on my PhD. The Head of Department at Manoa was Professor Kiana Lau.

The first morning was an induction day, learning the layout of the campus, where we could go, where was out of bounds. We had the freedom of the national parks, since we could be trusted not to destroy anything of value. Safety warnings were in place for certain craters and slopes, and we'd just have to work around the activity. Volcanoes were no respecter of schedules.

In the afternoon a small party gathered, with coffee and cookies. I took the opportunity to get to know Dr Halabi. I'd read his paper on the recent rise in activity of Anatahan, in the Northern Mariana Islands. He didn't seem all that keen on talking about it, though. I saw in him the traits of a passionate researcher – that paper done, his mind was already on the next thing.

'Have you seen what's happening in Turkey?'

'The Cos complex? I know there's a big study on there but I

don't think I'm right up-to-date with the findings.' Some academics would hide their ignorance, play along. I'd found that admitting ignorance meant I learned faster.

'Some fascinating data coming out. I'd love to be on the ground there but...' he stiffened at something over my shoulder. 'Professor Lau,' he said, 'may I introduce you to Doctor Caroline Fraser?'

I took a breath. Controlled myself. 'Professor Lau, it's an honour to meet you.'

'Fraser? Otago, yes?'

'That's right, Professor.'

'Yes, I read your paper on mapping. Very good. Meyer must be proud to have such a young star in his department.'

She'd read my paper. *My* paper.

'How is Christopher?' The blockage in my brain shifted. Chris Meyer. My Head of Department.

'He's fine, Professor. I'll pass on your regards.'

'Please do, not that he'll welcome them.'

Dr Halabi had made his escape and was standing next to Professor Seung waiting to be noticed. I tried to find something, anything to say. How do you make small talk with your hero? 'Professor, if...could I...one moment, please.' I got my bag and returned brandishing the battered paperback and a pen. 'I was wondering if you'd sign this for me.'

'My, that has seen better days. Well-loved or mistreated?'

'Well-loved.'

'A good answer.' She signed it, a simple *best wishes, K Lau* and handed it back. 'It's been nice meeting you, Doctor Fraser. Welcome to Hawaii.'

I could've just died, right there.

After the three-day conference, listening to papers by postgrads and postdocs, things quickly relaxed into a routine. The first month I was assigned an area on the west side – on the southwest rift zone – of the Kilauea summit caldera, the most active volcano in the Hawaiian islands, to set up and monitor magnetotelluric instruments. Kilauea is a shield volcano 1247 metres high but which rises only gradually above the big island of Hawaii. Rather than shuttle back and forth between the islands, Beth and I would stay in the national park's visitor housing and return to Honolulu only when necessary.

Kilauea is the centre of volcano tourism and the first stop for visitors. It was weird to be working under the ever-present gaze of tourists, to know that when they got home their photos would contain a figure in the background digging holes. Kilauea had broken out in May, small tongues of lava creeping down the seaward side. Things were calm now, though the image I'd had as a child on Sakurajima of the lava bubbling away under my feet never left me, the ground beneath me never as sure as it seemed.

Every morning I'd park at the side of Crater Rim Drive, the Kilauea Visitor Centre or the Thomas A. Jagger Museum where the Hawaiian Volcano Observatory was based. We were working alongside the US Geological Survey, but as they only hired US citizens Beth and I couldn't actually join their team. I'd hike into the next zone, my tools, water and food in my canvas backpack, and I'd spend the day walking over lava flows from 1919, 1921, 1954 and 1961 or the lush greenery on the eastern side. At the end of the day I'd return home exhausted.

Beth wasn't as easy to share with as Mike, and wet towels, used coffee cups and spat-out toothpaste quickly became a part of my day. I discovered a campsite near Kilauea, Kulanaokuaiki, and scrounged a tent, a sleeping bag and various bits of camping gear from people in the department. I thought Beth might be offended but she obviously wasn't too happy with my whining about cleanliness, so by the start of the second week I slept every night on the edge of the volcano. Just me and the mountain learning about each other.

Towards the end of that week I was working in the zone around the Visitor Centre and took advantage of that to hide from the midday sun. Initially I'd tried to eat on a bench in the public area but it was too busy. Gillian, a woman in her fifties who had moved to Hawaii from Ohio in her twenties, took pity on me and invited me into their staff room. It was Gillian who reminded me of something I'd failed to connect. She came in with a coffee and dropped into the seat opposite me.

'Oh, I need this. I've had to listen for the last twenty minutes while some Englishman bent my ear about Tennyson, as if working here all this time I'd completely failed to learn about Tennyson's poem.'

'Lord Tennyson? What's his connection with Kilauea?'

'You scientists, no time for the arts. You're going to make me go through it all again, aren't you?'

'If you don't mind?'

She sighed but I could see she really didn't mind. Gillian was one of those people who loved teaching others but hated to admit to the pleasure. 'Tennyson wrote a poem called *Kapiolani* about a High Chiefess who helped convert the islanders to Christianity. She descended into the crater to prove that Pele didn't exist and came back unhurt. A missionary wrote about the event and Tennyson read it.'

Someone called from outside, 'Gillian, the line's building up.' She took a big gulp of coffee as she rose. 'There's a book about it in the shop if you're interested. It's quite a story.'

Pele. I knew she was from Hawaii but I hadn't connected her with the volcano I was working on. Kilauea was her volcano, the Halema'uma'u pit crater was her home. In a flash the memory of Sakurajima, I felt again the warmth of her fire, saw her high above the magma chamber, passionate and fiery.

When I finished my lunch I went through to the bookshop and found what I was looking for, a thin paperback about Pele. That evening I sat on a rock near my tent with a cup of camomile, a soft sea breeze blowing over the island and the smoke from Halema'uma'u rising into the twilight and renewed my acquaintance with the goddess.

There were a few versions of her origins, but my favourite was this: Pele lived with her parents, Kanehoalani and Haumea and her siblings. Her older sister, the sea goddess Namakaokaha'i, feared her ambition would smother the land so Pele was banished.

She set off in a canoe for Hawaii but Namakaokaha'i wasn't satisfied with exile and chased after Pele, tearing her apart. Her bones became a hill, her spirit fled to the big island of Hawaii.

The story Gillian had told me about came much later, in 1824. Kapiolani was the daughter of a chief and one of the first to embrace Christianity on the island. With true born-again zeal she decided to smash once and for all the worship of Pele so she set off for Kilauea. A couple of missionaries heard what she was doing and tagged along. To go near the crater was to anger Pele but Kapiolani was determined. The lake of lava must have been terrifying but she climbed down into the crater and there prayed to her God. She returned unhurt and, as Tennyson put it, 'drove the demon from Hawa-i-ee'.

Each day as I walked the trails, Mauna Iki, Byron Ledge, Halema'uma'u, Kau Desert and Crater Rim, planting my devices, I was aware of the spiritual power of the land under my feet. I was lucky to be allowed to walk there. Until Kapiolani, it had been forbidden for fear of angering Pele. Now it was closed to the public because of Health and Safety. Fences and taboos, the fear of Pele's anger, give it any name you want, you get the same result. And I was able to walk over it freely, day after day, alone with my memories, Pele's fire burning beneath me.

A month passed and we were called back to Honolulu. At Beth's insistence we decided to make a weekend of it. We could've got a room through the university but Beth wanted pampering so we booked a twin room in a beach front hotel. I wasn't all that keen but after weeks in a tent I could see the attraction of a real bed.

We checked in and Beth went off to find a shopping mall. I threw my sunscreen and book into my bag and checked my emails in the lobby. There were a load from Graeme, a couple from my postgrads, a couple of old ones from Hannah I hadn't bothered replying to, and a new one from my dad. I left them unread, glancing only at the names and vague subject titles and logged out, walked onto the beach.

Sand in my toes, that smell of salt. The beaches I'd seen in my life, all those shores heavy with memories. Wild beaches on the west coast with Dad and Hannah, camping. Sicily, with the local boys posing. Aberdeen beach with Graeme, hot chocolate in Café Continental. Bouldering on Long Beach in Dunedin, pushing off sea kayaks. The sea had played such a part in my life. The night of Piper Alpha, I remember standing on the grass outside the hospital thinking about how grass meant home to me after all those holidays to dry, dusty places. But it's not grass, it's sand and sea. The boundary between the two. Land and the oceans between us.

I sat back in the sand and breathed deep, filling my lungs with the Pacific air. For a volcanologist, Hawaii is the hub of the ring of fire. Four hundred and fifty-two volcanoes in a twenty-five-thousand-mile belt, seventy-five percent of the world's volcanoes and so much we still don't know about them. I could spend a lifetime there and not even scratch the surface. But that was the way of science. If I could move us one step closer to predicting eruptions, it would be a life well spent.

If I could just work without distractions.

Emails from Graeme, from Hannah.

From Dad.

'Beautiful, isn't it?' I squinted up into the sun at the silhouette that spoke. Female, long hair and a silk scarf floating in the currents of wind. 'I never tire of it,' she continued. 'I get sick of all that, sure enough,' she gestured at the cafés and bars, the hotels and tourists, 'but it's worth it. You look like you need a drink.'

'I don't drink.'

'See, told you. Come on, I hate drinking alone.'

I watched her walk, the beckoning curve of her hips, followed her up the steps to a hotel. She picked a table where we could both sit under the parasol and ordered a bottle of Mâcon-Villages, two glasses. She was a bit shorter than me with long, auburn-tinted hair, a round face, mostly hidden by large sunglasses. Her clothes were expensive, tailored and even in the wind it was clear her hair was salon-styled.

'So, what's your name?' she said. A New York accent, but not strong.

'Carrie,' I said. 'You?'

'Ashley. Ash. You're Scottish?'

'Yes.'

'Well that's just perfect.'

The wine came and the waiter poured two glasses. Ash raised hers in a toast. I looked at it, looked at her, the sand sloping down to the sea, the oceans between us. I picked up the second glass. 'What should we toast?' she asked.

'The South Seas.' We clinked. I sipped. It was fresh and light, floral and fruity.

'So, Carrie, what are you doing on the other side of the world?'

'I'm in exile.'

'Banished from the kingdom?'

'Self-enforced, but yes, something like that. How about you? Do you live here?'

'I wish. I live in New York but I try to come here as often as I can.'

'You don't like New York?'

'I like it fine, but it's not like this. Besides, New York is work. Hawaii is only pleasure. Are you here for pleasure?'

I still couldn't see her eyes but there was no doubting the glint in them. Her whole face shone, her mouth upturned in a playful smirk, laughter lines beginning to show. I told her about my work on Kilauea, about taking the weekend off.

'So you are here for pleasure, but only until Sunday night? Me too, I fly back Sunday afternoon. I do like coincidences.'

She moved to top up my glass. I flinched, arm already jutting out to stop her, but the glass was empty, I'd finished it without realising. The shush of the breakers, the rustle of wind in the palm trees. I dropped my hand in my lap, let her pour. 'Why did you come and talk to me?'

'You looked lost.'

She took her sunglasses off. I looked at her over the rim of my glass as I drank.

It was dark outside. We lay in bed, worn out, happy. Ash flicked the news on, nothing but SARS and Iraq. 'There's Monday morning, right there waiting for me,' she said.

'How do you mean?'

'I'm a lawyer at the UN. This whole Iraq war is, as our beloved army would say, a clusterfuck, and a lot of it has landed on my desk.' She switched the TV off. 'But it's Saturday, that's Monday. You want to grab something to eat or would you prefer to love me and leave me?'

A twin room with Beth. Emails from Graeme. 'I assume the room service here is good?'

The walk of shame might be easier to pass off when you were wearing beach clothes the day before and have short, mussed up hair anyway but it's impossible to fully pass off when you share a room with a nosy Kiwi.

'What sort of time do you call this young lady? I was worried sick about you.' She was sitting up in bed reading her book. 'Did you get some? Look at that smile, you got more than some. Tell me all about him.'

'I need a shower.'

'I bet. You hungry?'

When I came out she was up and dressed. I quickly towelled my hair, threw on a pair of combats and a strappy top, threw everything into my backpack and followed her to the lifts. 'What did you do yesterday?' I asked her as we waited.

'Nothing like you. Did a tour of the malls, got some real bargains, came back here, waited for you and went out to a couple of bars when you didn't show.'

'Sorry, it wasn't planned. It just sort of happened.'

'Hey, don't apologise, I'd have done exactly the same. I still want all the gory details though.'

We filled our plates from the buffet and got a seat by the window. The fresh orange juice tasted gorgeous. 'So what have you got planned for today?' I asked her.

'No idea. Some sightseeing maybe. Do you want to hang out

or are you rendezvousing?'

We had swapped mobile numbers, but Ash was leaving for the airport at one o'clock. 'We might have lunch, but after that I'm definitely free.'

'We fly back at six?'

'Yeah, though I could do with it being later. I'm on the seismics from tomorrow.'

'Night shift. Lucky you. Are you moving back in or keeping your tent?'

'Back in if it's okay with you. A campsite during the day isn't the ideal place to get a good night's sleep.'

'Sure, I guess we'll pass each other morning and night. So, what's he like, this man of yours? Lunch the day after means it's not a one-nighter. Is he local?'

'No, from New York.'

'A holiday romance, how sweet. What does he do?'

'A lawyer.'

'A step up from a snowboarder.' Her face portrayed sweetness and light. 'No wonder you stayed over. His hotel must be better than this place.'

My phone chimed with a message. 'Speak of the devil?'

It was Ash. I arranged to meet her at eleven thirty.

'Well,' said Beth, 'do you fancy doing some sightseeing with me in the meantime?'

'Where are you going?'

'I haven't decided. The art gallery is near here but it seems a shame to be inside.'

'We've seen nothing but outside for the last month, the gallery sounds good.'

'You're not going to see much sun for the next month. Are you sure?'

'Yeah. Let's go.'

The gallery was a good choice as there was an exhibition of students' work. I always prefer students' work to the 'masters' because you come at the piece with no preconceptions beyond the connotations of the word 'student' – still learning. Before I went to an exhibition by Picasso say, or Monet, I already knew what to expect and the experience either satisfied my expectations or disappoints them. You never hear someone coming out of a Van Gogh show saying, 'I had no idea he could paint sunflowers so well, I'm quite flabbergasted.' The work was mixed, some moving, some baffling, some funny. One student, a Japanese woman judging by her name, had taken the *ukiyo- e* style of Japanese art and used it to portray modern women, so you'd get a stylised Japanese woman with pale skin, kimono and hair done up in the old fashion, but using her cellphone, or watching TV, using hair curlers. Another had a series of almost impressionistic paintings of police chasing a naked man through streets, parks, up mountains and along beaches. We both really enjoyed it, commenting on the work, collecting postcards and flyers when they were available. One day when I finally settled somewhere and bought a house, I'd like to fill it with this kind of art. Originals, but not by names, by artists still learning to express themselves. Flaws are more beautiful than perfection.

It was just after eleven when we came out. 'I'd better be off. See you back at the hotel after lunch?'

'What about checking out?'

'I hadn't thought of that. Sorry to be a pain, can you do it? My stuff's all packed. Can you leave my bag with yours behind the desk? She has to leave at one so I'll be back just after.' There was a pause. 'Is that okay? If not I'll come back with you now.'

'No, it's okay. Off you go. I'll see you later.' She left me at the crossing.

I picked an olive out of the salad while Ash fixed her hair. Her bags stood ready by the door next to my shoes and trousers. 'Do you want some of this?'

'No, you go ahead. I'll get something on the plane.'

'This is better than airline food.'

'Not in business class. How long are you in Hawaii for?'

'Two more months. End of June.'

'I'll be back in six weeks. I'd like to see you again.' She slipped a thin black coat on and checked her bag.

'I'd like that, but I don't know if I can come back to Honolulu then.'

'Then I'll come to you.'

She tossed my trousers at me. I scooted to the edge of the bed and pulled them on. The phone rang bright. It sparked something, a memory.

'My taxi's here. What were you going to say?'

Phones ringing in hotels. 'I'm in a relationship. In New Zealand.'

'You don't want to see me again?'

'I do.'

'Well then.' She took an olive and popped it into my mouth.

I picked up my bag from reception and called Beth. It rang out. I found a park near the hotel and walked through it, the chirrup of insects and the squawk of birds fizzing the air, the deep, rich scent of the flowers enveloping me in cocoons. I wanted to hang onto that mood for as long as possible. The weekend, the whole month had been a break from reality. Emails from Graeme. An email from Dad. My mobile rang and the memory surfaced. That night, the night, standing in the hall with the phone to my ear.

A voice, male and full of sleep, 'Yes, Frank Carpenter, what is it?'

Graeme.

The missed call was from Professor Seung. He followed it with a text. A few folk were meeting at the Hard Rock Café for a drink before Beth and I went to the airport. Directions included. I looked around the park. The colours were garish, gaudy, the fritz of bugs set my skin on edge. I turned my back and left, waved down a taxi and went to the airport.

The first night was tough. I hadn't been able to sleep much during the day and I needed to be sharp. Setting off explosive charges in the ground is not something you want to be dozy for but it had to be done at night to minimise contamination of the readings by things like traffic. When I got back to the house I couldn't even manage a shower before collapsing on my bed. I woke late afternoon and, still groggy, got a bottle of water from the fridge. It took a minute or two for the haze to lift. Beth's stuff was gone.

She'd arrived at the airport, all beer-merry and clutching souvenir bags. I thanked her for leaving my bag at reception and she said, 'you're welcome.' I asked her if she'd gone straight to the Hard Rock Café but she went off to the bathroom and never replied. On the plane she sat by herself. When we got back she went to bed and when I woke in the morning she had left. I had no idea when she took her stuff. I ran through the list of my possible misdemeanours, striking out until I remembered the conversation outside the gallery. Despite my best effort to play the pronoun game, I'd said 'she'. Was this really because of Ash? Because I'd used the female pronoun? I sat on the bed and ran both hands through my hair. A bitter taste dripped down the back of my throat and burned in my stomach. I wasn't going to let her get to me. Of all the things that were wrong with sleeping with Ash, the fact that she was a woman wasn't one of them.

I'd just showered and dressed when my phone rang. It was Professor Seung. 'How did the first night go?'

'Looks good,' I said to him. 'Everything coming through okay?'

'All within expected parameters.'

'Great. What's up?'

'Two things. Professor Lau asked to join you. I said it wouldn't be a problem.'

'No, that's fine. Did she say why?'

'I think she's just nosy.'

'Fair enough. Tonight?'

'Yeah. Can you pick her up? She gets in at seven thirty.'

'No problem. The second thing?'

'Delicate. I hear there is some issue between you and Beth.'

I took a breath. 'I haven't spoken to her since we left Honolulu,' I said. 'At least, she hasn't spoken to me.'

'I want this fixed. This is science, not a soap opera.'

'Yes, Professor.'

'Will this affect your work?'

'No, it won't.'

'Well then.'

'Thank you.'

I had a couple of hours before work so I had 'breakfast' and stocked up on rations to get me through the night. After my coffee I sucked it up and logged into my email account, dealt with the ones from my postgrads first – none of them had any real issues, just needed hand-holding – and a few other work-related ones. Then I went through Graeme's increasingly irate messages and replied as quickly as I could. *Having a lovely time, Hawaii lovely, people lovely, work going well, miss you.* As I typed this string of platitudes, the memory of Ash's fingers in my hair, her lips on my neck, signing off with a *love*. How easy it was to lie. I'd always been astounded at the way Hannah could lie about conferences and meetings and consultations but it really wasn't that difficult, not when your priorities were different. I guess that's what I never understood. Frank Carpenter was her priority. Dad was different, for all he screwed around. He never really lied about anything, he never had any relationships. He just fucked a cabin attendant or a woman in the hotel bar and the next day it might as well never have happened. His family was still number one. Not for Hannah. I thought about replying to her as well, but what would I say?

One email left.

Professor Lau was waiting by the car, hiking boots and a warm checked shirt, ready for the mountains. I threw my bag in the back and got in behind the wheel. The professor kept her bag on her lap.

'Where to?' I asked.

'Have you been to the Mauna Loa Observatory yet?'

'No, I haven't.'

'It's just a weather and CO_2 measuring station but the view is superb. Let's start there.'

I eased out into the road. The car wasn't in the best shape, an old Toyota that had been offroad more times than was good for it. It was like driving a tank.

'So what do you think of our university, Doctor Fraser?'

'Please, call me Carrie.'

'Then call me Kiana.'

'I don't think I could do that, Professor. I'm very impressed with the set-up you have here and getting practical experience with the equipment and techniques is invaluable.'

'How do you like Otago?'

'I like it very much, it's a good department and there are some very beautiful volcanoes in New Zealand to work on.'

'How do they compare with ours here?'

'I don't think I can compare them. For beauty you can't beat majestic snow-covered peaks but Hawaii is...Hawaii *is* volcanoes. There's something more...spiritual about the volcanoes here.'

'You've been reading about Pele?'

'A bit. I read about her when I was a girl.'

'Me too. I've been reading more of your work as well. Your paper on degassing rates is very impressive.'

'Thank you, Professor. Coming from you that means a lot, but it's little more than a series of questions, none of which I've answered yet.'

'But you raised them. That's often more important. Turn here.'

I was driving into the setting sun, the clouds turned rusty crimson, the horizon a strip of terracotta between the slopes of Mauna Kea and Mauna Loa, and turned off onto a single track. The rock and scrub terrain looked Martian in the light as the Toyota struggled up and around the twisting road. I hoped we wouldn't meet anyone coming the other way. The last of the daylight faded fast and I needed all my concentration to keep us on the road, the headlight beams like searchlights through kicked up dust. Any one of the jagged rocks along the side could rip the chassis out from under us.

We found the observatory perched on the shoulder of the volcano, a chain of one-storey buildings like teeth against the sky. As I got out and opened the gate a memory flickered up of watching Taka do the same thing at Sakurajima. I meant to go back to that volcano one day, go back as a professional. I wondered if Taka was still there. If he was still in touch with my dad. I parked the car and retrieved my bag.

'You look adventurous, Carrie, how would you like a hike to the North Pit?'

'Isn't it a bit dangerous at night?'

'Very. Any flashlights in that rust box?'

I got two from the boot, plus some spare batteries and jogged after her. 'Professor, I thought you wanted to see our work?'

'Ben needs things to be straightforward and logical, so it's best to tell him what he wants to hear.'

The flashlights were expensive, powerful ones and the beams, sharp and tight, showed the path clearly. As I walked behind Professor Lau, the ground around my feet bright, I wondered if there were there any snakes in Hawaii. One of the downsides of being a volcanologist, one I hadn't appreciated until my first field trip outside Europe, is that volcanoes tend to be in countries with a high number of dangerous animals, insects and spiders, many of whom live on the slopes waiting for unsuspecting geologists. I kept the light low, searching for any movement, anything coiled. I could ask Professor Lau, of course, but something in the atmosphere hinted at silence. The stars were coming out and, despite the light pollution from Hilo and the observatory, the sky was glittering. If I hadn't gone into geology, astrophysics would've been my second choice. To try and explain the universe, that was the point of science, and what bigger mystery than the beginning of everything? But geology was always first. As much as I loved physics at school, I'd never be able to visit another planet or galaxy. I'd never be able to touch anything I was studying. As a geologist, I could hop on a plane and in a few hours be in Iceland or the Philippines or Chile. It would take many more lifetimes before astrophysicists could visit Andromeda. Even a field trip to the moon was off the table. I did harbour a fantasy when I was much younger of being the first volcanologist to visit Olympus Mons, the shield volcano on Mars. It stands three times higher than Everest. Imagine mapping that.

We'd been walking for more than an hour, climbing slowly, stopping occasionally, following the twisting trail through stacks of black volcanic rock, when we reached the summit and the quality of the ground changed. In the torchlight it glinted, smooth curves, almost liquid. It had been, I realised. We were standing in the North Pit, part of Moku'āweoweo, the summit caldera of Mauna Loa, on hardened magma. The lip of the crater and a higher ridge beyond it blocked much of the light from below, and the sky opened up even more. There was a new moon and a perfectly clear sky. I stood, head back, staring at the ungraspable infinity of it, the stars, the galaxies, all those worlds and the space between them.

'We're not there yet.' The Professor was already metres ahead of me moving across the caldera on a deliberate path. For the second time I had to jog to catch up. It was obvious I shouldn't speak. We walked across the vast rock lake. I could almost be walking on the back of a dragon, so scale-like were the cracked plates. When we seemed roughly in the centre of the caldera, Professor Lau stopped, placed her bag down and began pulling things out of it. I wanted to offer to help but it felt like intruding. I put my own pack down and sat on the crater floor, running my hands over petrified lava.

Candles. She had big church candles, the size of two food cans one on top of the other. She lit each one with matches, managing two, sometimes three before the match burned down or blew out. She struck ten matches. Once the candles were lit she placed them in a wide circle around us. I felt maybe I should retreat and leave her alone with whatever ceremony she was about to perform, but she'd asked me to come, in fact she'd demanded it of Professor Seung, and I was already within the burning circumference. Whatever was going on, she wanted me to be part of it.

Once the circle was complete she came over and sat cross-legged in front of me. 'Don't worry,' she said with a small laugh, 'I'm not going to sacrifice you to Pele or anything like that. You've read my book?'

'Many times.'

'What happened on June first, nineteen fifty?'

'God, I remember. I'm sorry.' Today was the first of June. Fifty-three years ago Mauna Loa erupted. Professor Lau's parents had died while trying to evacuate. The Professor had been four years old and was carried to safety by her grandmother.

'Every year, assuming Loa is sleeping, I come up here at night – the eruption began during the night – and pray for them.'

'I'm sorry Professor, but I feel like I'm intruding. Maybe I should—'

'No, I want you here. I did a bit of research into you.'

'Into me?'

'Don't worry, not spying or anything. Papers, posts, that kind of thing.'

'Oh.'

'Yes, you're thinking what has this got to do with that. There was another Scottish geologist called Fraser came up in the results.'

'My father.'

'I met him once.'

It took a moment to process. Professor Lau and my father, in the same room? 'He never mentioned it.'

'He wouldn't remember me. Indeed I didn't remember him. It was when we were both postgrads. He delivered a paper and I was on after him. We exchanged a few words and that was that. I'd even forgotten about the conference but it all came back when I saw his name.' She paused. 'We're not at work. I'm not your boss. You can tell me to fuck off.' She took a deep breath. 'I saw what happened. He survived Piper Alpha but it broke up your family. I...' I'd never seen her so hesitant. She seemed to have shrunk. 'I thought you might get something out of this.'

I had to breathe. I counted to ten. 'I...thank you, but...my parents aren't…aren't dead. It wouldn't be appropriate to intrude on your memorial.'

'If you wish to leave, I'll take no offence, but I said, I want you here. I have no parents. I have no children. The last of my family died with my grandmother. When I come here, when I sit under the stars in this place of destruction and creation, I am communing with my family. In one month it will be fifteen years since Piper Alpha. It's fifty-three years since my night. One night, for each of us, changed everything. Up here, I acknowledge that. Then tomorrow I go back to work.'

'What do I have to do?'

'Nothing. Sit. Listen to the mountain. Listen to the stars. Just sit.'

I forced myself. If she thought I had some mental scars that sitting on Mauna Loa surrounded by candles would magically heal, then fine. I could humour her.

So we sat. Smooth as the ground was compared with outside the caldera, it was still rock. Soon my bum started to hurt, and I began to shift around. It was a warm night, so I took my jumper off, folded it up and pushed it under me. How long did she intend to sit there? What did she expect me to get out of this? Mourning dead parents was one thing but mourning living parents – that was daft. Dad was still there, in Aberdeen, in God knows what kind of self-inflicted state. Hannah had moved to France with Frank Carpenter. I hadn't gone to her wedding and hadn't met my step-brother and step-sister. She didn't need me. I didn't need her. We didn't even share a name anymore.

Fifteen years. 1988 to 2003. There'd be a service in St Nicholas Kirk, something in Hazelhead Park at the memorial statue. Fifteen years. One hundred and sixty-seven dead. One hundred and sixty-five from Piper Alpha and two from the rescue vessel. Their families would be looking at the calendar, July again, steeling themselves, getting ready for the wave of grief they knew was coming, the upsurge of pain the anniversary brought. Would some stay away? Dad wouldn't go. He never went. But were there other survivors who, fifteen years later, still couldn't…

what? Couldn't cope? Couldn't move on? Professor Lau was right. Those nights were fixed points, event horizons.

The tears came, silently at first, my face wet before I realised it. Then more and more, sobs, my palms slamming onto the rock, the volcano, the caldera. I wanted to see him. His email. He was getting married again. It was time to go home.

It was time.

We hugged each other, Professor Lau and I, both tear-stained under the stars. Thanked each other. Blew the candles out one by one, wrapped them in plastic bags and put them back in the professor's pack, scaled the sides of the caldera in the creeping dawn and made our way along the rocky path home.

The weeks passed, the night shifts continued and I didn't see Professor Lau again. June moved into July and the field work was done. The long-term readings could be trusted to continue mechanically without anyone watching over them. Everyone was back in Honolulu analysing data and imbibing caffeine. Beth and I were put in a flat together. I shrugged at the news but Beth brought the issue up with Professor Seung while I was in the room.

'If it's all the same with you, Professor, I'd rather make alternative arrangements.'

'Well it isn't all the same with me. I told you two to sort this out.'

'I've tried,' she said, which was news to me. Ben Seung looked at me. I shrugged.

'What's the problem, Caroline?' he asked.

'No problem, Professor. I've got no problem with the arrangements.'

'I bet you haven't,' said Beth.

You see, I said silently.

'Doctor Osbourne, do you have a specific objection to Doctor Fraser?'

'We are incompatible as roommates.'

'Why?'

'A difference of outlook.'

I could've watched her squirm all day, but I had other things to do. 'Beth learned that I am bisexual. She has a problem with that. I think. She hasn't spoken to me since she found out so I don't really know. I can only assume that's what the problem is and that she thinks it might be contagious and therefore doesn't want to be near me. Or maybe she thinks I'm going to jump on her in the night. You'd have to ask her.'

'Beth?'

She wasn't stupid. She knew any admission of prejudice would make its way back through the grapevine to her department. 'I have no problem with Doctor Fraser's lifestyle choice.'

'Fine. That's decided then.'

I thought about changing my flight home so we wouldn't have to fly together, but then thought, why bother? She was the one with the problem. At least we had separate bedrooms. A lot of American universities went for sharing in a big way.

The results were flowing in, everything working as predicted, more or less. I had to write a report for the department and for the funding body in order to justify the time away and the money spent, what I'd learned and how I could use it to benefit Otago. I was sketching it out on an A4 pad when my phone bleeped.

Remember me? I'll be back in Hawaii next week. Hilo or Honolulu?

Adrenaline like a flame shot through me, warmth and energy. Had I been looking forward to this that much?

Have you ever seen Kilauea? No. Show me. See you there, xx.

The intimate casualness of it. Two kisses. What could I say back? *Ok.*

Looking forward to fucking you.

The curse of Gregor Mendel: some things run in the family.

I put the phone away and went back to the notepad. Mapping the volcanoes in the North Island of New Zealand could provide the basis for a number of PhDs. My green pen flying across the lined paper, ideas unspooling from my mind, images of magma chambers, subterranean plumbing stretching out under the majestic New Zealand landscape, out under the oceans, down towards the core.

Was I that easy to please?

I needed a break so I changed into my running gear and set off through campus, down East-West Road onto Dole Street, left onto St Louis Drive and followed its meandering route to Peter Street, Ruth Place and up onto the Wa'ahila Ridge Trail. I'd found this place on one of my many runs since we were recalled. The wide paths and tree cover were perfect for summer jogging. I ran every morning, used the university gym at lunchtime and took a long walk after dinner, but I missed the big island and my campsite. The university was inland and, though vital and verdant, was too built up for my tastes.

When I was young I thought exercise helped me forget. The concentration, the effort pushing the negatives aside. Now I realised it distracted the conscious enough to let the subconscious do what it's good at: sorting and filtering.

As my steps kicked up dry dirt and twigs lay snapped in my wake, the white noise of my mind settled into a snowfall, then steady calm.

Dad's email, the wedding in December. It was time to go home. Not just Dunedin. Scotland. It was time.

On the way back through campus Professor Lau spotted me, called me over. 'How are you getting on?'

'Good, Professor, thanks. Kind of winding down really.'

We walked along the paths between departments, mostly empty with the students on holiday. I'd spent more of my university life as a student than as staff, and the spirit of a campus for me was still young people with bags and books sauntering from class to library, crowding green spaces when it was warm, crushed into stairwells to hide from bad weather. Without them campus felt hollow.

'Are you looking forward to getting back?' I hesitated too long. 'No? I thought you liked Otago.'

'Just some personal issues I'll have to deal with.'

'We all have those. Have you enjoyed your time in Hawaii?'

'I'll be sorry to leave.'

'You'll have to come back and visit us sometime.'

'I'd like that.'

Ash arrived Friday afternoon and we spoke briefly on the phone. Hilo didn't have much in the way of hotels so she rented a one-bedroom villa between the town and Kilauea, set back in a lush forest of palms and ferns, but because of work I couldn't island-hop until the next morning. I arranged to be there for breakfast.

It was her first time on the big island, so I offered to drive her around, show her the sights. As I went to meet her, the old Toyota rattled down the dirt track, the chassis skiffing the grass strip in the middle of the road. I could almost feel the forest hold its breath as it coughed past. The trees fell back and the villa appeared in a teardrop-shaped clearing. I shook to a stop in what looked like the most unobtrusive spot. Ash was sitting outside in one of four wicker chairs at a round marble table with a pot of coffee, plates of fruit, pancakes, eggs, bacon, a basket of bread and a jug of fruit juice.

'I didn't know what you'd want so I ordered everything.' How to greet her?

Like an interpretive dance portraying 'awkwardness', we half-hugged, kissed a bit of cheek, a corner of mouth. Her smell, coconut milk. 'Sit. Eat.'

'You look good,' I said. 'How was the flight?'

'Long. Not bad. I don't let myself complain about air travel.'

'I'd imagine not in business class.' I took a rasher of bacon, a bit of focaccia, slices of pineapple, poured some juice.

'It's not that. I pay for that, so it's not like it's a luxury.' I raised an eyebrow. 'Okay, it is a luxury but not a gift. No, I mean air travel itself is a luxury. Being able to get on a plane in New York and a few hours later be in Hawaii.'

'How long is the flight?'

'About twelve hours including the change.'

'Not bad for an entire continent and half an ocean.'

'One hundred years ago that would've taken months. It drives me mad when I hear someone bitching that their flight is thirty minutes late, like thirty minutes is such an inconvenience.'

'Still, it's a long way for a weekend.'

'A week.'

'Oh, you've got the week off?'

'No, but I've got phones and the internet and a bag full of papers.' My face must have betrayed me. 'Is that okay with you?'

'Okay? No, it's... I mean yes, it's just I leave on Tuesday.'

'Project done?'

'My part in it.'

'Well, that gives us four days.'

'Three and a half.'

'You're a glass half-empty girl.'

'I try not to be.'

'Pessimism's good if it motivates you.'

I finished off my breakfast and Ash drained the coffee pot, which must have held at least a litre, if not more. 'You never drink coffee?' she asked.

'It really messes with my sleep cycles.'

'That's the point. I couldn't survive without it.'

'Sounds like an addiction.' It came out harder than I meant, a tone of accusation that crept in. She cocked her head and looked at me. I couldn't meet her eye.

'You might be right,' she said after a pause. 'But if you'd had the week I've had, you'd need a caffeine kick in the ass.'

'Sorry. Work?'

'Yeah. Not talking about it.'

'Secret?'

'Depressing. So. Are you going to show me this island?'

'You'll need some sturdy shoes.'

'I thought I might.'

The villa was only a ten-minute drive from the Kilauea Visitor Centre so we started there. As it was a Saturday, it was pretty busy inside so I quickly said hi to Gillian and some of the others, told them if they saw two strange people in the restricted zone, one of them would be me. Ash didn't seem too disappointed at not seeing the displays, but then we were going to see the real thing, and from much closer than the tourists. We set off down the trail, my pack full of water and fruit I'd pinched from her villa.

'Kilauea is a shield volcano. They look a bit like a warrior's shield lying on the ground.'

'I was just thinking that.'

'They're built up mainly of lava, rather than being mountainous like stratovolcanoes. This one is the most active volcano on Hawaii and the second youngest. It has a caldera at the summit and two rift zones heading out that way and that.' She followed my finger east and west. 'You'll notice that this direction is like a desert but when we were driving up it was all lush and green. That's because sulphur dioxide can cause acid rain. This is known as the Ka'ū Desert. There's a campsite over there where I camped for a few weeks. It's really beautiful. Peaceful.' We turned off the main trail directly towards the Halemaumau Crater. 'Where we're going is Pele's home. Do you know Pele?'

'Personally?'

'I mean have you heard of her?'

'Just the tourist stuff.'

'Well Pele was—'

'Carrie?'

'Yes?'

'Are you going to lecture all day?'

'Sorry, I thought...'

'You switched into teacher mode there.'

'Sorry.'

'Hey.' She grabbed my shoulders and turned me towards her, took my head between her hands, palms soft on my cheeks, fingertips gliding over my ears, and kissed me. I kissed her back, the anger at myself, the hurt melted.

164

'Sorry, I—' Kissing again, silenced by her tongue, the scent of coconut, the fine strands of her hair rolled under my thumb. 'Point taken.'

A barrier crossed. We held hands as we climbed the gentle slope, the kilometres of piping underneath us thrumming with gallons of molten rock, vibrations rolling up through our legs, caressing our bodies, a current passing through our clasped palms. We sat on the ground, the rocks too jagged, sipped water, scanned the horizon. From that angle we were alone in the world, a low ridge hiding us from the viewpoint. I breathed the air, filtered earth through my fingers. 'I don't want to leave.'

'Hawaii?'

'Yeah.'

'No one does. I never do. But that's what makes coming back sweeter.'

'I suppose.'

'Are there any jobs open?'

'I don't know. I haven't checked.' Why not? It was obvious. I'd always wanted to work in Hawaii. Professor Lau knew me, knew my work. I'd been in Otago long enough that jumping ship wouldn't be too much of a surprise. 'I will though.'

I leaned towards her, she leaned, we kissed again, the heat between us, bubbling inside me, hands over clothes, the shock of skin on skin, under my shirt, under her top, my lips on her neck, tongue behind her ear, her hands moving down, skimming my stomach, her tongue in my mouth, a button, a zip, and her hand, her hand, my back against my pack, her hand, her mouth on mine, her hand, the rocks under me, the ash, the earth, the volcano, Pele deep under me, in me, the warmth, her hand and I came, twitching, catching my breath, my face buried in her neck. 'I missed you.'

'You too. Shall we go back?'

'In a minute. Where's the water?' She pulled back, rocked into a squat and handed me the water. I drank, straightened myself out and we walked back to the car. She laughed, looking back. 'What?'

'I'll never look at a volcano in quite the same way again.'

'Me neither.' I gunned the engine and swung out into the road.

Using one of the internet stations in the airport, I checked the Manoa website. There were no jobs going but I set up an alert just in case. The idea flitted round my head like a caged bird, flapping and disrupting all my other thoughts. If the pieces fell into place it would be possible. To move from the rim to the hub. A house along the coast from Honolulu, away from the tourists and the buildings and the traffic, sea views out the front, mountains out the back. No sharing. Just me, my life set up the way I wanted it. An escape from the Dunedin weather.

I sat at the gate listing changes to my CV, publications to add, crafting a statement of intent, where I wanted to go from here. I kept half an eye on the people around me. Perhaps Beth had changed her tickets. From my backpack I pulled out a paper I'd printed off before leaving the university, about the study in Turkey Dr Halabi had mentioned. He seemed very interested in it. Perhaps if he decided to go to Turkey, that would leave an opening in Manoa. I'd email Halabi and stay in regular contact with him.

They called my flight and I gathered my stuff together, everything in its place so I could easily find it while we were airborne. As I slung my backpack over my shoulder, Beth appeared beside me.

'Are you going to tell him?'

'Who?'

'Graeme. Are you going to tell him?' She wasn't keeping her voice low, assured in her righteousness.

'Which do you have a bigger problem with? That I cheated on Graeme or that I did it with a woman?'

'One just makes the other worse.'

'That's bullshit. You were all for gossiping when you thought I'd spent the night with another man. You're a bigot, don't hide it.'

'I don't intend hiding. But it's that poor boy I feel sorry for, deluded into thinking you care for him.'

'I'm sure you'd care for him much better.'

'Oh, I would.'

'Well you can fucking have him then. Only he doesn't go for the fat ones.'

That was childish and I hated myself for saying it. But she deserved it. I handed over my boarding pass, praying Beth wasn't seated anywhere near me. Would she tell him? I wouldn't put it past her.

As we lifted off the Hawaii tarmac there was more than gravity pushing me into the seat. I was leaving the sunshine behind and heading for winter.

I got back to my house in Dunedin late, exhausted after the flights, the waiting, the taxi driver who wouldn't shut up. Dropping my bags inside the door of my room I grabbed a towel and my dressing gown. Shower. Bed. The lights were on in the living room so I stuck my head in to say hi to Mike. Graeme was sitting next to him on the couch, both playing a football game on Graeme's Xbox.

'What are you doing here?'

'Oh, hey sweetheart. Just playing some…hey, no fair, I wasn't paying attention.' He paused the game, stepped over Mike's outstretch legs, arms open. 'Welcome home.'

'I'm going for a shower.'

The hot water battered my scalp. I scrubbed hard, my skin red, the plane, the recycled air, the plastic food, getting it all out of my pores.

I towelled off, brushed my teeth and put the robe on. My bed was a mess. How many nights had Graeme stayed here? I climbed in, his smell, sweat musk. On my side, back to the door. This was where I'd run to. Where I'd built a home. He got in beside me, a hand on my hip, moving down. I shoogled it off.

'You okay?'

'Exhausted.'

'I've missed you. You hardly replied to any of my emails.'

The scent of coconut still filtering through my blood.

In the morning I slipped out while he was sleeping and went for a run along Portobello Road, the wind off the ocean hard in my face, muscles pushing to counter it. Graeme was awake when I got home. He came through to the kitchen as I was draining a pint glass of water.

'Are you not working today?' I asked.

'Got the day off. So I could be here.'

'I've got to go into the office.'

'You're joking.'

I shook my head, refilled the glass from the tap and drank, the cold water rushing through my hot, tired body. I needed a shower but there was no point. I'd cycle into campus, use the showers in the gym.

'But you just got back. I haven't seen you for months. Haven't heard from you hardly.'

'I know, but I'm not on holiday. I have work to do. Lots.' In the bedroom In emptied out my backpack on the bed, pushed in clean clothes and a towel. 'You're going now? Carrie, come on. I got today off specially.'

'I didn't ask you to, Graeme, and you didn't ask me.' I could hear the words coming out louder, faster than I meant. 'If you'd asked me I'd have told you.'

'I did ask you. I emailed you on Saturday. You never answered. I have a whole day planned.'

'I'm sorry. Look, I'll be done by threeish. Meet me on campus then.' In the hallway I changed into my cycling shoes, put a pair of trainers in my bag, opened the door.

'Carrie.'

I looked back. He lunged at me, a kiss, and I jerked away. A second passed. Hurt in his eyes. Pathetic. 'Sorry. You startled me.' I kissed him, quick, on the mouth, stubble scratching.

At my desk I wrote out the to-do list that had been lengthening in my head and set about completing it. Emails to everyone who needed to know I was back. Emails to Professors Lau and Seung thanking them. An email to Dr Halabi thanking him for bringing the Turkey study to my attention, over-egging how interesting it was, hinting that I might be thinking about heading that way myself. Nothing motivates an ambitious scientist more than the thought of a peer getting there first. I made the changes to my CV and made a second list, this time of papers and reports to write.

Just after eleven o'clock Jeannie Parker opened my door, knocking as she did.

'Morning,' she said. 'I heard you were back.'

'Got your spies out?'

'Claire saw a sweaty mess whizzing by on a bike. We figured it must be you.'

'Guilty as charged.'

'I'm just off for lunch. Coming?'

'Definitely. Where to?'

'Staff club?'

'Done.' I followed her out, locked my door behind me.

'So how was it?'

'Great. All according to plan.'

'Any mysteries solved?'

'We'll see. Piles of data collected.'

'Papers?'

'A few.'

'That's what it's all about. Funding, papers, funding, papers.'

The staff club was quiet so we took a table by the window, filled our plates at the buffet. Jeannie nodded at my plate. 'Something you want to tell me?'

'What do you mean?'

'Looks like you're eating for two.'

'God no. Airline food and jet lag. Forgot breakfast.' I popped a cherry tomato into my mouth. 'So what's been going on while I've been away. Any scandals?'

'My side of the building's been pretty quiet but it's all been kicking off on your floor. Have you heard about Paul?'

'Paul Harding?' Paul was taking up the slack while I was away. 'What's happened?'

'He's off. University of…can't remember. India.'

'His dream job. When?'

'End of the semester.'

'Good for him. Anything else exciting?'

'No, that's it.' I breathed easier. If Beth had started spreading rumours, Jeannie would know all about it. 'So tell me about Hawaii. I've never been. Is it as gorgeous as they say?'

'Sun, beaches, tropical climate. Okay if you like that sort of thing.'

Back in my office, my mobile rang, snapping me out of a dwam. Graeme. 'Hi.'

'I'm downstairs. Are you done?'

'Downstairs?'

'Remember. You said to meet you on campus at three.'

'I did. Hang on. I'm not…I'll be a couple of minutes.' I took all my things with me, I wouldn't be coming back to the office that day.

Graeme was sitting on a bench across from the entrance, hands in his jacket pocket, legs stretched out in front of him, staring at his feet. His lips were moving a little, like maybe he was talking to himself, or singing under his breath. I dropped down by his side, startling him.

'Hey. Sorry I kept you waiting. Head up my bum all day.'

'No problem. I've always got plenty of time for you.'

Did he mean that as reassuring or was it a dig at me? 'Sorry about last night. This morning. Jet lag.'

'No worries. Feel better now?'

'Yeah. Still a bit spaced but much better. So what have you got planned for us?'

'You sure you've got the time? You're not going to say you have to go back to the office later?'

I showed him my bag. 'Got everything with me. I'm all yours.'

'That's what I like to hear. There's something I want to show you then we can get dinner. Plato's okay?'

It had become something of a regular haunt for us, the associations with our reunion. 'Sounds good. What do you want to show me?'

'A surprise. Let's go.' He jumped up, suddenly full of life.

'My bike.'

'Bring it. We're not going far.'

Pushing it along, we walked up Albany Street and turned left onto George Street. It was a bright sunny day and as we walked I remembered the first time we'd met up in Dunedin and I showed him around the town. Now he was leading me somewhere.

'So, I was pretty busy while you were away.'

'I saw. You and Mike were certainly busy with that Xbox.'

'Very funny. Life got boring without you around so I joined a cricket team.

He's on it too.'

'So how were you busy? Cricket doesn't count.'

'I got working on the designs. The guys in Fife loved them and we're going forward.'

'That's great.'

'Big load of cash coming my way. Up front and royalties.'

'So do you have to go back?'

'At some point but it's still early days. They'll send me some prototypes to test first.'

'Snowboards?'

'Everything. Boards, skis, gear, trainers, basically head to toe in Graeme Anderson kit.'

'That's amazing, congratulations. It's great what you can get done when I'm not here.'

We waited for the traffic to stop, then crossed the road. 'So what's next? More designs?'

'This.' He stopped in front of a closed shop. It had been a shoe shop, the kind that sold cheap imitations of brand trainers.

'This?'

He took a set of keys out of his pocket and unlocked the door, pushing it open against the weight of junk mail. I wheeled my bicycle inside and leaned it against a shoe rack. All the stock had been cleared out but the shelves and stands remained. It must have been closed a while, a layer of dust on everything. I followed Graeme through, past the cash register still in place.

There was a second room in the back with a mini kitchen, a big stock cupboard and, beyond that, next to the back door, a staircase.

'You're opening a shoe shop?'

'A skate shop. Skating, surfing, snowboarding. The works.'

I didn't know what to say. 'You really have been busy. Have you signed a lease?'

'Got the keys today.'

'Can you afford it?'

'I can now.'

'And a business plan?'

'I've been working on this for years, of course I've got a business plan.'

'Sorry, you didn't seem to be doing much.'

'What does coming up with a business plan look like? Sitting in the library all day? I know what I need, I've been in touch with suppliers, Gabe's sister has come up with a logo, the sign's been ordered, I'll get the flyers printed before I go back to the slopes, next couple of days off the lads are coming round and we'll gut this place, redecorate.'

'Sorry, I just...'

'You just didn't think I'd do it. Listen Carrie, I'm not an idiot. I know I've spent the last wee while flaking around but I needed to do that, you know? But now I'm in business, my name will be on gear all over the world, the money will roll right in.'

'I'm really happy for you.'

'Are you?'

'Of course.'

'You don't seem very...enthusiastic.'

'Jet lag.'

'Come on then, I'll show you the rest.' He took my hand and led me out into the street and unlocked the next door along.

'Have you rented upstairs as well? Makes sense. I was wondering how you'd get all the gear in downstairs.'

'Oh, we'll knock the staff room and the stock room through, make it one big open plan space.'

'Are they not load-bearing walls?'

'I've had the builders in, they can do it.'

'So what's up here?'

It was a flat, two bedrooms, living room, kitchen, bathroom. It clearly hadn't been used for a while either and smelled musty and damp. He slid the living room window open, went through to the bedrooms and did the same. 'The same guy owns both. When I asked him he gave me a deal on the whole building.'

'Good idea, save on the rent from where you live now.'

'Exactly. And the commute to work isn't so bad.'

'Beat the traffic.'

He went into the kitchen and came back with a bottle of champagne and two flutes. 'I know you don't but I thought you might make an exception. This is a special occasion.' I took the glasses from him, there was no place to put them down but the floor. He unwrapped the cork and got his thumbs in position.

'Careful.'

'I've done this before.'

'You're not on a podium now. You could take an eye out.'

'Yes, Mum. Here's to *Board Stupid*.'

'You're not calling it that?' The cork flew out, cannoning off the roof, hitting the floorboards and shooting out the open window.

'Shit.' We ran over and looked out. No smashed windows or car crashes.

He poured out two glasses.

'To your new place,' I said. We clinked and drank. The bubbles fizzed into my head, tickling my nose.

'Our new place.'

'What?'

'If you want. I thought, this place is big enough, it's right in the centre of town, it's near campus and, well, we've been going out for three years. I thought it would be, you know, a good time to—'

'You decided we're moving in together? Without asking me?'

'I'm asking you now.'

'But where did this come from?'

'It's hardly an idea out of the blue.'

'It's right out of the blue.'

'It never crossed your mind?'

'No, never.'

'Oh.' He put his glass down on the floor, sat down with his back against the wall. 'But we've been together three years. We've known each other for twenty years. We love each other. We're over thirty. I mean, I'm not saying it's time to get married and have kids, but it's really never occurred to you that you might want to live with me?'

'We knew each other when we were kids, Graeme, for ten of those years we didn't even see each other. You make it sound like we've been a couple for decades, like this is fate or something. We've only just started going out. We're still getting to know each other. If it wasn't for the coincidence of your coming to Dunedin, we'd probably have gone another decade without crossing paths.'

'Do you really think it was a coincidence I ended up in Dunedin? I love you, Carrie, and I came to find you.'

'You said you were here on holiday.'

'I was on holiday. I quit the circuit, I told you all that. But of course I chose Dunedin because you were here. I had the money, I could've gone anywhere. Your dad told me you were here. I found you on the website and emailed you.'

'My dad?'

'I was having a pint in Under The Hammer last time I was home and he was there. We got chatting.'

'Oh great. A campaign, a whole fucking conspiracy of people sitting around in pubs in Aberdeen discussing me, passing on information about me.' I was getting shrill, the champagne sloshing out of the glass as I gestured with it. 'And you came over here with what, the idea that you'd get me into bed, we'd move in together above a fucking surf shop and then what? Married? Kids? I'd give up my career and cook and clean for you, get fat while you fucked teenage skate girls? Yeah, I know all about you, it's not that hard really, but you know nothing about me, fucking nothing.' I tried to put the brakes on, failed. 'Well here's some things you don't know. I'll never get married. I'm never going to have kids. You know my background. Do you really think I'd make the same mistakes my parents did? Here's something else you missed. I'm bisexual. While I was in Hawaii I was fucking an American woman who made me come more in two long weekends than you have in three years. Didn't know that, did you?'

I stopped. He was frozen, a pale statue.

'Is that all true?'

I nodded. I took my glass through to the kitchen, put it in the sink, leaned against the counter. In his face the hurt turned to anger. 'Look,' I said, 'obviously I didn't mean to say all that, to tell you in that way. It was wrong of me. Horrible. But you, all this, took me by surprise. That's not an excuse, it's just... Fuck. I don't know, Graeme. I can't do all...this.'

'You make it sound like you've been tricked but everything we did, everything between us, you agreed to. After three years I thought maybe we could take the next step. We spend most nights together anyway. But I get it now, you're with someone else.'

'It just sort of happened.'

'You don't fuck other people by accident. Do you know how many offers I get up in that resort every fucking day? And I've never said yes, not once.'

'I'm sorry. Perhaps it's for the best. Now you can screw all those piste girls.'

'Fuck you. You're right about one thing, Carrie. You are damaged. You're fucked up and you fuck up everything you touch. I should've seen that. I guess love is blind. Blind and fucking stupid.'

Aberdeen,
June 2013

Marcus walked up Schoolhill, pushing through the shoppers heading for the Bon Accord centre, St Nicholas Kirk imposing above him. The Piper Alpha chapel in there he'd never seen. In a week it would be the twenty-fifth anniversary. Isobel was on at him to go, but he couldn't. After all that time, he still couldn't face seeing his pain in the eyes of others.

He ran through the pubs in his immediate vicinity, the Prince of Wales, O'Neill's, Ma Cameron's, the Hogshead, Triple Kirks, Slain's, all of them open, all of them with a decent Guinness on tap, all of them with a paper, a bar you could stand at in the gloaming and ignore the daylight. But no, he would drink after, not before. It wouldn't be his fault this time. He'd try to make peace and if it didn't work he'd go and get properly fucked.

His hip ached a bit from the walk yesterday, a couple of hours around the flatter parts of Bennachie. The top of the Mither Tap now out of his reach, that pin in his hip a permanent reminder of being a drunken fuckwit. Without a helicopter or slaves to carry him, he'd never stand on the top of a mountain again. Still it had been a lovely walk, just him and Isobel out amongst the pines and the wildlife, a good steak and ale pie on the way home, warm enough for sitting in the garden in the evening. They talked about getting a dog, a Labrador maybe, something from a shelter, but it would be a shame to leave it when they were both working. When he retired, which wasn't that far off. He was looking forward to it, truth be told, being a house husband while Isobel still worked. Do the cooking and cleaning, get the garden sorted finally.

He followed Skene Terrace, commanding his legs not to take the stairs into North Silver Street where Under The Hammer was, kept on up the incline, looked up at the flats on his right. He'd once had a one-night stand with a woman who lived in there, a long time back. He took Summer Street, Huntly Street,

Rose Street, Thistle Street, Rubislaw Place. Until he came out onto Albyn he could pretend he was just out for a walk, but Albyn made it real. He was walking to Carrie's hotel. He was going to walk in and call her room. In a matter of minutes they'd be standing face-to-face. He could go into Number Ten, he hadn't had a pint in there for years. Nostalgia took his legs in that direction but no, come on, Marcus, after. Deal? Deal. He crossed onto Queen's Road and made his way to Malmaison, slowing his pace, letting the prickles of sweat dry. Getting his speech straight in his head.

In reception there was an Eastern European woman behind the desk. A memory flitted by, a few weeks back, in Budapest with Isobel, a city break, sunlight on a church wall.

'Good afternoon, how can I help you?'

'My daughter is staying here. Caroline Fraser. Could you call her room and tell her I'm here? She isn't expecting me.'

'Yes, sir. One moment.'

His throat was dry. Even a shandy would've helped. You can't smell a shandy.

'I'm sorry Mr Fraser, but she is out at the moment.' She held the phone away from her mouth, hand over the receiver.

'Oh.' Of course, that was always going to happen but he hadn't wanted to take the risk of calling in advance.

'But her partner is there. She says if you can wait, she'll be down in a minute.'

'Her partner?'

'Can I tell her yes?'

'Um. Yes. Sorry. Yes.'

She relayed his consent. 'You can wait here in reception or in the bar.'

He was halfway through his pint when the receptionist led a woman with long auburn hair into the bar and pointed her towards him.

'Mr Fraser? I'm Ashley Wolfe but you can call me Ash. It's a pleasure to meet you.' He shook her hand. 'Carrie is down at the university just now but she should be back after lunch. Ah yes,' the receptionist had reappeared behind the bar, 'a gin and tonic please and another pint for Mr Fraser, charge them all to my room. Thanks. Are you happy sitting at the bar or should we get a table?'

'You are...' he started, couldn't find the words. 'Carrie's...'

'Yes. Perhaps a table is best. Thank you.' She picked up the drinks and walked to the far corner. He drained his pint and followed her. The receptionist returned to her desk. They were alone.

'Did you know Carrie was bisexual?' Her voice was soft, sympathetic, but he could tell there was a fierce intelligence opposite him.

'Yes, sorry. I knew, she told us. I just...'

'You just didn't expect her lover to be here.'

'Sorry. I shouldn't have dropped by. I...'

'It's no problem, Mr Fraser, I just didn't want there to be any misunderstanding. I was in our room catching up on some work. I didn't want to turn you away.'

'So you and Carrie? How long have you been...?'

'We've been together for ten years.'

'My wife and I have been married for ten years.' He had no idea why he said that. The coincidence. The timing.

'Congratulations. She and I had just got together when she came back for your wedding.'

His wedding. The last time he'd seen her.

'Thank you. I had no idea.'

'Is it a problem?'

'You're very direct, aren't you?'

'I'm a lawyer. I'm sorry, Mr Fraser—'

'Call me Marcus.'

'I'm sorry, Marcus, but I know something of the situation with you and Carrie. I assume you've come to effect a reconciliation. I think that's something worth pursuing but if you have a problem with Carrie's sexuality we should deal with that immediately.'

'You mean am I homophobic? No, it's not that. Carrie and I…it's been ten years and the last time wasn't…it didn't go well. I was psyching myself up to speak to her. It never occurred to me that her, that you…' He took a drink. 'Carrie and I haven't been close for a long time.' He took a moment, another mouthful, tried to organise his thoughts. 'Do you think she'll see me?'

It was Ash's turn to pause, the ice in her gin and tonic rattling as she drank. 'I don't know, Marcus. She hasn't contacted you. She hasn't said anything to me about wanting to see you. However being home has unsettled her. It's easy to maintain a policy of non-contact when you are on the other side of the world.'

'Aberdeen is a long way from Hawaii.'

'Yes. Can I get you another?'

'I shouldn't. I don't want to be drunk when I see her.'

'No, probably not a good idea. However I don't think you should see her today. She's preparing for the conference, she delivers her paper tomorrow. You know that's why she's back?'

'I work at the university now.'

'It seems Carrie's out of touch as well. The paper is important to her, and it's her *alma mater* so she wants to do well. However, we're here all week. Once the stress of the conference is out of the way we can arrange a meeting.'

'I'm worried if you tell her she won't come.'

'So am I, so I won't tell her.'

'She really hates me.'

'She's been hurt. But so have you. I think this is worth a try but it might not work.'

'You know our history?'

'Some of it.'

'Why do you want to help?'

'I've seen the way she's been since we arrived. If you'd turned up in Hawaii I may have reacted differently, I don't know. We went to the Piper Alpha memorial yesterday. Even if it fails, even if you two can't resume a relationship, I think it might be good for her to try. I'm guessing it would be good for you as well.'

Marcus nodded. 'Her mother and I, we did so many things wrong. But you never stop loving your daughter.'

'You'd be surprised, Marcus. Some parents find it all too easy.' Her voice caught as she spoke, she took a deep breath. 'I'm having another. Will you join me?'

'I'll get them.' He rang the bell on the bar, ordered another round. 'She'll bring them over,' he told Ash.

'Do you like the great outdoors, Marcus?'

'I do. Carrie and I used to go climbing together.'

'She's planning to take me to somewhere called Loch More... Loch Morch...Loch—'

'Loch Morlich?'

'That's it.'

'The Cairngorms. We used to camp there every summer.'

'Are you free at any time this week?'

'I can be.'

'And your wife?'

'Isobel? I'd have to check.'

'Okay, here's what I'm thinking. We're staying at the Hilton there.'

'Coylumbridge?'

'I think so. I have to admit these Scottish names defeat me. If you and your wife could also book in there, then we could arrange to meet.'

'Make it look like a coincidence?'

'She won't fall for that. But if we get her out amongst the mountains, away from negative memories, she might be more relaxed.'

'When are you booked in?'

'Thursday and Friday night.' Her phone bleeped. 'That's Carrie. I should go.'

'Okay, I'll get the hotel booked. I should give you my number.'

'Take my card, send me a text when you're fixed.'

He drained his pint, took some money out of his wallet.

'Don't worry about the drinks, they're on me. You can buy a round in Loch Morlich.'

'Thank you for this.'

'I'm glad to help, Marcus.'

'I really miss her, Ash. When I was out there, during the disaster...'

'I understand. I can't guarantee anything, but we can try.' She stood, they shook hands again. 'I look forward to your text.'

'Thank you. And I apologise for my reaction when we met.'

'No need, Marcus. Take care of yourself.'

He left her to finish her gin and crossed the street, heading straight for Number Ten.

Aberdeen,
June 2013

The morning was a meet-and-greet, geologists from all over the world coming together to exchange ideas, dirt and, by tonight, bodily fluids. The bars of Aberdeen would be packed over the next few days with scientists trying to reclaim their student days. I was staying well out of it. In and out. Tomorrow I'd deliver my paper, drop my conclusions like a grenade, clear out. Then we were off to Skye, the Cairngorms, then back and flying home. A week, in and out.

'Carrie, it's wonderful of you to come. We're all looking forward to your paper. The prodigal returned and all that.'

'Professor Boyle, you're looking well. The weight of administration suits you.'

'An act, Carrie, all an act. Inside I'm drowning. How are things in Hawaii? Professor Lau still as terrifying as ever?'

'Still fighting her corner, if that's what you mean. How are things here?'

'I'm not sure I have the strength for the winters anymore. I never seem to get the chill out of my bones.'

'I can't say I miss that.'

'No. I envy your position in Hawaii. Do you think you'll ever move back to this part of the world?'

'I can't rule it out, but to give up Hawaii it would have to be one hell of a job offer.'

'Well, with your reputation and publication history, you must get offers all the time.'

'Some, it's true. But I imagine after tomorrow...'

'Yes, your paper. *Geothermal Energy Extraction and Collateral Seismic Events*. I've been hearing some interesting things about it and I'm curious why you chose to come all this way to deliver it. Care to elaborate?'

'You've read the abstract?'

'I have. Bit vague.'

I tilted my head and smiled. I knew he'd heard about my conclusions. There were only two reasons why someone would turn up in the European oil capital and deliver a paper on *Geothermal Energy Extraction and Collateral Seismic Events* – if their conclusions would be warmly welcomed by the oil industry or if their conclusions would spark outrage. 'No spoilers, Professor Boyle,' I said. 'But I am expecting a lively debate afterwards.'

'I'll make sure I don't miss it, then.' He looked around at the other groups, people mingling, and eased me into an empty adjoining room. 'Changing the subject, I need to have a word with you.'

'This sounds serious.'

'Not serious, just personal.'

'My father?'

'Have you spoken to him?'

I took a deep breath. This was bound to happen sooner or later, I just thought Boyle would wait until he had a few drinks in him. 'No. We haven't been in touch for a while.'

'Then I should tell you. Your father works for me now.'

'For you? Here? In the department?'

'Yes. Part-time, teaching.'

'I...I had no idea. Will he be—'

'At your paper? I don't think so. I advised against it, at least without speaking to you first. Not an ideal place for a reunion.'

'No. Thank you. And thank you for warning me.'

'Carrie,' he put a hand on my shoulder, his soft eyes all saggy concern, 'you should see him. While you're here. He's changed. He's less troubled.'

'Is he still drinking?'

'You know as well as I that nothing could keep him away from the drink for long. But it's under control. I have no complaints about his work, he is punctual and prepared, which is more than I can say for many others in this department. Carrie, your father will never be the way he was before all that horror, but he's about as healed as he's ever going to be.'

Who was this old man to interfere? I sipped my orange juice, trying to quench the burn. 'Professor Boyle, I thank you for your concern and I appreciate you telling me about my father's employment situation, but I'd ask you not to get involved with my private life.'

'Carrie, if I've spoken out of turn and offended you, then I apologise. Marcus is one of my oldest friends. I know much of his behaviour was inexcusable, and PTSD is only a label that covers a lot of hurts, but I just want to say this and then we will never speak of it again. He understands the hurt he has caused and he is truly sorry for it. Is there no part of you left that loves him? That can, if not forgive him, then at least see him and let him apologise?'

We returned to the meeting and he left me to catch up with Dr Halabi, who had left Hawaii for Istanbul, opening up the position for me. I put myself on pleasantries auto-pilot, reminiscing about shared colleagues, listening to the abstract of his paper, but I wasn't hearing, wasn't caring. I kept expecting my father to come around the corner any moment, to come into the room. I'd hardly slept and everything felt woolly.

As soon as Boyle left I made my excuses and texted Ash. I'd agreed to show her the campus and then the beach but I just wanted to go back to the hotel and hide.

I met Ash's taxi outside the English department. She hugged me as it drove off. There was a coffee cart inside the Taylor building that hadn't been there before but otherwise everything was the same.

'This is gorgeous,' she said. 'It's one of these proper Harry Potter ones.'

'It was founded in fourteen ninety-five, three years after Columbus found America.' I couldn't help having a dig.

'A good time to be a geography student.'

'Third in Scotland, fifth in Britain.' I took her through the quadrangles, the granite towers with crowns perched on top, the battlements and ornate arched windows, Bishop Elphinstone's tomb, the chapel. When I'd been a student I'd taken all of these buildings for granted. King's College wasn't an architectural masterpiece then, it wasn't a piece of history, it was where I had classes, did exams. Elphinstone Hall was the site of anxiety attacks, the lawn the setting for a messy break-up. Now the towers, the ancient blocks, the quads, glowed in the sunlight.

'How was this morning?'

'Oh, you know. Shake hands, repeat the same four pieces of information, move on. Did you get much done?'

'Yeah, it was a productive morning.'

We walked through the quad behind Elphinstone Hall where the drama society did plays before the summer holidays. I'd seen *A Midsummer Night's Dream* and *The Tempest* there. We crossed King Street, passed the pill box- like Golf Road flats where there'd been plenty of parties, and cut across the golf course, turning right when we reached the sand.

'It must have been great having the beach so close to campus,' said Ash.

'We didn't come down as often as you'd think. It's cold here, pretty much all year.'

'I can see why you prefer Hawaii.'

The beach was almost deserted, a few dog walkers, kids playing. One man doing tai chi.

'What's that?' said Ash, pointing at a building.

'Leisure centre. I used to work there.'

'Lifeguard?'

'General dogsbody. I got to climb for free though.'

'Good perk. Are you okay?'

I sat down hard on the sand, felt the prick of tears, tried to fight them but couldn't, I was too tired. Ash put her arms around me, pulled me into her shoulder. Why had I come back, why now? The pain of it all, I could vomit, I could scream.

I emptied. When the aftershocks subsided, Ash gave me a tissue. Her shoulder was soaked.

'Sorry.'

'It's okay. I was wondering when you'd do that.'

'Cry?'

'You were going to break eventually.'

'I should never have come.'

'You had to, sometime. You can't keep running forever.'

'Watch me.'

'You can but you shouldn't.'

'He works at the university.'

'Did you see him?'

'No.'

'Maybe you should.'

'I can't.'

'You can. I think it's time, Carrie.'

'I don't want to.'

'You're scared.'

'No, I'm angry.' I swallowed. Blew my nose. 'Sometimes I wish he'd died out there.' She didn't reply. 'A hundred and sixty-seven men died that day. He survived but for what? Everything afterwards was horrible. Maybe someone else would've done something more worthwhile with their second chance.'

'You don't mean that.'

'If he'd died that day I could've mourned him and moved on. It would've been finished.'

'You think you'd have been any happier?'

'Probably not. But another family would be.'

'It was a disaster, Carrie. You were all victims, but he will die someday. He might get hit by a bus tomorrow, he might live to be one hundred. But one day he'll be gone and so will your chance to see him. Trust me, Carrie, that hurts a whole lot worse than the anger you're feeling now. Even after all the hurt, even through all the anger and hatred, I'd give anything to see my dad one more time.' Now she was the one crying. My turn to hold her. A tanker was leaving the harbour to our right, slipping by the lighthouse.

186

We had an early night but I woke at three o'clock, bright-eyed and full of energy in the dark. Ash of course had no problem. Her regular breathing was a metronome I timed my own breathing against, trying to lull myself back to sleep. It was no use. I slid out of bed, wrapping a thick dressing gown around me, got my laptop and took it over to the desk, thinking I could read over my paper one last time, hoping it would send me back to bed. I tweaked the ending, adding qualifiers, deleting them.

Even at that hour I could hear traffic outside, Saturday night taxis, trucks, people who worked in the night, people who hid in the night. This end of Aberdeen was quiet, pretty safe, far from the pubs and clubs. The only people who drank this far up were the oil executives, bankers, lawyers and accountants who had offices and huge detached granite houses in the area, whose kids went to private schools like Albyn. Dad used to drink up here, Hannah too when she went out. Maybe he still did. Someone's retirement party, leaving do, they'd both get dressed up, a taxi would come, I'd be left with the Galloways or, eventually, on my own, then they'd come back reeking of alcohol, not talking to each other or pretending not to fight until the Galloways had closed the door on us. He'd been flirting. She'd been rude. The usual. Then it all stopped.

Skye,
December 2003

I wanted to leave New Zealand immediately but my new flat in
Hawaii wouldn't be ready until the new year. I could be at Dad's
wedding, then fly out again. I'd take a holiday, get the last few
months out of me, forget all about Graeme.

We had a small leaving party, Jeannie Parker and some others
from the department, though Professor Meyer didn't come,
petulant at Paul and me leaving at the same time. I said goodbye
to Mike after arranging for one of the PhD students to move in
and shipped my belongings off to Hawaii. I'd been in Dunedin
for nearly five years but there was little melancholy in the taxi
to the airport. Hawaii, and Ash, beckoned. But first.

The wedding was on Skye, just four of us, me, Dad, Isobel and
Isobel's brother, Gavin. Bride, groom, two witnesses. The bare
minimum. We were booked into the Flodigarry Hotel, a large
country house at the north of the island. They invited me to
drive over with them but I declined, rented a car and drove
myself. From Glasgow, I took the road along Loch Lomond and
through Glencoe. After the jagged peaks of New Zealand and
the bubbling calderas of Hawaii, there was something stately
and distinguished about the ancient mountains of Scotland,
worn down by millennia of weather, ice ages, scarred and ripped
by glaciers. They'd borne it all with gentle majesty. Names on
the map, on the signs rang with the music of history, mine and
ours, snatches of songs, *Loch Lomond*, Ben Vorlich which Dad
and I climbed when I was eleven or twelve, Ben More, the Crian-
larich hotel, the Green Welly, Loch Tulla, Loch Leven and the
burial island of the MacDonalds of Glencoe. I took a break at the
museum, the hills around us dowsed in thick snow but the sun, for
now, shining, and I wallowed in the melancholy of my nation.

Ben Nevis covered in mist, Fort William dismal in the gloom
and then Eilean Donan Castle, Dornie, Kyle of Lochalsh. My

childhood dripped from these names.

I'd forgotten about the bridge, had never seen it. Last time, every time, we'd taken the ferry. I was looking forward to standing on deck, the wild wind whipping over me, but I rolled easily onto the bridge and minutes later was on Skye, the glamour, the romance of it taken from me. But the sun came back, some of the mist cleared and my spirits rose with the slopes, the scree and the scrub, through Portree and onto the single-track roads. I was almost disappointed when the hotel came into view.

I parked, stretched. An Alfa Romeo was the only other car in the car park, black, splashed with mud, the engine still ticking as it cooled. I took a few steps towards the view, the rich green lawns of the hotel, stepping down towards the sea, two small islands offshore, the sea scattered with boats.

'Carrie.'

He was standing in the doorway, like the Laird, green Barbour jacket, slacks, a beard. He'd filled out, had colour in his face, though that could've been the wind. We stopped a few paces from each other.

'What way did you come?'

I told him.

'A beautiful road.'

'I don't like the bridge.'

'No, not the same.'

'This must be Isobel.' Behind him a small woman appeared, a similar outfit to Dad, her hair a curly black helmet rippling like a bush in the wind. We shook hands.

'Pleased to meet you, Caroline.'

'Likewise. Please, call me Carrie. Only my mother calls me Caroline.'

'Carrie.' She put her hand on my father's arm, the move almost aggressive, protective. 'Marcus, the room is ready, would you like to unpack and freshen up?'

'Good idea. Carrie, why don't you check in and we'll meet you in the bar in half an hour?'

'Sure.'

A man in a purple psychedelic shirt was leaning on the counter chatting to the receptionist. He had a similar hairstyle to Isobel, wild curls, and a beard, jeans and sandals. 'You must be Gavin,' I said, 'Isobel's brother?'

'Ah, and you must be young Carrie?'

'I'm Carrie, yes. Pleased to meet you.' I held out my hand.

'Och, none of that, we're near enough family.' He pulled me into a bear hug, gave me a kiss on my cheek, managing to catch a bit of my mouth.

'I suppose so,' I said, freeing myself. 'I'd like to check in, please,' I said to the receptionist. 'Carrie Fraser.' Gavin stood back, waiting, whether for me or for the girl to be free again I couldn't tell. Now I had arrived, tiredness caught up with me. The wedding was first thing the next morning at the Portree registry office and there'd be little chance of an early night. I got my key. 'We're meeting in the bar in half an hour,' I said to Gavin. 'I'll see you there.'

'Best dump the bags then.' He followed me through the lobby and up the stairs. On the first landing we looked at our keys. 'Looks like this is you,' he said pointing to the left. 'And this is me. Just across the way.'

'Okay then.' I closed the door, backpack, jacket and suitcase slipping into a heap, stripped down to my underwear, the stink of travelling released into the room. They could start without me.

I tidied myself up, the room, made it temporarily mine. Books by the bed. Alarm set for six. Shoes ready by the door. Gifts prepared. Dirty clothes into a plastic bag. Half an hour. Forty-five minutes. I'd have to go down eventually.

They were waiting for me, finishing their first drinks. I sat in the empty seat beside Gavin, a waitress came over. Another young girl, late teens, early twenties, another Eastern European accent. She smiled at me, looked at Gavin with a wary eye.

'Do you have camomile tea?' I asked her. She nodded.

'Tea?' said Gavin in mock disgust.

'Carrie doesn't drink,' said Dad. 'Another pair of pints, and another wine, oh my love?'

'No, this island air is making me thirsty. I'll have a half of the same beer and a Talisker.'

'You don't drink?' said Gavin. 'Ever?'

'Occasionally. I have a very low tolerance for alcohol.'

'A cheap date, you mean?'

The waitress brought our drinks over and we toasted the wedding.

'Isn't it bad luck to toast without alcohol?' said Dad.

'It's bad luck with water, but not with tea. Dad said you are a lawyer,' I said to Isobel.

'A solicitor, yes.'

'In what area?'

'Employment law.'

'My friend is a lawyer.'

'In New Zealand?'

'In New York. The UN.'

'Wow, bigshot,' said Dad. 'How is life in New Zealand?'

'Over,' I said. 'I've got a new job at the University of Hawaii.'

'Hawaii? I know who I'm going to be visiting on my holidays,' said Gavin. 'Hawaii?' said Dad. He gave me a strange, searching look. 'I thought you were settled in Dunedin.'

'Five years is long enough.' He looked like he wanted to say something else but I cut him off. It was beginning to feel like an interview. 'So, Gavin,' I said, 'what do you do?'

'I'm a musician. And a historian of music.'

'What does that involve?'

'I collect and archive the folk music of Scotland so it can be preserved for posterity. Have you any idea how much of our culture has been lost? In places like Shetland we've been lucky, being isolated, but the closer you get to the central belt, the more has been lost.'

I wondered how he'd feel in Dunedin, whether he'd appreciate it as a living lineage or a pastiche. He seemed the type of man who could happily have a party on his own but was all the livelier in company. Dad and Isobel seemed a good couple.

There was a calmness between them, like a beach the morning after a storm.

I was struggling, wanted to go back to my room and get a nap. I thought Dad should do the same, the drinks he was putting away, but I kept that to myself. We agreed to meet again for dinner at seven. He followed me out into the lobby while Isobel and Gavin stayed at the table. I noticed he was limping.

'It's good to see you, Carrie. It's been too long.'

'Durham,' I said.

'Not my finest moment. I've changed since then, Carrie.' He was holding a present in his hand, wrapped in shiny green paper with a white ribbon. 'I got help.'

'You're still drinking.'

'Not like I was.'

A member of hotel staff walked by, gave us a 'Good afternoon.' We waited until he'd gone.

'Dad, if you want to talk maybe we should go upstairs.'

'I don't want to talk, I mean, not now. After tomorrow. It's great to see you, Carrie, but this is a wedding party. Digging up old hurts would spoil the mood a bit, don't you think?'

Pretend it was all fine? Well, I was used to that. 'What have you got there?'

'For you. No, open it upstairs.'

'Thank you. I have presents...'

'Tomorrow, this is something aside from the wedding. You'll be back down for dinner?'

'I will. You won't get too drunk before then?'

'I will.'

From the landing I saw him return to the bar, swaying slightly like he was pivoting around something. Once in my room, I kicked my boots off, lay down on top of the bed and fell fast asleep.

When I woke I guzzled half a bottle of water, dropped an effervescent vitamin C pill into the rest and shook it up. A cabin attendant once told me that vitamin C is a great help for jet lag and whether it's true or just a placebo effect, I'd followed her advice ever since. It was six o'clock, I still had an hour until dinner. I knew I wouldn't sleep more but it was nice just lying on the bed, not having to do anything. There was a warm hum in the room, the heating probably, and the muffled sounds of a hotel at work. I found my hand resting on the present Dad had given me. I picked it up and eased the wrapping off. When I was a kid Dad had got frustrated every Christmas morning by the slow, methodical way I'd unwrap my presents, picking the tape, folding the empty sheets before turning my attention to the present. He wanted to see my face, wanted me to rip the paper off in excitement.

It was a book, a paperback, cheaply bound. There was no cover image, just white card with *Piper Alpha and Me* by Marcus Fraser. I dropped it onto the bed, my fingers burnt. He'd written a book. Not a real book, this looked like he'd had it printed and bound himself, but it was his story. Our story. He'd written it all down.

Downstairs in the bar pouring alcohol down his throat. Why had he given me this? Why now? Why today?

I picked it up again. He'd written inside. *Carrie, I'm sorry for everything.*

Is that what this was: his explanation? His apology? I flicked, stopped at random.

I was still going into work every morning though to this day I've no idea what I did when I got there. For a while they kept my desk clear, then they gave me redundant work, checking calculations, going back over old projects and tying up loose ends. Nothing that could cause any problems. Nothing where decisions had to be made. No one knew what to do with me. A geologist, usually working in the office, being out there that day was the unluckiest of timings. The other survivors, they worked offshore every day, were only back between contracts or on leave. There was a split between management and offshore workers, the management, those at the sharp end of the oil industry.

I flicked again, back, forth. He went into details, the levels, the separation. Things I'd picked up over the years, things I hadn't known. Decisions about safety, budgets, cuts, were made onshore by people who would never be put in danger. *We treated them like faceless drones there to keep profits up and problems down. Piper Alpha ripped that wall to shreds. For weeks, every night you turned on the TV there they were, the survivors, the families, not faceless, not nameless. There they were. In the offices they couldn't hide from it. Reality wouldn't leave them alone with their balance sheets and legal loopholes.*

While Red Adair was offshore putting out fires, capping wells and eventually sinking Piper Alpha to the bottom, I went into the office every day, the scars on my hands, the stink of drink off me, the chance that I could lose it at any moment, that was so much worse than any Grampian TV report or Newsnight interview. Every day they saw me, every day they had to face it again.

He was angry. He raged. They were afraid of him. He hadn't spoken to anyone, professionals, journalists, no one, but people were always calling, asking. Maybe that's why they didn't let him go. Fear of what he might say if he did speak to the press. But he was useless. They shunted him sideways, moved him off important projects. He spent his time reviewing other people's work, possible fields, ways of getting more oil out of known sites.

Was it all about work? I flicked again but there was no contents page, no index. Isn't that what everyone did in these situations, checked the index for their own name?

We both had affairs. Cabin crew. Waitresses. Whoever I could find on business trips. She had Frank Carpenter in Bristol for years.

I flicked, rifled.

When I went down to Durham for Carrie's graduation I was near bottom.

That night, Hannah, me and Carrie... I left, ran off into the Durham night, drank all night, picked up my bags and took the first train home in the morning, slept then went straight to Under The Hammer. I could see myself there, holding court in

the corner with the other regulars, life and soul, hiding the pain.
And then the fall.

Hospital. His hip replacement. I knew none of this.

*It was Carrie leaving that was the final straw. I hadn't known
how much she held everything together. She had to leave. I'm
glad she got away. But it nearly killed me.*

That taxi. Leaving him on the doorstep.

Carrie was in Durham. Carrie was in New Zealand.

But Isobel was there. The only one who never left me.

I'd stayed in Aberdeen so I could look after him. He'd made
me go to Durham. He'd given me the money to do whatever I
wanted when I graduated. I'd been there, six years I looked after
him like his carer.

The only one who never left.

Seven o'clock flickered by on the LED clock. Gavin knocked
on my door, called through to me, his voice distant as the wind,
just another muffled sound from the hotel. I kept flicking.

Isobel, how she nursed him, helped him, put him back
together while his daughter got on with her own life. The
cooking – my dad cooks? – the walking to rehabilitate, then it
became a love story, a proposal under a meteor shower in
Findhorn.

I closed the book. All those things I never knew. All those
thoughts, the pain. He hadn't talked so I hadn't talked. But in
his words it seemed so much worse. He couldn't talk. I didn't
want to. I was selfish. I was cruel. I ran off like Hannah. My
mother's daughter. I left and Isobel picked him up.

The only one who never left.

Even before Piper Alpha, Hannah had one foot out the door.
But I stayed. I stayed until I couldn't stay anymore.

He'd given me permission. Told me to go. After the day at the
memorial I thought he'd turned a corner.

I didn't know any of those things because he'd kept them
from me.

To my daughter, Carrie, I'm sorry for everything. A PS. An
afterthought. I threw the book across the room. It hit the wall

and dropped down behind the chest of drawers.

This was all Isobel knew of me, sitting downstairs, judging me.

They'd have eaten by now but they'd still be sitting around the table, bottles of wine, discussing me. The girl who ran away, hiding in her room.

I paused in the lobby, rearranged my face. Hands raised in apology, 'Jet lag,' I said, taking my place, 'caught up with me. I was on the other side of the world yesterday. Or the day before. I'm not even sure what day it is.'

'You missed dinner,' said Gavin. 'I think the kitchen's open. We don't mind watching you eat if you don't mind watching us drink.'

'I'm okay, thanks.'

'You sure?' said Dad. 'You haven't eaten since you arrived.'

'I had a good lunch on the road.'

Isobel was watching me, the lawyer in there, the look I could recognise from Ash.

'I've been meaning to ask,' said Dad, signalling to a waitress, 'did you ever see Graeme Anderson in New Zealand?'

'Graeme? Yes, I saw him.'

He ordered another round for them all. I ordered a glass of lemonade.

'I know his dad. Used to anyway. I saw Graeme in Under The Hammer...och, it must be three years ago, maybe four. Quite the celebrity, he was. This is a boy Carrie went to school with,' he said to Isobel and Gavin. 'Professional snowboarder, bronze in the Olympics.'

'How did you know he was in New Zealand?'

Dad looked shifty, embarrassed. 'I didn't. I thought he might be. We got drunk that night. Very drunk. End of the night it was just us two. He was staying in a hotel, didn't want to stay with his folks you see, so we ended up in the bar there. He was asking about you all night. Talking about you. How you helped him out, helped him realise his dream, how he owed it all to your advice. Seemed to have a thing for you. Anyway, he was going through something, a crisis, midlife crisis he called it, not even thirty and he's having a midlife crisis.' Gavin and Isobel rolled their eyes. Kids these days. 'Anyway, I told him you were in New Zealand. I got the feeling he intended on using that information.'

Graeme. Just like he'd said. Turning up in Dunedin wasn't an accident. I could see him, standing in that flat as I yelled at him. 'He did, yes. He's still there now.'

'Young romance rekindled, that's lovely,' said Gavin.

'He's not moving to Hawaii with you, is he?' said Isobel.

'You definitely are a solicitor,' I laughed, feeling no mirth. *The only one who never left.* 'He's running a shop in Dunedin, teaching snowboarding in the season, designing equipment for a company in Fife. We were going out for a while but it didn't work out.'

'Why not?' said Gavin. They were all drunk, the three of them, not an ounce of diplomacy between them. I was trying so hard.

'He wanted a housewife, Gavin, he wanted someone to do his washing and have his kids. That's not me.'

'You don't want kids?' said Isobel.

'No,' I said. 'Do you have kids?'

'No,' she said. 'Never wanted them either. More trouble than they're worth.'

'I wouldn't swap having a kid for anything,' said Dad.

'Yes, but you're talking about Carrie,' said Gavin. 'I have kids,' he said to me. 'Off somewhere with their mother. No idea where. When you talk about not having kids, you have to imagine not having Carrie, imagine her never having been born. For Carrie and Isobel it's different. They're imagining not having abstract kids with no names, no faces, no memories attached to them. It's much easier.'

'It's not easier,' said Isobel. 'There are still biological urges, but you make a choice. Abstract kids or current life. I've never found myself in the position of weighing one against the other and finding that kids would make my current life better. I assume it's the same for Carrie.'

'Not really.' *I'm not like you.* But what reason could I give? That when I thought about kids I imagined someone else with my childhood, someone else living through what I did? That if I brought a child into this world and they suffered it would be my fault? I couldn't say that to Dad, however true it was.

'So why don't you want kids?' said Gavin.

'Because I'm bisexual.'

There was silence for a moment, and I'm sure the hotel staff and the other guests were staring at our table. I drank my lemonade, the bubbles fizzing inside my throat.

The thing with problems, with issues as Ash would call them, is that there's only space for so many inside you at any one time. If you push down one problem another pops up somewhere else. Something's got to give, something's going to come out.

Gavin was the first to react. He laughed, a big belly laugh that reverberated off the stone walls. 'That shut everyone up. Well done, Carrie.' Dad looked stunned, his forehead wrinkled like he was working something out. Isobel finished her wine, watching me as she drank.

'But Graeme?' said Dad.

'God, Dad. I'm bisexual.'

'Still hope for me then,' said Gavin.

'Gavin, if you have nothing useful to contribute...' said Isobel.

'Sorry, Gavin, but no. I have a partner.'

'In Hawaii?' said Isobel.

'We met in Hawaii.'

'The lawyer?'

'Yes, actually.'

'So you're leaving Graeme for another woman?' said Dad.

'Yes. Well, that's what I do, isn't it? Leave.'

I could see the blow land, him flinching. The air fuzzed as we looked at each other, love and hatred sparking between. He was trying, pushing down anger, pushing back tears. Part of me thrilled that the power wasn't one way. But the pain was palpable. Hating an abstract past from the other side of the world was nothing like hating your father sat in front of you. I looked down, away, catching Isobel's eye in the motion. His defender was ready to pounce, *the only one who never left.*

'Just like her mother.' She stood up, lifted her bag. 'Looks like these scientists are right. Perhaps there are genes for certain characteristics. Marcus, I'm going to bed. Don't be long.'

I watched her weave through the tables.

'I thought we could make it through one night,' said Dad. 'You read the book?'

'I flicked through it. Enough to get a good impression of myself.'

Dad seemed to shrink back in his seat. 'None of us come out of this smelling of roses.'

'She does.' I nodded at Isobel's empty chair.

'I shouldn't have shown it to you. I didn't think you'd read it tonight. I thought it might help. Clarify things. I want us to start again.'

I felt dry, parched, I sipped my lemonade but it felt flat, weak. I caught the waitress's eye. 'A Mâcon-Villages please.' I didn't want to look at Dad.

It was Gavin who broke the silence. 'Well, when families get together, it's never boring.'

My drink came. I sipped. It tasted of Ash.

I went for a walk before bed, the bitter chill a slap in the face. One of the audiobooks I used to block out the sound of them fighting when I was a kid was *Robinson Crusoe*. Hannah's parents had given it to me as *a change from those boring science ones.* Alone on that desert island, starting from nothing, building a home, scratching out a life, each day, each month, each year a progression. I'd imagine myself there, making rope out of vines, reinventing fire, pulling fish from the sea. I was always almost disappointed when Friday came along. I looked out at the bruised sea, the salt in the air, the rumble of hidden power.

Jet lag. At half four I finally dropped off into a fuzzy doze, woke lost at six to some ungodly beeping. In the shower with my head against the tiles, water drilling into my skull. The face in the mirror needed make-up, eyes like an owl, pallor of pizza dough.

They were waiting in the restaurant for me, three well-dressed hangovers. I took my seat next to Gavin, ordered some camomile, some orange juice and a few pieces of fruit. Gavin had a full Scottish, Dad and Isobel both clasped cups of coffee. We all stared at the grease, bean sauce and tomato juice swilling around Gavin's plate. The vitamins sank through my body, sparking synapses and cells. I wasn't going to let Isobel think she was right. I wasn't going to let her win. For one day I could put the past aside and play happy dysfunctional families.

Dad and Gavin were kilted. Dad's was Fraser of Lovat tartan, a green, red and purple pattern. He was a good man for the kilt: thick, hairy legs, the stomach and beard of a feudal chief. Gavin's was green and blue checks with marked red and white lines. 'What clan is that?' I asked him.

'Sutherland,' he said. 'We're Mowats,' he nodded at Isobel. 'An old branch of the clan.'

Isobel was wearing a white skirt suit that looked expensive, definitely not off the rack. 'You look lovely,' I said to her. 'Where did you get it?' Like I'd recognise the shop. Sure enough she said a woman's name like I should know it.

'Is that in Aberdeen?'

'Edinburgh.'

It was going to be a long day. 'So, what's the plan? Dad?'

He looked rough. 'I was thinking about getting married.'

'Not too hungover for sarcasm then. I meant—'

'We'll drive into Portree, registry office, I do, sign here, witnesses sign here, some photos, back here for the party.'

'Do you want me to drive?'

'Aye, could you? We've a bottle of champagne but we need a driver.'

'That's me. We'll have to take your car though, my rental isn't big enough.'

'You're a star,' said Dad, perking up. 'In that case, Bloody Marys?' The other two nodded.

'I'll see you by the car.'

I took a walk across the lawn towards the sea and really wanted to go down to the beach but this wasn't the day for crunching through pebbles and poking things in rock pools. When I was in second year the Geology Society organised a trip out this way. It was partly a serious trip to try out some of the techniques we'd learned in the classroom and partly an excuse for debauchery.

It was the first time I'd left Dad alone for more than a few hours. I called a couple of times but he never answered. On the Sunday night we had a party. The stress of worrying about him all weekend got to me and I had a drink, then another. We started playing games, truth or dare, that kind of thing.

That was twice now I'd come out on Skye.

By the time they appeared the vodka had done its work and spirits were reviving. They were much livelier as we got underway, Dad up front with me, Isobel and Gavin in the back. The single-track road was empty apart from a couple of locals who waved as the brush scraped the side of Isobel's car.

'I love this countryside,' said Dad. 'So dramatic. All the stories, Highlanders fleeing English soldiers, hiding from traitorous Scots, Alan Breck and his like, lads amongst the heather.' I had an image of Dad, a memory from when I was ten or eleven, the two of us on the ferry from Kyle of Lochalsh, him with one hand on my shoulder telling me about Flora MacDonald and Bonnie Prince Charlie. 'Talking of Alan Breck, they're thinking about renaming Edinburgh Airport, Robert Louis Stevenson Airport,' he said.

'Nice,' said Gavin. 'Waverley Station, Stevenson Airport. Wonder what they'll name the bus station?'

'How about Aberdeen Airport?' I said. 'What could they call that? Annie Lennox Airport?'

'Lewis Grassic Gibbon Airport?' said Gavin.

'Knowing that city,' said Isobel, 'it would end up Sir Alex Ferguson Airport.'

'Like George Best Airport in Belfast,' said Dad. 'Football trumps everything.'

'Liverpool is now John Lennon Airport, isn't it?' I said.

'Yes,' said Dad. 'It was the first place he went when he got some money.'

I was a fully paid-up atheist but there was something about weddings in places other than churches that seemed bereft, the religious underpinning of the ceremony removed. Stripped of the 'standing before God' element, it really was just a confirmation of ownership for property purposes. Legal marriage, legitimate offspring, hereditary rights, inheritance. Could love not just be love?

Gavin and I stood back and watched them exchange self-penned vows, holding hands before the registrar.

'On the ocean of life our rafts met. I pledge myself to you, that we may sail together for the rest of our days.'

It was awful. At least I'd never have to go through anything as sickening as that. If Ash and I ever could get married it'd be, 'Do you?'

'Aye.'

'And you?'

'Why not?'

And done with. Take the fear of God out and all you're left with is sentimentality.

They signed their names. Gavin signed below, then I added my name, official witnesses.

Rings exchanged. 'I had them made by a jeweller in Shetland,' she said. 'My own design.' They looked like every other Celtic pattern I'd ever seen.

We drove back towards the hotel and stopped at Mealt Falls. A famous tourist spot, it was deserted as Dad and Isobel posed for photos in the unhelpful wind, Kilt Rock as the background, the stunning ninety metre basalt columns on a sandstone base that resembled the pleats of a kilt. As the light shifted the colours occasionally resembled a tartan. 'A geologist's wedding photo,'

I said, and Dad laughed. Gavin and I took it in turns to take photos, set the timer up for a couple of group snaps. Dad popped the champagne, filled four plastic flutes. 'I'm driving,' I said but he handed me the glass anyway.

'We're just up the road and that's all you're getting. You're not going to refuse a drink on my wedding day?'

So I took it, the bubbles flushing my nose like wasabi. The shifting sunlight caught the white of Isobel's clothes and I felt something like warmth towards her. It was strange seeing my dad like this, part of something that had nothing to do with me. He was a different person, a new person. I raised my glass to them.

A car drew into the car park and an elderly couple got out, wrapped up sensibly. They offered to take photos so the four of us posed, serious, silly, ready, caught out. They were retired, touring Scotland now they had the time for it. Dad invited them back to the hotel but they declined, a schedule to keep. We waved them off as if a happy retired couple was the best omen a wedding party could see.

'I'm getting hungry. What time's lunch?' I asked.

'Whenever we get back. You seem happier today,' said Gavin.

'Just exhausted yesterday. I still am but it's nice to see him so happy.'

'Isobel won't apologise for last night,' he said. 'That's not her personality. But she is sorry.'

'I wish I had a brother like you.'

'You have an uncle like me now.'

'Step-uncle.'

'I used to wish I was an only child, like you,' he said. 'Isobel and I fought through our childhood. But the older we got, the more we realised how much we had in common.'

'When I was really young I was so happy I didn't have a brother or sister, I could have my parents all to myself. After what happened – you know all about what happened, I assume?'

'Aye.'

'After that I wished I had hundreds of them, a whole army of siblings to look after Dad.'

'It must have been hard.'

'It was what it was.'

Back at the hotel Isobel went upstairs to change while the three of us went through to a private room. Dad and Gavin ordered gin and tonics and, the bubbles from the champagne still pinballing around my head, I joined them. Dad sat in a plush highbacked armchair and sighed, a content, satisfied exhalation. He looked over at me, smiled.

'We've come a long way, Carrie. Long fucking way.' I nodded, bubbles trying to push out through my eyes.

'So, this lawyer of yours,' he said. 'What's she like?'

As I told them about Ash, her auburn hair and tailored clothes, her trips to Hawaii, how we met, the clean version. Isobel returned wearing a turquoise dress in a 1960s Jackie Kennedy style, with a white cardigan. 'Not ideal for the time of year,' she said after we'd all commented on how much it suited her, 'but we're not going out again.' Gavin went to the bathroom and the rest of us sat at the table with open menus in front of us. I was suddenly ravenous. 'So what does she do at the UN?' Isobel asked, her own gin and tonic appearing through the swing door with our second round. 'Human rights,' I said. 'Just now it's all Iraq.'

'Any idea what?'

'Not really, she usually wants to forget about work.'

Gavin came back in looking excited. 'Have you seen the news?' he said. 'They found Saddam.'

'What will they do with him?' I said.

'Back to America for the show trial of the century,' said Dad.

'No, they'll hand him over to the Iraqi administration with instructions: death penalty.'

'So they can find one guy in the desert but not a supposed stockpile of WMDs?' said Gavin. 'They found the oil okay.'

'That's not difficult. I can do that. Carrie can do that,' said Dad.

'I thought you were volcanoes,' said Gavin, 'not oil.'

'You don't study geology at Aberdeen without learning a thing or two about oil.'

'Why did you choose volcanoes?' asked Isobel. 'Not many of them in Aberdeen.'

'Part of the appeal, I'd imagine,' said Gavin.

'Partly, but almost all branches of geology require international travel. It's a global business.' Dad snorted, laughing while taking a drink. I smiled, pleased he'd got the joke.

'Harry Boyle,' he explained to them when he caught his breath. 'An old friend of mine. He made that same joke a thousand times.'

'Do you still see Harry?' I said.

'Harry now is it? It was always Professor Boyle before. Aye, I see him once in a while. He's a busy man. Do you come across him at all? Conferences and things?'

'His name, sometimes, but never the man himself. I used to meet a lot of his PhD students and one of his collaborated with one of my former students on a paper.'

'You're supervising PhDs now?'

'Have been for years.'

He raised his glass. The waitress came and took our order. I went for the venison. The rich dark meat seemed just the thing for the atmosphere, the location. 'Harry's going to be the next Head of Department,' said Dad.

'Old Cameron is retiring?'

'Ill health. Lung cancer I think, but that's just a rumour.'

'Seems likely.'

'Would you ever take a job at Aberdeen?' Isobel asked me. Our food arrived, two soups, a crab, a Cullen Skink and the scallops, and a bottle of Sauvignon blanc. We each had order envy.

'What, leave Hawaii for the bottom of King Street? She'd have to be mad,' said Gavin, filling my wine glass.

'They wouldn't have me,' I said. 'I'm so out of touch on petroleum geology and as you pointed out earlier, there's not much use for my specialty in Aberdeen.'

'You never did explain why you chose volcanoes,' said Gavin.

'Two reasons,' I said, the crisp yellow flavour of the wine on my tongue. 'Firstly if you don't want to work for the oil industry, if you want to pursue geology academically you need something with a lot of unanswered questions, something that needs research. Secondly, volcanoes are amazing. They're just so cool. When I was a kid, Dad and I would go on trips, Vesuvius, Etna, Sakurajima in Japan. It was on Sakurajima I got this scar,' I said, pulling back my hair to show them. 'They're probably the most dangerous places on the planet but also the most fertile, people live on them, farm on their slopes despite knowing that any minute it could erupt and kill them all. We know more about space than we do about what goes on under the ground beneath our feet.' I was rambling, talking fast. 'Volcanoes got under my skin, literally,' I rubbed the scar. 'Mum and Dad had been arguing all through the trip up Sakurajima so I ran up the mountain, tripped and hit my head. Later I passed out and had a kind of vision.' Dad was looking at me, something in his face. He hadn't heard my version of the story. I'd never told anyone about it. 'I'd been reading a book Mum gave me on goddesses and it had a chapter on Pele, the Hawaiian volcano goddess. While I was unconscious I had a vision, a dream really, vision makes it sound grander, madder, but anyway I had this dream where I saw Pele sitting inside the volcano quietly powerful, controlling the magma. If she lost her temper the volcano would erupt but as long as she was happy, calm, pacified, everything would be okay.'

Everyone had stopped eating, they were watching me. It was a weird story, I knew, but I was caught up in the memory.

'In the hospital later, with Mum and Dad still arguing, I could still remember it, that warmth, the fire, the hidden strength, the violence waiting below the surface ready to explode. That's when volcanoes got into me. It's funny, I suppose, if Mum and Dad hadn't been fighting all the time I'd never have got this scar or had that vision. I'd maybe have gone into petroleum geology and never left Aberdeen.'

I stopped. They were staring at me. I took a sip of wine, my throat dry.

Well done, Carrie. A story about your parents at your father's wedding. Ten out of ten for appropriateness. I bent my head to my soup, started spooning sour broth into my mouth.

The venison was chewy, hard to swallow. We moved onto red wine with the main course, the Pinot Noir mixing with the juice of my rare deer steak, the potatoes islands in a river of oily blood. Gavin had started talking about the difference between the western islands and the northern ones. As a Shetlander he held their culture to be separate from the rest of Scotland – Norse rather than Celtic, more part of Scandinavia than a pre-Roman Britain. 'When I was in the Merchant Navy I had a map of the world on my wall next to my bunk. One of my roommates was a Mexican. He told me to turn my map upside down. At first it looked wrong. But you know what? It totally changed my perception of the world. The map finally looked how I'd always thought the world to be. In Shetland we never looked south for our culture and influence. Greece, Rome, Paris, London. We look north. Turning the map on its head made that clear.'

'The first time I saw a map in New Zealand,' I said, 'I thought it was so badly drawn.' I drank a mouthful of wine. 'We're used to the map with us in the centre. You don't see how the Pacific dominates the planet. Obviously in that part of the world the Pacific is at the centre of the map. Hawaii at the centre. It took me a while, like you were saying Gavin, to realise the problem was with me. My thinking was Eurocentric and Anthrocentric.'

'But maps are there for our use,' said Isobel, looking at Dad instead of me. 'It makes sense for them to reflect the information we need.'

'But maps are supposed to reflect reality,' I said. 'Otherwise what use are they? If I want to climb a mountain or drive from Glasgow to Skye I need to know the truth of the landscape, where the roads go, where they don't.'

'But weren't you and Gavin just saying that reality is how you perceive it?' She finally looked at me. There was something in her eyes, hard and soft. Maybe it was the drink. She'd had a lot, we all had. 'You turn the map upside down, put the Pacific in the middle, look at it from someone else's perspective and suddenly you realise reality is what you make it.'

'Spoken like a true lawyer,' laughed Dad. 'But you're right. It's relativity. Reality changes depending on where you are observing from.'

'No, no, no. Nonsense. That's okay in physics,' I said, 'where it only has to work on a blackboard. If they get it wrong it doesn't stop them from getting home at the end of the day, if they postulate a multiverse and there isn't really one, nobody dies, nobody's village gets washed away. You're all missing the point. There is a solid reality that exists independently of us and our observations and it comes along with hideous regularity and smashes anyone who gets in its way. The laws of nature weren't drafted by Newton and Copernicus and Darwin and the rest, they were there while we were shrews hiding from predators and they'll be true once we've reduced this planet to a lifeless rock. You can talk about perception and Einstein all you want but when the ground underneath you blows up, when the world around you is nothing but falling debris and fire, you have to deal with reality head on. You can't run from reality.'

'You did.' Isobel slammed down her knife and fork, startling me out of my speech. 'You and your mother.'

I looked at her, a little woozy. I'd been lost in pictures I'd seen of eruptions, the stumps of houses, the smoke and ash.

'In front of your father talking about falling debris and fire, like the wisest voice in the universe.'

Hollowed, everything emptied out of me. Gavin was looking at his plate. I looked at Dad.

He held his hands up. 'Okay,' he said, 'we've all had a drink. Let's call a ceasefire and calm down.'

I wanted to explain, tell them I was speaking about myself, not them, not him, not what they thought I was talking about. Not Piper Alpha. But the words weren't there. I couldn't reach out to them, couldn't reach them. We were too far apart. Too many oceans. I should never have come.

'I'm sorry,' I said, slowly, quietly. 'I didn't mean any of that the way you took it but it's too late. I've ruined your day. I'm quite drunk and I never normally drink. Not an excuse but there you go. I'll leave you to it. Sorry.' I got to the door and looked back at Dad. 'I shouldn't have come back. I'm sorry.'

On my bed I cried. I cried all the wine out, all the gin, all the champagne, red tears, white tears, bubbly tears, quinine tears. I cried until I fell asleep. When I woke it was dark out and I had a splitting headache. I took three painkillers and drank water straight from the tap.

I packed my bags. Changed into proper clothes. Real clothes. Back into myself.

The hotel was quiet. I reached over the desk and left my key. The book still behind the chest of drawers.

The scrunch of gravel under my wheels, the sweep of my headlights across the trees.

Loch Morlich,
June 2013

Marcus sat on the beach at Loch Morlich, the thick scent of pine from the arc of trees behind him, the glutinous seeping resin heavy in the air. To his left the river that ran into the loch where Carrie had once seen a pike and been scared by the picture in the *Usborne Spotter's Guide*, all those prehistoric teeth. To his right the water sports centre where they'd rented kayaks, dinghies, windsurfers. Ancient and worn, the peak of Cairngorm, the Ptarmigan restaurant on top, the spikes of the chairlift, the swoop of the ski runs. They'd changed it, added a funicular railway, guided walks. Tamed it and corporatised it. He took a swig from the wine bottle, screwed it back into the sand.

This area was haunted by his past. Ghosts of himself, of others.

Isobel had warned him but he'd gone ahead, booked the room like Ash suggested.

He pushed his hands into his jacket pockets, found the box of matches and his cigarettes, lit one and watched the exhaled smoke whip away in the wind. They used to have bonfires on the beach. Marcus took great pride in fires, manly pride, all natural materials apart from the match – one match, any more was cheating – to go from scattered wood and leaves to a roaring fire. Your own resources, your own wit, you against nature, you with nature. That Christmas he'd spent up near Ullapool, the fire he'd lit had burned all day and all night, he'd kept it going the whole time he was there, sheltered from the wind, he tended it, prodded it, coaxed it, controlled it and let it loose. He'd seen himself in it, in that fire, as he stared into the flames, saw himself surrounded by other flames, running, diving, swimming. As long as he kept that fire going, he was alive. If it had gone out, he'd have given up.

Suicidal. He held a vigil for himself.

He'd left that out of the book. Written it all down, everything, but he cut that out. Cut other stuff too. But left a lot. Maybe too much. Had it been a mistake to give Carrie the book? To give it to her then and there? He'd been carried away, hyped up and happy, his wedding, his daughter there. Gavin had gone to wake her up and found the staff cleaning her room. The car gone. Not a word for ten years. Only the steady tick of published papers, conference appearances to let him know she was alive.

That was another mistake. He shouldn't have gone to the conference.

Marcus waited for her to start before sneaking into the MacRobert lecture theatre. It was a huge, soulless hall with bleacher-type seating that was pushed back at exam time. From his own lectures here he knew there was no way in or out without being seen by the speaker. He could come in at the top, behind the back row, or he could come round the side and walk right by her on his way to a seat. Neither would keep his presence secret so he stayed on the side, hidden from view. He'd promised Harry Boyle that he'd stay away but curiosity got the better of him.

On the surface *Geothermal Energy Extraction and Collateral Seismic Events* seemed pretty straightforward. Using the internal heat of the earth to create electricity wasn't a new idea but the side effects were often disastrous, causing earthquakes and sinkholes. Like fracking, it was risky and not something most people wanted in their backyard. Unlike fracking, it was clean and renewable. Finding a way to reduce the risk would constitute a massive step towards a carbon-free energy source. There were only two reasons someone would travel to the oil capital of Europe and deliver a paper on the subject. Either way, Carrie's paper was attracting attention.

In the ten years since the wedding, Marcus had kept a loose check on her career. Since Harry had given him the job at the university it had become much easier to access her published papers. Initially an expert in mapping volcanoes, she had expanded her interest into general subterranean mapping and at some point had become involved in climate science. It was clear from the direction her research had taken that Carrie was trying to make geothermal energy extraction work. She'd come to Aberdeen to deliver bad news to the oil industry in person. That, Marcus had to see. Judging by the crowd in the hall, he wasn't the only one.

From his shadowy corner he couldn't see her, but he could see the projector screen. As she took them through her research, the relevant images flashed up, raw data on one side, a three-dimensional computer map on the other. Her voice was calm, steady, strong, carried well by the radio mic. Marcus found himself trying to pick apart the strands of her accent, the Scottish Rs, the Kiwi EE, the I changed to U, an American twang over the A. She carried a souvenir of every place she'd lived. Perhaps more surprising was the depth of the voice, the years behind it. She was forty-one, he realised. How could his daughter, his little Carrie, be forty-one?

He was in danger of getting emotional, of doing something daft like stepping out into the light. He leaned his back against the wall, sheltered in the shadows.

How much things had changed. When he'd first got into the oil industry a lifetime ago, the only two questions asked about potential oil fields were 'how much oil?' and 'how cheap to extract?' Safety was never mentioned, except by the unions and they weren't in the room when important decisions were made. The Cullen Inquiry into Piper Alpha had made a hundred and six recommendations for changes to safety procedures, all of which were adopted. Yet accidents still happened. Only three years before, the Deepwater Horizon fiasco had taken place in the Gulf of Mexico. A year later the triple disaster in Japan had turned the world more strongly against nuclear power than before. Now fracking was the enemy. Like it or not, the industry had two new questions to answer – 'is it safe?' and 'is it clean?'

He tried to focus on what Carrie was saying. It sounded like she was approaching her conclusions.

'What the data show is that scientific and technological solutions are here. For widescale geothermal energy extraction, it's no longer a matter of if, but when.'

Marcus peeked over the side of the seating, looking over someone's foot and through a table support. She was talking almost without reference to her notes, looking directly at the room. She knew what she was doing. Her body language was confident and confrontational. Her shoulders squared, arms by her side, her head raised searching for any challenge. He risked a step forward so he could see the audience.

'Projects are being rolled out around the world. Places like Kenya, Tanzania and Ethiopia are already pursuing geothermal energy production and even the World Bank is starting to take notice. When it comes online, it will be cheap, it will be clean and it will be safe.'

He smiled at that, in the shadows. Her echoing his checklist. She'd done her homework, knew where to hit them. She was off the science now, off the hard facts and into interpretation.

'This is a challenge to everyone in this room. To the academics and the industry representatives. The oil industry is in its endgame. Fracking? Drilling in the arctic wildlife refuge? These are stopgaps, quick fixes. They are dangerous, unpopular and expensive.'

Behind her, on the projector screen, oil spills, sealife coated in crude, protestors against fracking, against BP, Deepwater Horizon, Seacrest, Ocean Ranger, Exxon Valdez.

'What my work shows, what the work of my colleagues shows, is that the age of petroleum is over. Geothermal energy extraction is no longer a dream. It's a reality. And that reality means the death of the oil industry.

'I've been asked why I came all this way to deliver this paper. It's because of where we are, where this conference is. Because of who is in this room. The oil industry isn't just an abstract entity, drilling over the horizon. It's the livelihoods of the people of this city and others like it around the world. Aberdeen is my hometown. When the oil goes, or when the market moves on, without an alternative industry, this city will wither. But it doesn't have to be that way. Together we can build a new industry, with the science I've outlined today and your expertise, your global networks and infrastructure, your knowledge and your money. We could make this city the centre of the world for sustainable energy, if only we can find the will and the courage to lead. Occasionally science gives you a glimpse of the future. It's up to you to be part of it.'

She closed her folder, pulled off her radio mic and dropped it on the lectern, walked out. She wasn't staying for questions, wasn't staying for the inevitable showdown. She'd done what she came to do.

Too late he realised she was coming right at him.

She saw him. Stopped. They looked at each other. He reached out a hand. 'Carrie, that was…'

She pushed by him and out of the hall. The door hissed closed. '…brilliant.'

Isobel was around somewhere, back at the tent reading. He wished she were there, just for a moment, next to him on the sand, so he could touch her, feel some tactile presence, a real human presence in amongst all these ghosts and memories. He let them come, he had to let them come, knew better than to fight, but it didn't make it any easier. Another slug of wine.

They'd moved out of the hotel after one night, after the fight, ran to the safety of Loch Morlich, the comfort of recognition.

Dr Shaw had encouraged him to face his past, to admit to his mistakes, to accept them for what they were.

You couldn't make others do the same.

Coylumbridge Hotel,
June 2013

'You had no right. No right.'

'No, but I was right to do it.'

'You ignored my wishes.'

'I did.'

'You're not sorry?'

'I'm sorry about the way it turned out. I'm not sorry I did it.'

Hotel rooms were not the place for fights. You knew everyone could hear everything. You couldn't take a step without hitting a wall, a bed, the other person. It was all too easy to block the only route of escape. Ash had put herself between me and the door and the only thing I could do was physically shift her. She was all but daring me to. I wanted past her. I wanted out. There was so much anger in me, so much fire that needed to burn. I was afraid of what would happen if I erupted in here. She knew that. She was pushing me.

'We're going to talk about this.'

'There's nothing to talk about. You knew my wishes. What happened was entirely your fault.'

'I don't deny any of that.'

'Good.'

'So now we can talk about what happened.'

'Fucking lawyers!' I took a step towards her but we both knew I wasn't really going to push her aside. I flung myself down into the armchair, exasperated, suddenly very tired. 'Fine. Explain.'

'You're an idiot.'

I waited for more. Nothing came. 'That's your argument?'

'You have no idea why you came here, why you agreed to that conference, do you?'

'To deliver my paper.'

'Why here? Why now?'

'I didn't decide the conference should be in Aberdeen this

year. If it were up to me it would've been somewhere I actually wanted to go.'

'What was in your paper that it had to be delivered in person? Why couldn't it be published in one of the journals?'

I hated arguing with her, I couldn't think straight when we fought but she had this irritating ability to cut her emotion out of an argument. I felt like cattle being pushed through the channels she wanted me to go through until I got to the abattoir.

'What's your point?'

'You chose to come here. Whether you admit it to yourself or not, it's true. You chose to come here. To deliver a paper attacking the oil industry twenty-five years after Piper Alpha. You really expect me to believe that's coincidence?'

'I don't care what you believe.'

'I know that's not true.'

'Okay, say I did do all that, consciously or not, one thing I definitely didn't do was get in touch with my dad and say, "Hey, let's meet up. Last time was such a blast, let's do it again."'

'You knew he was friends with Harry Boyle. You knew he'd find out.'

'He's known where I am for the last ten years. You think proximity was the problem?'

'He came to the hotel. In Aberdeen. He came on Sunday when you were on campus. I spoke to him.'

'And hatched this plan.'

'Yes. I told him not to go to the conference, that it would be better for everyone to meet somewhere else.'

'He didn't listen to you. He came anyway.'

'I know. I underestimated how much he wanted to see you.'

'And how much I didn't want to see him.'

'No, I knew that. I just don't want you to end up like me.'

'What does that mean?'

'I never saw my father again.'

'I know. I'm sorry, but this is different.'

'No, Carrie, it's not. The only thing that's different is that I didn't try. And now I can't.'

'So you decided for me?'

'Yes.' She came over and sat on the edge of the bed, at a right angle to me, our knees touching. 'Look, Ash, I know you had good reasons. But they were *your* reasons.'

'What are your reasons? Tell me why you'll never see your father again until it's too late.'

'Too much—'

'Too much what? Anger? Bitterness? Shame?'

'Time. Too much time. All of those things and more but too much time. I made my choice. My life. It was with you in Hawaii.'

'Was? Oh no you don't. You won't run from me, Carrie.' But I was already out the door.

I walked from the hotel into the forest. Something in the Speyside air, something that I recognised from my childhood. Pine, maybe, or resin. All the open space, the mountains, the sky, golden eagles, the osprey nest nearby. My memories were all green and brown, rushing water and rocky roads. When Dad and I walked the Lairig Ghru, the mountain pass that runs all the way to Braemar, we started from here, taking the Chalamain Pass. I'd been looking forward to showing this place to Ash. I'd wanted to camp at Loch Morlich but it would've been too much hassle to get all the equipment together and she got a discount at the Hilton.

When I was a kid we'd come to the Coylumbridge for an evening. I'd swim in the pool, Hannah and Dad would sit in the bar. Last night Ash suggested a drink and for nostalgia's sake we went down. I realised straight away it was a set-up. No coincidence involved in Dad and Isobel sitting at a table for four. I nearly walked out. I should have.

He'd been drinking.

I ordered an orange and lemonade, waited for an explanation.

I'd never thought Ash would do that. Would take his side. Their side. She was supposed to be different.

Why couldn't people just leave me alone?

One glass of orange and lemonade. The time it took to drink one glass of orange and lemonade. Must be some kind of record. Zero to sixty in whatever seconds. I wasn't even listening. I was watching the ghosts. Graeme and I, his father and mine. That summer we'd bumped into each other at Loch Morlich, we'd gone to the hotel. Teenagers by then, we hung out in the games room, played *Pac-man* while our fathers drank. Graeme played *Street Fighter* and I wondered which of them would drive us home. Whether that would be the night we died in a car crash, startled by the machine gun chatter of the cattle grid, off the road by the clay pigeon lodge, upside down in the trees, tyres spinning, lights blinking.

Those ghosts, the bar was full of them, the hotel. Dad said something. Isobel, something. And I was on my feet, shouting something, Ash holding my hand, trying to make me sit but I was off through the hotel, out into the car park and down through the trees to the river.

Ash described me like one of those wind-up cars, the ones you pull back along the floor so the mechanism primes then when you let go it zooms off. A wind-up toy, permanently primed, ready to go.

But the world wasn't big enough, wasn't flat enough. I'd run around the world and there I was, back in Scotland, back at the start. If I set off again would I ever be back? Would I die in Hawaii, be buried in the ground I'd spent so much time mapping? My ashes scattered over Pele's domain. Would I move on, some of the projects I had in mind, Indonesia, the Philippines, Chile?

Ash in the room. 'You won't run from me.'

She was right.

Loch Morlich,
June 2013

Marcus kicked sand onto the fire, the flames smothered, the empty bottle in his hand. Sand turned into glass at temperatures above 1700 degrees Celsius. The charred wood, singed rocks, all of it buried, the last of the smoke drifting into the twilight air. The gentle lapping of the loch. When he died, he wanted to be scattered there.

At rest.

The pine resin, the peaks. He'd been happy here. Before Piper Alpha, before everything. He'd been happy. He no longer wished he'd died that day, was thankful for the days he'd been given, hard as they were.

A figure stood in the shadows between two pines. He kept walking towards whoever it was. Maybe it was no one, just someone there to watch the sunset. She stepped out onto the beach, walked down to the shoreline, pine needles and twigs pushed up the sand. Carrie. He followed her to the edge, stood beside her looking out over the shimmering mirror of the loch, the last of the sun blazing on the hills, the ground beneath their feet.

Acknowledgements

I was born and raised in the Aberdeen area and vividly remember July 6th 1988 and the weeks and months that followed. There isn't a family in Aberdeen from that time that does not have some connection with someone who was on Piper Alpha that night. It was a tragedy that scars the city to this day. The decision to write this book was not taken lightly.

There were 226 souls on Piper Alpha that night, of whom 165 died. Two members of the Sandhaven crew also perished, sacrificing their lives to save others. 167 men. Richard Common, unable to cope with the guilt that he had survived while so many others hadn't, took his own life in 1994. Out of respect for the memories of those who died and the privacy of those who survived, I chose to create a fictional 227th man, Marcus Fraser. He never existed and is not based on, or an amalgam of, any real people related to Piper Alpha. His presence on Piper Alpha within these pages is an anomaly to allow the story to be told.

This book is a work of fiction. For those who wish to learn more about the tragedy, there are three non-fiction books on the Piper Alpha disaster from which I drew my research. *Piper Alpha: A Survivor's Story* (Star, 1989) by Ed Punchard, *Fire in the Night: The Piper Alpha Disaster* (Pan Books, 2008) by Stephen McGinty, and *Death and Oil* (Pantheon, 2011) by Brad Matsen. The documentary *Fire in the Night* (2013) based on Stephen McGinty's book was also invaluable.

While researching PTSD and alcoholism I learned much from the following two papers:

Sudie E Back *et al*, 'Use of an Integrated Therapy With Prolonged Exposure to Treat PTSD and Co-morbid Alcohol Dependence in an Iraq Veteran', *The American Journal of Psychiatry*, 169:7 (July 2012), pp688-91.

Alastair M. Hull *et al*, 'Survivors of the Piper Alpha Oil Platform Disaster: Long Term Follow-up', *British Journal of Psychiatry*, 181 (2002), pp433-8.

Help, advice and corrections were kindly provided by Professor Susan Klein at the Aberdeen Centre for Trauma Research; Patricia Inglis, Advanced Nurse Practitioner, Aberdeen Royal Infirmary; Dr Liam McIlvanney; Professor Thor Thordarson; Carol Whitney Thordarson; Dr Jonathan Todman. Any lingering mistakes are entirely my own.

Great Britain didn't enter a snowboard team in the 1998 Olympics. The bronze medal in the Halfpipe went to Ross Powers of the USA.

This book was first published as *The Waves Burn Bright* by Freight Books in 2016.

With thanks to Bernard Chandler, Sarah Dobbs, Rodge Glass, Molly Greenshields, Robbie Guillory, Patricia Inglis, Vicki Jarrett, Duncan Lockerbie, Alex Lockwood, Matthew Mackie, Alison Miller, Michael Maloney, Judy Moir, Paul S Philippou, Adrian Searle, Ryan Vance.

For Minori, with love always.

TIPPERMUIR BOOKS

Tippermuir Books Ltd is an independent
publishing company based in Perth, Scotland.

Publishing History

Spanish Thermopylae (2009)

Battleground Perthshire (2009)

Perth: Street by Street (2012)

Born in Perthshire (2012)

In Spain with Orwell (2014)

Trust (2014)

Perth: As Others Saw Us (2014)

Love All (2015)

A Chocolate Soldier (2016)

The Early Photographers of Perthshire (2016)

*Taking Detective Novels Seriously: The Collected Crime
Reviews of Dorothy L Sayers* (2017)

Walking with Ghosts (2017)

No Fair City: Dark Tales from Perth's Past (2017)

*The Tale o the Wee Mowdie that wantit tae ken wha keeched
on his heid* (2017)
SHORTLISTED FOR SCOTS CHILDREN'S BOOK OF THE YEAR 2019

*Hunters: Wee Stories from the Crescent: A Reminiscence of
Perth's Hunter Crescent* (2017)

A Little Book of Carol's (2018)

Flipstones (2018)

*Perth: Scott's Fair City: The Fair Maid of Perth & Sir Walter
Scott – A Celebration & Guided Tour* (2018)

God, Hitler, and Lord Peter Wimsey: Selected Essays, Speeches and Articles by Dorothy L Sayers (2019)

Perth & Kinross: A Pocket Miscellany: A Companion for Visitors and Residents (2019)

The Piper of Tobruk: Pipe Major Robert Roy, MBE, DCM (2019)

The 'Gig Docter o Athole': Dr William Irvine & The Irvine Memorial Hospital (2019)

Afore the Highlands: The Jacobites in Perth, 1715-16 (2019)

'Where Sky and Summit Meet': Flight Over Perthshire – A History: Tales of Pilots, Airfields, Aeronautical Feats, & War (2019)

Diverted Traffic (2020)

Authentic Democracy: An Ethical Justification of Anarchism (2020)

'If Rivers Could Sing': A Scottish River Wildlife Journey. A Year in the Life of the River Devon as it flows through the Counties of Perthshire, Kinross-shire & Clackmannanshire (2020)
SHORTLISTED FOR 'NEW BOOK OF 2021', SCOTLAND'S NATIONAL BOOK AWARDS (SALTIRE AWARDS)

A Squatter o Bairnrhymes (2020)
by Stuart A Paterson, **Scots Writer of the Year 2020**

In a Sma Room Songbook: From the Poems by William Soutar (2020)

The Nicht Afore Christmas: the much-loved yuletide tale in Scots (2020)
SHORTLISTED FOR SCOTS CHILDREN'S BOOK OF THE YEAR 2021

Ice Cold Blood (2021)

The Black Watch and the Great War (2021)

The Perth Riverside Nursery & Beyond: A Spirit of Enterprise and Improvement (2021)

Beyond the Swelkie: A Collection of Poems & Writings to Mark the Centenary of George Mackay Brown (1921-1996) (2021)

Dying to Live: The Remarkable True Story of Scotland's Sickest Survivor of Covid-19 (2021)

The Shanter Legacy: The Search for the Grey Mare's Tail (2021)

Fatal Duty: Scotland's Cop Killers, Killer Cops & More... from 1812 to 1952 (2021)

A Scottish Wildlife Odyssey: In Search of Scotland's Wild Secrets (Keith Broomfield, 2022)

Sweet F.A.
(Tim Barrow, Paul Beeson and Bruce Strachan, 2022)

A War of Two Halves
(Tim Barrow, Paul Beeson and Bruce Strachan, 2022)

Forthcoming

William Soutar: Collected Poetry, Volume I and Volume II
(Kirsteen McCue, Philippa Osmond-Williams
and Paul S Philippou (editors), 2022)

William Soutar: Collected Poetry, Volume III (Kirsteen McCue, Philippa Osmond-Williams and Paul S Philippou (editors), 2023)

Berries Fae Banes: An owersettin in Scots o the poems bi Pino Mereu scrievit in tribute tae Hamish Henderson
(Jim Macintosh, 2022)

Perthshire 101: A Poetic Gazetteer of the Big County
(Andy Jackson (editor), 2022)

Perth City Activity Book: Exploring the Past and Present
(Felicity Graham, 2022)

The Whole Damn Town (Hannah Ballantyne, 2022)

Balkan Rhapsody (Maria Kassimova-Moisset, translated by Iliyana Nedkova-Byrne, 2022).

All Tippermuir Books titles are available from bookshops and online booksellers. They can also be purchased directly (with free postage & packing (UK only) – minimum charges for overseas delivery) from **www.tippermuirbooks.co.uk**.

Tippermuir Books Ltd can be contacted at
mail@tippermuirbooks.co.uk.